THE SPACE
BETWEEN US

ALSO BY JESSICA MARTINEZ

Virtuosity

THE SPACE BETWEEN US

JESSICA MARTINEZ

Simon Pulse

New York London Toronto Sydney New Delhi

SIMON PULSE

An imprint of Simon & Schuster Children's Publishing Division
1230 Avenue of the Americas, New York, NY 10020
First Simon Pulse hardcover edition October 2012
Copyright © 2012 by Jessica Martinez
All rights reserved, including the right of reproduction
in whole or in part in any form.
SIMON PULSE and colophon are registered trademarks of Simon & Schuster, Inc.
For information about special discounts for bulk purchases, please contact
Simon & Schuster Special Sales at 1-866-506-1949
or business@simonandschuster.com.
The Simon & Schuster Speakers Bureau can bring authors to your live event.
For more information or to book an event contact
the Simon & Schuster Speakers Bureau at 1-866-248-3049
or visit our website at www.simonspeakers.com.
Designed by Mike Rosamilia
The text of this book was set in Janson Text LT.
Manufactured in the United States of America
2 4 6 8 10 9 7 5 3 1
Library of Congress Cataloging-in-Publication Data
Martinez, Jessica.
The space between us / Jessica Martinez.
p. cm.
Summary: Seventeen-year-old Amelia feels like her life might be getting back on track after
a bad breakup when her younger sister's pregnancy gets them both banished to Canada,
where new relationships are forged, giving Amelia a new perspective.
ISBN 978-1-4424-2055-7 (hardcover)
[1. Sisters—Fiction. 2. Pregnancy—Fiction. 3. High schools—Fiction. 4. Schools—Fiction.
5. Calgary (Alb.)—Fiction. 6. Canada—Fiction.] I. Title.
PZ7.M36715Sp 2012
[Fic]—dc23
2011038019
ISBN 978-1-4424-2057-1 (eBook)

FOR ALL THE GOOD SISTERS
IN THE WORLD, BUT ESPECIALLY
FOR MY OWN, AMANDA

Chapter 1

Charlotte Mercer, please report to Principal Blackburn's office. *Charlotte Mercer* to Principal Blackburn's office."

Static crackled, then the PA system cut out. I could feel all twenty-two heads turn, but I kept my eyes on my paper and gripped my pencil just a little tighter. Even Mr. Mason stopped taking the derivative on the board and glanced over his shoulder at me.

I forced myself to keep writing. *Move along, nothing to see here.* As it was, the minute class was over I'd be fielding questions about what she'd done. Like I knew.

Mr. Mason went back to the problem on the board,

and one by one, the weight of the stares lifted.

Please don't be another frog.

Last week she'd taken a huge bite out of one of the formaldehyde-soaked frogs in the biology lab. She couldn't have just nibbled off a tiny piece and spit it out. No, of course not. Apparently the dare stipulated chewing and swallowing, and Charly took her dares seriously. With half the class watching, she'd sunk her teeth into its torso, ripped off the entire left leg, then chewed and swallowed.

When Ms. Dansk realized what'd happened, she freaked out and sent Charly to the nurse, who determined Charly was physically fine (psychology report pending) and sent her along to Principal Blackburn. The whole thing resulted in a two-day in-school suspension for Charly and an hour-long assembly about lab safety for the entire school. Oddly enough, people were so impressed by the whole repulsive stunt, they weren't even mad about having to sit through the assembly.

Charly missed it. Dentist appointment.

I wasn't ready for another incident. I'd just decided I was going to hit the next person to ask me what frog tasted like.

The bell rang and Savannah met me at the doorway with an arched eyebrow. She knew better than to ask, but I answered anyway. "I have no idea. Let's go eat."

"Hey, Amelia," someone yelled from behind as we

pushed through bodies packing the hall. "Why's Charly in the office?"

"Don't know," I called without turning around.

Dean met us at the top of the stairwell, looking like someone stole his puppy. "Is she getting busted for the toaster oven thing?"

"What toaster oven thing?"

He glanced around for teachers. "You know . . . the toaster oven in the staff room . . ." He fiddled with the button on his shirt pocket and frowned, clearly trying to decide whether telling me was ratting her out or not.

Dean is one of a hundred guys at Primrose High who would follow Charly to the ends of the earth if he thought there was a chance she might accidentally touch his arm or something. The only difference between Dean and the others is that Charly actually likes him. It's the platonic sort of like she reserves for the cute, clean-cut boys, but it's enough for me to make a point of putting up with him.

"I have no idea what you're talking about and I don't care. Are you coming to lunch?"

He hesitated.

"Come on, baby face. She'll probably show up," I said.

That did it.

The three of us sat at our usual table by the window with the scenic view of PHS's asphalt parking lot. Charly didn't show, but a handful of her minions did: Harrison,

Dean's slightly less intelligent wingman, Asha and Liam from drama club, and some tall guy with a dimpled chin whose name I can never remember.

"So what's the plan for homecoming?" Savannah asked between carrot sticks. For reasons unknown she'd bought a homecoming dress one size too small and stopped eating normal food. I'd already warned her the beta-carotene overload was going to turn her skin orange, but she didn't seem to care. Apparently super-skinny and orange was preferable to regular-skinny and human-colored.

"No plan for homecoming. I'm going to Atlanta with my dad," I said, eyeing the door. No Will yet, but it was Wednesday. He had debate team meetings on Wednesdays. Or he used to. Now Wednesdays were probably reserved for making out with Luciana in his car.

"We talking about homecoming?" Sebastian asked, putting his tray down next to Savannah. "Hey, sugar." He put his chin on top of her head and gave her a quick squeeze that looked disturbingly like a headlock.

"Hey, baby."

Sugar, baby, honey, cookie, sweetie pie. Good thing I was friends with them before they started going out. Otherwise I'd have to hate them for being so annoying.

"No, Savannah was talking about homecoming. I was talking about going to Atlanta."

"Enough of the too-cool-for-homecoming act,"

Savannah said. "You're not. And it's our senior year, so you have to come."

"Wrong. I don't. I've been the last three years. I already know exactly what happens. *You* have to go to collect your little princess tiara, but I am free to do whatever I want."

"So, why is your dad going to Atlanta?" Dean asked.

"He's giving some presentation at a conference."

Dean nodded and chewed slowly. "So, uh, your whole family's going?"

Poor Dean. It would be better if Charly was going to Atlanta so she wouldn't have to reject him outright again.

"No. Just me and my dad."

He took another bite of his sandwich and chewed with renewed enthusiasm. I was about to tell him to be careful not to bite his cheek or choke, when Savannah leaned over her tray and whispered, "You know that if you don't go to homecoming, *he* wins."

I glared into her big, concerned eyes. Could she not see the entire table full of people listening? "No. I really want to go to Atlanta. At the Coke museum they let you sample different Coke formulas from all over the world. Think of the buzz. A whole world of sugar and caffeine."

She sat up straight again. Then, rather than going along with my lame change-of-subject like any decent best friend would, she elbowed her puppet.

"Oh, yeah," Sebastian said, "I've got this friend I'm going to set you up with."

As if his brain produced its own thoughts in Savannah's presence. "I don't want to be set up with anyone."

"But you don't even know this guy," he argued. "He's cool."

I knew every man, woman, child, and dog in Tremonton. Very few of them could be classified as cool. "Where's he from?"

"Tallahassee. I roomed with him at soccer camp. And he'd just come from Bible camp too, so he probably wouldn't be too freaked out about your dad being a pastor."

I cringed. "If I was going to homecoming, a Tallahassee import would definitely have potential. But I'm not. Really. I'm going to Atlanta."

I hope. Dad had been noncommittal last time I brought it up, but he was more distracted than against it. He definitely didn't say "no."

So I'd started working on Grandma instead. I told her I wanted to research the Campus Missionary program for next year when I was at college, and what better place to start than the Southern Methodist Pastor's Conference? Plus I'd have plenty of downtime to work on my SAT prep book and do my homework. She'd been skeptical. She was *still* skeptical, but I had time to win her over, and as soon as she was on board, Dad would cave.

Atlanta was the perfect excuse to get out of town. I could spend the entire time studying by the pool and watching pay-per-view movies in the hotel room, both of which would be ten times more enjoyable than going to homecoming, or sitting at home thinking about previous homecomings.

Last year I went with Will. And the year before.

A group of skinny little freshman boys in baggy jeans with tough-guy chains shuffled up to the table.

"Hey, has your sister ever eaten roadkill?" the closest one asked.

I stared into the kid's eyes, trying not to be distracted by the whole face full of zits needing to be squeezed. Did he not realize I was a senior?

"Do you, um, think she'd eat roadkill if I dared her?" he continued. His friends had started to inch backward.

"Please go away." I turned back to my turkey sandwich.

"*Denied*," one of the friends muttered as they wandered off.

Savannah pushed her plate of carrots aside and put a sympathetic hand on my arm. "Are you sure about homecoming?"

I closed my eyes, and willed myself to not flinch. She meant well. And she was right, if he showed up at homecoming with Luciana and I stayed away, I'd lose. People would assume I was sitting in front of a TV with a bag of powdered-sugar mini-donuts.

But did it matter? They all assumed that *he* dumped *me* last April anyway.

"I'm sure," I said, and took a bite out of my apple.

Savannah didn't know why we'd broken up, and I couldn't explain it to her. I couldn't even explain it to Charly. And I was guessing the gorgeous Brazilian rebound didn't know either.

Will knew. And I knew.

"SHAZAM!" Charly's tray clattered as it hit the table across from me, fruit punch sloshing over the lip of her cup. She didn't notice. "I just survived a trip to Blackburn's cave."

I dropped a napkin on the juice spill. "Dare I ask why?"

"I put my bra on over top of my shirt after PE, and Señora Lopez freaked when she saw me in the hall."

"Why?"

"I don't know. Probably because she's mean and uptight."

"No. Why would you wear your bra over your shirt?"

She frowned. Clearly *why* had not come up yet. "Because I thought it would be funny. And it was, by the way."

"I'm sure Blackburn thought it was hilarious."

She put a fry in her mouth and grinned. "I told him I

was protesting sweatshop labor in India and wherever else they make bras, and it was like he'd been hit by a tranquilizer dart. He started talking about protesting the Vietnam War when he was young and some other crap I wasn't really listening to."

Dean and Harrison laughed. The thespians and the kid with no name followed, while Sebastian applauded. At least Savannah rolled her eyes.

"That's great," I said. "I'm sure all the little children hunched over sewing machines would be thrilled to know they've helped you out."

"And I will be forever grateful to them for saving me from an in-school suspension. He didn't even threaten to call home." She pulled the pieces of her grilled cheese apart and held one in front of my face. The mass of congealed orange cheese product was sweating. "Think this is organic?"

"Yeah," I said.

"Seriously? You think?" She wrinkled her nose.

"Of course not. Unless space-age polymers are now falling under the organic label."

She closed the bread around the greasy cheese and took a bite.

"Since when do you care about eating organic?" Savannah asked suspiciously. She thinks she has dibs on living green since her stepdad bought her a hybrid. She's gone as far as to lecture strangers at the mall for tossing empty soda cans in the garbage.

"Since today," Charly answered. "Now that I'm a protestor of sweatshop labor in . . . Amelia, where are the sweatshops?"

"China, Malaysia, Guatemala, the Philippines, Thailand . . . should I keep going?"

"No, that's good."

"Wait a second," Savannah jumped in, jabbing a finger dangerously close to my face. "You *can't* go to Atlanta. You guys have a big game! Ha!"

I knew it was only a matter of time until that hit her. "I'll have to miss it." The words felt wrong even as I said them. I'd never missed a field hockey game. Not even when I'd had mono.

"What? The team captain can't just skip out on the biggest game of the season."

"We'll beat Baldwin whether I'm here or not."

That wasn't true. I took another bite of my apple and stared at the core to avoid eye contact. Baldwin beat us last year, and was rumored to be even stronger this year. Something about a new German coach and brutal three-hour practices.

"What did Coach Hershey say?" Charly asked.

I glared at her. Whose side was she on? "I haven't told her yet. Today. At practice."

Coach Hershey is like a stick of dynamite: small, tightly packed, and deadly. I was still trying to come up with the right way of phrasing it so she wouldn't explode in my face.

"Homecoming is about football," I said. "Nobody cares about girls' field hockey."

"Apparently not," Savannah muttered, and folded her arms.

"Hey, speaking of Baldwin," Charly said, "can you give me a lift out there tomorrow night?"

"Why, so you can spend the evening stealing stop signs?"

Charly had come away from her summer job mowing greens at Baldwin Country Club with a paycheck, a tan, and a pack of total morons she now hung out with. Most of them were dropouts or just going nowhere. Unless there was a possibility of keg stands—then they were definitely going *there*.

"We didn't steal them. We borrowed them and then we put them back. Mostly."

"I won't even be home from practice until after five and then I've got homework. Plus, I need to practice for my choir audition."

She closed her eyes and shuddered. "You should *not* be auditioning for choir."

"I'm doing choir."

"But you have a terrible voice. No offense."

Sebastian and No-Name stifled laughs. Savannah coughed.

"Thanks a lot, guys," I muttered, then turned back to Charly. "Offense taken, and I know I don't have the best voice, but choir will make me look well rounded."

"But you're not."

"Conversation over."

"Does that mean you're not driving me to Baldwin?"

"You need to get your driver's license."

That shut her up. She'd already failed the road test twice.

"You don't want to go out to Baldwin tonight," Dean jumped in. "They're the enemy. Come with us to DQ after football."

If Charly answered, I didn't catch it. I was too busy watching Will.

He was coming through the doorway to the cafeteria, Luciana in tow, her pearly pink nails and brown skinny fingers curled around his bicep. He was talking, and she was laughing. No, her whole body was laughing—her head thrown back and her other hand touching her throat.

Please. Will is a lot of things, but he's not that funny.

Adrenaline screamed through my veins, but I didn't move. I gave myself three seconds. Three seconds to see how happy he looked, still tall and skinny, those same brown eyes and curly brown hair. Three miserable seconds, then I looked down.

Thankfully, Savannah was too busy canoodling with Sebastian to notice. Her sympathy is my kryptonite.

Charly pushed her pudding cup toward me. "Butterscotch. You can have it."

She gave me a crooked half smile, crooked because when we were ten she'd been standing on the wrong side of my swing during a softball game.

Butterscotch is her favorite.

"Thanks."

Chapter 2

Come out to the tree with me," Charly whispered, pushing just her head through my open door.

I didn't look up from my calculus. "I've got to finish this. Why are you whispering?"

"I don't want Grandma to hear me. She's still pissed about those jelly jars I borrowed."

Borrowed. Charly had taken ten of Grandma's canning jars and used them as pins for watermelon bowling at the drama club's back-to-school party. None survived.

"I've really got to work on this," I said. I did. In the

last hour I'd accomplished nothing—just stared at numbers, and copied out problems, my brain abandoning every effort before I could find the derivative of anything.

I couldn't stop thinking about the fact that next year at this time I'd be in New York, in a dorm room at Columbia, listening to indie music with roommates who wore funky scarves and glasses and got straight As and had Ivy League boyfriends who played lacrosse. Maybe *I'd* have an Ivy League boyfriend who played lacrosse. Somebody I'd met in one of my political science classes. Then we could go to Yale Law School together and—

"What are you thinking about?" Charly interrupted.

World domination. "Calculus."

"Tragic." She shook her head. "You looked so happy."

Charly pushed the door open all the way. She was already wearing pajamas, a pink tank top and shorts with white eyelet trim, and she'd knotted her hair into messy pigtails.

"You look like you're five years old," I said.

"I've got snacks." She lifted a bowl of strawberries in one hand, then two Cokes in the other.

I closed my textbook.

"Are you going to finish my math for me?" I asked as we tiptoed downstairs.

"The answer is *c*."

"It's not multiple choice, idiot."

I elbowed past her at the landing, kept my lead through the kitchen, and slipped out first, the moist night air swallowing me whole. That air. Warm and wet and suffocating.

It can't be like this up north. I've seen pictures of New York in the fall. People wear sweaters. *I* could wear a sweater.

The screen door banged shut behind Charly. "Shhhhh!" I said, and turned to see her sprinting down the steps, giggling as she passed me.

"Don't shake the Cokes!" I called, breaking into a run. Frogs screeched in the dark and I tried not to think about stepping on one. The crabgrass felt like a carpet of dry sticks beneath my bare feet, but I ran anyway, passing her easily. First one to the tree gets the best seat.

The black walnut is ours, mine and Charly's. Grandpa carved our names into it after we—the three survivors— came here to live. I was a toddler, so I don't remember anything, not the name carving, not the crash, not the funeral, not my mother. I think us living here was supposed to be temporary, but then Grandpa got sick so Dad had another reason to stay. And after Grandpa died, we just never moved out.

The tree is the perfect distance from the old plantation-style house for us to sit in its branches and chuck the green walnut hulls at the windows. Five points for a wooden shutter, ten points for an actual windowpane, and fifteen points for the French doors or any piece of the veranda furniture. Then there's the impossible: the rooster-topped weather vane on the roof. Fifty points for the vane, but neither of us has hit it yet. Not for lack of trying.

We're taking a break from it though, since last week Grandma promised if she saw one more walnut hull on the porch we'd be polishing silver till Christmas.

I swung myself up onto the lowest branch, then reached down to take my Coke from Charly.

Can in hand, I made my way down the branch to the first fork. It was too dark to see, but I know every knot and branch and mossy patch on that tree by touch. I didn't say anything, just settled with my back against the trunk. Charly found the second-best spot farther down the bough, where it forks again and flattens almost enough to resemble a seat.

Charly opened her Coke. I opened mine too. All around us fireflies glowed and sank into the darkness.

She broke the silence first. "Do you think I should dye my hair red?"

"*What?*" I stared at her pigtails. Charly has the kind of buttery-blond hair people spend fortunes trying to imitate. "That would look so bad."

"You think? Ty and Mitch said I'd look sexy with red hair."

"Ty and Mitch are idiots. I'm telling you, those Baldwin guys have the collective IQ of a chimp. And why do you even care what they think? Dad would kill you."

"No, *Grandma* would kill me," she said. "Dad would cry."

She was right. According to photographs, Charly looks just like Mom—the blond curly hair, the blue eyes, the freckles. Dad really might cry.

My hair is nut brown and I have all of Grandma's angles, from chin to hips to knees. If I dyed my hair red Dad would be disappointed in me. Grandma would probably ground me, but only because seventeen is too old for the paddle.

When we were younger, sixteen was the legal age for everything fun: boys, pierced ears (one per ear), cell phones, etc. But now that we've both passed that mark, the list of forbidden activities has only shifted: drugs, skipping church, sex, etc. We can't do any of those until Dad dies. To my knowledge, hair dying hasn't been discussed, but Charly is a believer in do first, ask later.

She'd earned two weeks of grounding for piercing her ears when she was fifteen. It was dumb of her. I don't know why she hadn't just waited three months and saved herself getting in trouble.

"So you're not over Will," Charly said.

I took a sip of my soda and held it in my mouth until

the bubbles stung my tongue and cheeks. When the fizz finally died, I swallowed. "Luciana can have him."

"But you're not over him."

She said it so matter-of-factly I almost couldn't deny it. "Am too."

"I still don't get why you guys broke up. A year and a half, and it's just over for no reason?" Charly flicked a strawberry top off her thumb. "I mean, something must have happened."

Of course something happened. You happened.

"Nothing happened."

"You didn't even have a fight?"

I accused him of being in love with you and he admitted it.

"No. We've been over this a million times."

"Yeah, and it still makes no sense—him just breaking up with you out of the blue."

I chucked a strawberry top at her, but it fell short. "*He* didn't break up with *me*. It was mutual. Why doesn't anyone believe that?"

"Okay, okay, I believe."

Charly had been oblivious. As usual. She hadn't noticed the way Will started looking at her last spring, the same way she doesn't see how Dean and entire legions of other guys look at her now. I couldn't even hate her for it. She was too clueless.

But hating Will didn't seem quite right either. It's

not like he'd actually done anything wrong. I could just feel it, the way his body turned to her when she was around, the way he watched the words come out of her lips when she spoke. He smiled for her like she was sunshine and oxygen rolled into one, like he just couldn't help it.

If I was mad at anyone, it was myself for not being more . . . something.

"What did Hershey say when you told her you're missing the game?" Charly asked.

"I chickened out. I'll tell her tomorrow."

She snorted.

"What? She worked us hard today. I'd like to see *you* kick that wasps' nest."

"I don't see why you don't stay here, and just go to homecoming."

"Why would I do that?"

"To have fun. Go with whoever Sebastian was talking about, and stop obsessing over Will and his trampy girlfriend."

"I'm not obsessing. I really do want to go to Atlanta."

"To quote Grandma, 'And all liars shall burneth with fire and brimstone in hell,'" she recited, then held out the bowl of strawberries.

I took one. "You're paraphrasing, but I'm pretty sure Grandma was quoting God anyway. And I'm not lying.

I'm finished with high school boys. This year is about getting into Columbia."

Charly shrugged. "Fine, but Luciana really is a tramp. She sits right in front of me in art, and her jeans were so low today she was showing about three inches of thong."

"Lovely." My last swig tasted more like metal than Coke. I propped the empty can beside me.

"Wanna hear my song?" Charly asked, and handed me the bowl.

"Do I ever."

I'd heard her sing it a thousand times, but *Wicked* tryouts were only a week away. So Charly poured her heart into "Defying Gravity," and I ate the rest of the strawberries.

In my opinion, *Wicked* is a little ambitious for a high school in the rural South whose talent pool consists of overly confident pageant girls. But Charly is better than all of them, so maybe she can carry the show. She has the kind of voice my choir director loves—clear and sweet and perfectly in tune.

Grandma objects to Charly's *Wicked* ambitions, but not enough to forbid it. It's a combination of the play's name and the fact that Charly's GPA is bouncing between embarrassing and fatal. I tried explaining that the play is a *Wizard of Oz* spin-off, but that didn't seem to make a difference to Grandma. And of course, grades are grades. No sugarcoating a 2.5.

"So how was it?" Charly asked, a little out of breath from the soaring finish.

"Great. You'll get the part." If I could just remember what part that was.

"I hope so. I feel like I was born to play Galinda."

Right, Galinda. The good witch?

I rubbed the branch beneath my fingers, feeling the spongy bark crumble. Dad said Mom had loved the trees in Florida. She grew up in the Canadian Rockies with giant fir trees and other evergreen trees too prickly to climb. I wanted to ask Dad if she ever climbed the trees around the house we used to live in, over on the other side of Tremonton, but I could never quite find the right moment to ask. Besides, grown women, *mothers*, don't climb trees, do they?

"I'm starting to feel kind of sick," I said. "Maybe strawberries and Coke isn't the best combination."

"I'll remember that next time I want to stay home from school."

A halo of fireflies lit above Charly's head. I reached out to catch one, but she was too far away. They scattered.

"You know what we discovered out at the golf course?" she asked.

"What?"

"When you light a golf ball on fire you'd think you could hit it and it'd look like a meteor, but it doesn't. The flame goes out right away."

"Scratch what I said about the collective IQ of a chimp. There are smarter chimps." I rubbed my temples, picturing the scene. "I can't believe you actually did that. I'm surprised the golf balls caught fire."

"Oh, we had to soak them in gas first."

"What?"

"It's not like it was my idea."

"Yeah, 'cause the cops *really* care whose idea it was when they're arresting everyone. You could have killed someone!"

"It was the middle of the night. It's not like some innocent golfer was going to get a flaming golf ball to the head."

Unbelievable.

"Oh, come on, Amelia," she said. "It was fun. Even you would have had fun."

"If this is the stuff you're telling me about, I can't imagine what you aren't telling me."

"I don't keep secrets from you."

I hesitated, but not because I didn't believe her. "I know."

"So will you drive me out to that party tomorrow?"

"No. Again. I'm not taking you out to Baldwin to get into more trouble. The summer is over, the job is over. You have no reason to hang out with those guys."

The mugginess and the croaking frogs were suddenly too much. I was being smothered.

"I'm tired," I said. The thought of tomorrow, of field hockey, and calculus, and seeing Will, and pretending to be above it all made me want to fall asleep and wake up next year.

I glanced over at Charly. She'd pulled her knees up under her chin and wrapped both arms around her legs, nothing anchoring her to the branch. Her pigtails shone yellow in the moonlight, falling on her shoulders. A gust of wind, or a sneeze from me, anything to shake the bough, and she'd fall.

She picked up the empty bowl from the branch where I'd propped it, and held it out to me. "You take it in."

I took it.

Charly went up to bed while I rinsed out the strawberry bowl.

The house was quiet except for the hum of the AC and Dad's voice floating down the hall. I put the bowl away, then followed his voice to the closed door of his den. The words were muffled, but I could tell he wasn't on the phone. It was his pulpit voice, or a quieter version of it, but with that same powerful mix of casual and caring he reserved for the Sunday sermon. People heard it and forgot they were sitting in church, not at Starbucks chatting with a friend. A voice like that could call people sinners and they'd still come back next week.

I knocked.

"Come in."

"Can I talk to you for a minute?"

"Of course." He stood in front of his desk, dog-eared papers in hand. "I'm just running through the conference presentation again."

"Do you need an audience?"

He took off his glasses and laid them on his desk. His face looked empty without them. "It's pretty late, isn't it?"

I crossed the room and climbed into the leather desk chair. "I guess."

"Is your sister in bed already?" He rubbed the angry red marks on the bridge of his nose.

"I think so."

"So, what was it you wanted to talk about?"

"Atlanta."

He looked confused, but said nothing.

"I just wanted to ask if you'd decided about me coming with you. You know, since we talked about it last week."

"To Atlanta?" He squinted, as if trying to remember a conversation from last year. "I don't remember discussing that."

"We did."

"Well, I'm sorry. I guess I forgot." He ran a hand through his silver-streaked hair. "Honey, I don't think coming to Atlanta with me is going to work. Presenting at this conference is a big deal—I'm not going to have time for sightseeing."

"It's not like I'm five. I don't need babysitting."

"I know you're not five, but you're not an adult," he said. "I'm sorry."

He sounded sorry. But he's good at sounding sorry, or inspired, or pensive, or joyful, or whatever. I stared at the grain in the hardwood floor. "You won't even notice I'm there. I promise."

"That's not the point. Besides, I've decided to go up on Monday, and you can't miss a full week of school."

"But . . ." He was right. He knew it. "Can I just fly up and meet you on Friday, then?"

He came over and hugged me, signaling the begging was officially over. "I really am sorry." He put his glasses back on, and looked instantly wiser.

As I stood up I felt the fight drain from my body. I should have known. Tremonton is a black hole of suckiness and it wasn't going to let me escape.

"Good night, sweetie," he said as I left the den.

"Good night."

I texted Savannah from bed:

> change of heart. can u still hook me up

It took all of five seconds for her response:

> done

Chapter 3

Against all odds, the state of Florida gave Charly a driver's license.

"Lord, protect us" was Grandma's response when Charly came running into the kitchen, waving the temporary license like a winning lottery ticket. Grandma went back to arranging her roses in a glass vase.

"Third time's a charm!" Charly sang, and turned to me at the sink. She held out her arms for a hug.

"I'm holding scissors." I snipped the stem of the last pink blossom and handed it to Grandma. Charly settled for holding the little piece of paper up close to my face, too close to even see the writing, like she thought I would want to verify it wasn't fake.

"Why didn't you tell me you were taking the test again?" I asked. "Who drove you?"

"Dean. I wanted it to be a surprise!"

She grabbed the Jeep keys—*our* Jeep keys now—from the hook, and swung them around her index finger. "How do I look?"

"Dangerous," I said. "Have you called Dad yet?"

"Nope. I'll call him tonight when he's back at the hotel."

His response would be like Grandma's, but with a smile. Charly amuses him.

"Let's go somewhere," she said, twirling around the kitchen, still swinging the keys. "Come on, Grandma, let's go get ice cream."

Grandma placed the vase of top-heavy blossoms on the table runner. "Are those centered?"

"A little to the left," I said.

She pushed the vase an inch.

"Perfect."

Charly grabbed my arm. "I'm serious! We're all going to Dairy Queen and I'm driving. You too, Grandma."

"I'm too young to die," I whispered to Grandma as we followed Charly out the front door.

"Pray, child. Pray."

. . .

Charly cut off two people on the way to DQ, an impressive feat in a town as small as Tremonton. "Holy crap," she shouted after the second time. The other driver honked and sped off, flipping us the bird. "He came out of nowhere."

"Feces are hardly holy," Grandma muttered. "You've got to be cautious, Charlotte."

"Sorry."

Grandma rubbed her temples for the rest of the ride, muttering, "Thank you, Jesus, for letting me live another day," as Charly swerved into the DQ parking lot.

"Or maybe she's already killed us, and this is actually heaven," I said from the backseat.

Charly pulled into a parking spot—two parking spots, actually—then we went in and ordered.

"Now that I have my license, I won't have to bug you for rides all the time," Charly said between bites of her banana split.

"Good. Here, eat this," I said, dropping my cherry into her ice cream.

"This *is* heaven."

"You've cheated on way too many math tests to end up in heaven."

Grandma raised an eyebrow at Charly.

"She was kidding," Charly said, sinking her red plastic spoon into whipped cream and fudge sauce.

Grandma turned her steely gaze to me. "Were you kidding, or does your sister cheat?"

I shrugged. Of course she cheated. I'd seen her spend more time copying answers onto the inside of Coke bottle labels than I'd seen her actually studying. "If she cheats, she does a terrible job. What's your GPA again, Charly?"

Another lie averted.

Charly smiled sweetly and narrowed her eyes at me.

I grinned back.

Savannah loaned me a dress for homecoming. We would've planned a shopping trip to Tallahassee, but we ran out of time—I had my last crack at the SATs to study for, and she had extra cheerleading practices. The entire cheerleading squad (Savannah included) actually believed the outcome of the football game had something to do with whether they shook their pom-poms in perfect unison. I'd learned not to mock her aloud.

I didn't really need a new dress, anyway. Savannah had a closet full of once-worn formals that nobody at school had even seen. Her dad was a judge and worked at the capitol building, which meant she got to dress up and eat lobster and crème brûlée at political functions in Tallahassee a few times a year.

"The green one with the pleats," she said, after I'd

tried on a whole pile of them. "It brings out your eyes and makes you look like you have hips."

"You don't think it's too low cut?" I eyed myself in her full-length mirror. I'd have to wear a shrug or something over it if I wanted Grandma to let me out of the house.

"Course not."

I took it home and hung it in my closet next to the pink dress I wore last year, forcing myself not to think about how Will had bought me a rose wrist corsage and told me I looked beautiful. But I failed. I couldn't not remember every second of that night. It was before things got complicated.

I was also actively forcing myself not to worry about my date. I'd talked to Nick twice on the phone, and he didn't seem too annoying, just typically self-centered. All guys are. He'd mostly talked about his chances of getting a football scholarship, but according to Savannah, I didn't have to actually like Nick or enjoy myself. The important thing was that people see me looking good, and looking happy.

Charly found Savannah's dress on Wednesday after school while rifling through my closet.

"Yowza, is this what you're wearing on Friday?" She wedged her head through the hanger so the dress hung over her T-shirt and jeans.

"No," I grunted between crunches. "I'm wearing it to the field hockey game tomorrow."

"Spaghetti straps, huh? Good luck leaving the house in this."

"I've got that angora shrug to put over it."

She twirled around, watching the finger pleats flare in the mirror. "Do you mind if I take the car tonight?"

My abs were on fire. Coach Hershey's conditioning program was a relentless progression of push-ups, sit-ups, and planks. She made it clear that if we didn't feel like puking at the end, we hadn't done it properly.

"The car?" Charly repeated.

I did my last crunch and collapsed on the carpet. "Take it. I'm going to bed early anyway. Where are you going?"

"That party at Mitch's I was telling you about."

"You're going all the way to Baldwin on a school night?"

"Yeah. Cover for me, will ya?" She pulled my new Abercrombie sweater over her head.

I rolled onto my side and started doing leg lifts. "What?"

"I said cover for me. Sisters cover for each other."

"I'm not lying to Grandma. She can totally tell."

"That's because you're a terrible liar."

"So don't make me. And I don't remember hearing you ask to borrow that."

"Can I borrow this?" she called on her way out the door.

I didn't answer.

• • •

After dinner I tried reading the short story assigned for English, but when I pictured the main character, it was Will's face I saw. I couldn't help it. And not just his face, but the way he looked at Charly the night I first knew.

I'd been late leaving my study group, and hurrying because Will was supposed to pick me up for a movie. He was always so anal about getting the best seats. But when I got home, he was already there, in the kitchen with Charly. She was wrapped up in telling a story, moving her hands and doing voices and laughing all at the same time. And he was just staring. Staring so hard he didn't even see me watching from the doorway. Neither of them saw me.

Why do I always end up there? My brain can hijack any line of thinking and force it to Will's face at that moment, all serious and fascinated and needing.

I hate that face.

I ran my fingers along the edge of my desk. It's Dad's old desk, an oak, antique-fashioned thing with lots of drawers and cubbyholes and the name of his high school girlfriend etched into the wood on the far left side— *Caroline*. Weird thinking of him as a teenager, hunched over his own homework. Even weirder to think of him carving some girl's name into the wood.

It'd never occurred to me to carve Will's name into anything, though at the beginning of last school year I'd written *Amelia Harmon* on the inside of my notebook in ink. Just to see what it looked like. Then I'd taken a Sharpie to it before anyone could see.

I glanced out the window to where driveway melted into darkness. Charly wasn't back yet, but she had thirteen minutes to make her ten o'clock curfew. *Come on, Charly.* I didn't want to see whether or not Grandma would actually ground her for homecoming. As expected, Charly had turned down Dean, but a big group of her drama friends were planning to go together. She'd be pissed if Grandma kept her home.

I tossed my English textbook on my bed and wandered downstairs to where Grandma was pinning pattern pieces to fabric, humming while she worked.

"Another apron?"

She took a pin out of her mouth and slid it through the tissue paper into the fabric. "For Myrna's daughter."

"Pretty," I said, running my finger along the floral print. Shalya would hate it. She's a hairstylist at Tremonton's one and only salon, and wears animal print and feather boas daily—not as a costume or a joke. But Grandma has always been better at buying fabric she thinks people should like than buying fabric that they actually like.

Grandma smoothed the wrinkles out of the last pattern piece, her face unusually soft under the yellow kitchen light.

Her chin-length silver hair was tucked neatly behind each ear, and her lips were pursed in concentration.

She motioned for the pincushion just out of her reach, so I picked it up and held it out.

"When did your sister say she'd be back? She isn't answering her phone."

Cover for me. Like it was that easy to fend off one of Grandma's interrogations.

"Eleven. She said she was going to ask you if she could stay out late to rehearse for play tryouts. Did she forget?"

Grandma frowned and took a pin from the cushion. "Yes. Eleven is way too late for a school night. She knows that. She's at one of those drama kids' houses?"

I nodded and started rearranging pins according to the color of the ball on the end. Avoiding eye contact was essential. "I think they're rehearsing lines."

"I'm not sure those kids are a good influence on Charlotte," she said. "If she spent half as much time doing her real homework as she does dreaming about *Hollywood* and *Broadway*, maybe her grades wouldn't be so terrible."

Grandma spat out Hollywood and Broadway like they were Sodom and Gomorrah, and I kept arranging pins. It was a stupid lie. Performing arts are not Grandma's thing. I should've said Charly was getting biology help—Charly *should* be getting biology help.

"I worry about that girl," Grandma mumbled, more to herself than me. Then her shears began slicing through the cotton.

It was my moment to say something.

I didn't.

I finished color-coding Grandma's pincushion and kept my mouth shut, because sisters cover for each other. Sisters lie.

Chapter 4

t didn't hit me till morning, till I banged on her door for the third time. Usually by the third attempt I got some sort of response, something along the lines of *go away* or *I hate you*, but not today.

I opened the door to find hurricane aftermath as usual: clothes strewn everywhere, the stench of Cooler Ranch Doritos emanating from an open bag on her dresser, and some kind of magazine collage project under way on her desk. But no Charly. The bed was unmade, but it'd been that way since the last time Grandma had forced her to wash her sheets. Her backpack sat unopened on her pillow, and my new Abercrombie sweater was nowhere to be seen.

She hadn't come home.

Panic pulsed through me like a current of electricity. I rewound to last night. Grandma had gone to bed, then I'd come upstairs and fallen asleep reading that short story for English. I remembered waking up to pee in the middle of the night, but it hadn't occurred to me to check on Charly. I'd just assumed she was back. Or maybe I'd forgotten she was even gone? Whichever. I was *asleep*. Was I supposed to be babysitting her in my sleep?

My hand trembled as I closed the door. Grandma was in Tallahassee. Dad was in Atlanta. And Charly was . . . somewhere.

I closed my eyes and there was the Jeep, crumpled and twisted and strewn across the highway, glass everywhere. And then I pictured blood. My mouth felt watery and the taste of vomit crawled its way up my throat. Why had I let her go? She was dangerous enough behind the wheel in broad daylight, driving through residential Tremonton. But freeway driving at night?

And I'd lied to Grandma.

I took a shaky breath. I had to slow down. This was Charly, which meant the list of possible explanations was long and crazy. No need to jump straight to dead in a ditch. She could easily have fallen asleep at the party, or gone home with a friend, or done any number of stupid but not life-threatening things that prevented her from coming home. She knew about Grandma's appointment, so maybe she'd even planned on staying out all night.

But she would have called.

If she showed up at school like nothing had happened, I was going to kill her.

I marched back to my room and looked out the window. No Jeep. Had Grandma's car been in the driveway last night? I couldn't remember. If so, Charly would've parked in the garage. I called Charly's number, but it went straight to voicemail. Not surprising. Charging her phone would have required a single functioning brain cell. I chucked my phone onto my pillow and it bounced off, clattering onto the floor. I ran downstairs to check the garage and confirm what I already knew. The Jeep wasn't there.

I got ready for school fast, forcing myself to think about my day. This was game day, not freaking out day. I had to focus. A bagel, orange juice, a hard-boiled egg, a cheese stick, pretzels, apple, nuts—I tossed the food in a bag, thinking carb, carb, protein, fat, carb, carb, protein. Fueling is a fine art, and I wasn't going to let Charly and her constant screwing around and inability to think about anyone else distract me.

I called Savannah.

"Can you give me a ride to school?"

"Sure," she said. "Jeep trouble?"

"No. Charly took it. She . . . long story." It didn't make sense, not wanting to tell Savannah. But she'd think I was a terrible person for not calling Grandma and Dad and the cops and the entire world. She didn't know what being Charly's sister is like. If I ratted Charly out now, then she just showed up at school, we'd both be in trouble for no reason.

I waited outside her first period algebra class, watching everyone go in until Ms. Barrett came over to close the door. "Amelia, don't you have a class to get to?"

"Yes, ma'am." I turned to leave.

I was halfway into the stairwell when Ms. Barrett called, "And where is your sister?"

I pretended not to hear.

I was five minutes late for Chem, but I may as well have not gone at all. I didn't hear a thing. The image of twisted steel and blood-soaked asphalt kept flickering in my mind, and my chest felt like someone was squeezing it. There had to be an explanation. She was somewhere, safe and oblivious in her self-absorbed little way.

She wasn't at her second period class either. Or third.

Tell.

But how much? And who? I was frozen, coasting toward a red light, and back when it was yellow I'd been too gutless to floor it or to slam on the brakes.

Savannah found me by my locker before English,

holding the lock but not turning the dial. One more class till lunch. Charly was not late. Charly was not coming.

"What's the matter? You look terrible. Are you going to throw up?"

"No. Maybe."

"Here, come with me." She pulled me into the girls' bathroom.

"I'm not going to throw up. I . . . I'm just sort of freaking out. I did something really stupid."

"Take a sip," she said, handing me one of the water bottles from her backpack. Hydration was key in her Operation Squeeze into Homecoming Dress. "You can tell me."

A timid-looking sophomore appeared from one of the stalls. Savannah glared at her and she skulked out, too scared to wash her hands.

"Charly's sort of missing." Hearing the words come out of my mouth made my chest tighten and my stomach drop. "I thought she'd be at school, but I can't find her anywhere."

"Wait, missing? What do you mean?"

"She didn't come home last night. And I didn't tell anyone."

The door to the bathroom opened and a couple of freshmen tried to come in.

"Out," Savannah ordered, then turned back to me. "Okay, back up. How'd she get past the jailer?"

"Grandma left for Tallahassee really early this morning for a doctor's appointment, so I didn't even see her. And last night I kind of lied to her about why Charly was out late. I said she was practicing her audition stuff. You know, for the play."

Savannah shook her head, eyes wide. I had to look away.

"So where'd she actually go?" Savannah asked.

I stared at the cracked white tile behind her. It looked like a spider web. Or a broken windshield. "To Baldwin. For a party. She took the Jeep and she's such a crappy driver and I just have this terrible feeling she, I don't know, crashed it, and she's hurt or worse and—"

"Stop!" Savannah's hands on my shoulders jolted me out of my babbling. Was she going to hug me? That would be weird. I'm not the hugging type. Then again, I'm not the on-the-verge-of-tears type either. "Take a deep breath."

I swallowed and tried, but my chest was too tight.

She swung her backpack off her back and pulled her keys out of the pocket. "Take my car. Drive straight home. Call your grandma on the way and tell her everything. If Charly isn't there when you get home, call the police. Got it?"

I nodded, gripping the keys so tight they dug into my palm. "But you aren't allowed to lend out your car."

"Amelia, your sister is missing. I'm pretty sure my dad would understand."

Of course he would. This was an emergency. Anyone would have seen that when they woke up this morning, or anyone who wasn't so self-absorbed as to think a field hockey game was more important than her sister's life.

"Go," she said.

I stumbled out of the bathroom, too dazed to say thank you.

I called Grandma from the road. She was driving too, and I could hear the murmur of Christian talk radio in the background as I stumbled through my confession.

I waited for her anger. That's what I wanted, to be yelled at. I deserved it.

But she didn't yell. Instead, she told me in a shaky voice to go home and wait for her, and that she'd call the police. From the woman who was scared of nothing, I got naked fear. Anger would have been so much better.

"What about Dad?" I whispered.

She exhaled into the phone, but it was more like a shudder. We both knew it. If something had happened to Charly, it would kill Dad. "I'll call him after we talk to the police. Pray for your sister."

I hung up.

When I broke my arm in eighth grade, I didn't cry.

And when I broke my heart in eleventh, I didn't cry then either. Charly thought there was something wrong with me, like my tear ducts didn't function, or I was part robot, but I was proud of it. It was a choice.

But suddenly my shoulders were shaking, and terrible animal-moaning sounds were coming out of my mouth. I couldn't even try to hold them in, and the tears burned lines down my cheeks while snot dripped onto my lip. I was barely aware enough to wipe it away with my sleeve.

What would my life be like without Charly? I couldn't imagine. But then I forced myself. It would be colorless. Pointless. Empty. If only I'd refused to let her have the car like I knew I should have, she'd be safe at school right now, cheating on a math quiz or belting out some show tune in the cafeteria.

The helplessness made me want to scream, but convulsive sobs had already stolen my body and I couldn't reclaim it. Grandma said pray. What kind of Christian was I? Why was that the last thing to come to mind? *Please, Jesus, save my sister. Let her not be dead. Let her not have killed herself in a car wreck, or have been abducted by a sicko, or hit by a drunk driver. Please don't take her like you took my mother. Dad will never forgive me.*

By the time I pulled onto our street, my jaw and neck ached from contorting my face, and I felt like I might throw up.

And then I saw the Jeep. Whole. Red paint shiny as ever, parked in the driveway beside the palmetto trees, exactly where it belonged.

For one second, all the terror burned away, leaving the sweetest, brightest feeling in the entire world radiating through my body. Charly was alive.

Two seconds, three seconds, four seconds.

By the time I threw Savannah's car into park, five seconds had passed, and I was homicidal. I sprinted two steps at a time up the front porch, up the stairs to the second floor, down the hall toward the bathroom and the sound of the shower.

The bathroom door was locked. I banged with both fists. She *never* locked the door when she showered, and she was obviously the only one home anyway. She must have sensed I was coming to kill her. I kept pounding on the door, fists clenched so tight my nails dug into my flesh. She could hear me, I *knew* she could hear me, but the shower just kept on roaring.

I stopped, took a step backward, and sunk to the floor with my back against the wall. My heart pounded in my ears as I struggled to catch my breath. Charly was in there. She was enjoying a leisurely shower. I'd just been to hell and back, and she was exfoliating.

Eventually, the shower stopped. She could hear me now if I yelled, but I wasn't going to. I'd wait. My fists were still sore from the banging and my head throbbed from the crying—I wasn't going to scream myself hoarse too.

When she finally opened the door, she was wrapped in her towel, hair a wet, tangled mess on her shoulders. She didn't even look at me, just stepped over my feet and started down the hall.

"Are you kidding me?" I shouted. "Where do you think you're going?"

"To my room." She sounded tired or bored. I was *boring* her.

"No, you're not. Where have you been?"

She turned around and stared at me. Her face was puffy, eyes bloodshot.

"Oh, I see. Under a keg."

"Whatever."

"Not whatever!" I stood up and followed her into her room. "I thought you were dead in a ditch somewhere! I spent all morning looking for you. I lied to Grandma!"

"You lied to Grandma?" Her eyes widened with relief. "Oh, thank you, Jesus."

"No, thank you, *Amelia*. And Grandma knows now."

"What? Why? You said you would cover for me!"

"I did! And then I realized I was covering for someone who was probably dead or kidnapped or who knows what and I got scared. Grandma is *totally* freaked out. She may have already called the police."

Charly slapped her forehead with her palm and moaned. "Why would you do that?"

"Savannah made me realize you might be in trouble."

"You're taking orders from Savannah? That girl is a fourth-generation cheerleader."

"Yeah, and she's ten times smarter than you! This is all your fault. *You* didn't come home, *you* didn't call, *you* didn't care about anybody but yourself—and now you're blaming Savannah? Unbelievable."

She winced.

"I'M SORRY, IS THE VOLUME OF MY VOICE HURTING YOUR ALCOHOL-SOAKED BRAIN?" I screamed.

She scowled. "Calm. Down. Amelia."

How dare she pretend I'm the emotional one. I took a controlled breath. "Fine. Explain."

A beam of sunshine sliced through the clouds and the glass, cutting her face in half. She squinted and turned away, like the light was piercing her skull. "I fell asleep. I forgot to charge my phone. That's it. I'm sorry."

It took everything in me to keep from reaching out and grabbing a handful of wet hair.

"*Fell asleep?* Are you kidding me? Is that what we're calling *passed-out drunk* now?"

She opened her mouth to respond, but the sound of tires on gravel stopped her.

I smiled bitterly. "Good luck."

"What's that supposed to mean?"

"Grandma's going to kill you," I said. "And you totally deserve it."

The front door opened and slammed. "Amelia?" Grandma yelled. "Charlotte?" Her voice sounded hard, not shaky like it had on the phone. She'd seen the Jeep out front.

"We're up here," I called.

Charly looked at me and I realized, too late, that the teams were all wrong. It was always us versus her.

Propelled by rage, Grandma climbed the stairs fast, and stood before us in pink lipstick and a floral dress—full doctor's appointment regalia. Anger pinched her thin face, making it even more severe than usual.

"This had better be good," she said, pointing a shaky finger at Charly.

"I was at a friend's house. I fell asleep."

"Not good enough. Whose house?"

"Katie. From work." Charly's words were quiet and empty, like they weren't coming from her. I didn't even think there was a Katie.

Grandma glared in my direction and I couldn't help it, I winced under it. "So not a friend from school? Not practicing for the audition?"

I opened my mouth to explain, or not to explain, but

to lie, except a plausible lie, like *that's not what she told me!*
didn't come. I just stood there, mouth open.

She turned back to Charly. "Why didn't you call? Did
you even think about how worried we would be?" Her
glossed lips trembled as she spoke.

"My phone was dead. I forgot to charge it."

"And this *Katie* has no phone at her house? How about
electricity? Running water? From the looks of you, she at
least had plenty of alcohol. Thank goodness."

"Sorry." But she didn't sound sorry. Charly usually
groveled her way through trouble, but apparently the
booze had drained the grovel out of her.

I closed my eyes to brace for it, but even still, the
crack of skin on skin, Grandma's palm on Charly's cheek,
knocked the breath out of me. Charly reached up to cradle
her face in her hand, and I couldn't not stare at the rash
that bloomed between her fingers.

"Not sorry enough. You're grounded for a month."

Charly didn't respond, just stood with her back bent
and her hand on her cheek.

"And you," Grandma said, turning to me. "One week
for lying."

"But homecoming," I sputtered. "I have a—"

"No homecoming, no play rehearsals, no sports, no
hanging out with friends for either of you."

"*What?*" I yelled, forgetting myself, forgetting Grandma,

forgetting Charly's flaming cheek. "I have a game today! You can't ground me from that!"

"Don't tell me what I can't do," she said. "And don't ever use that tone with me again. I expect more from you."

"But I'm team captain," I said, bringing my tone down to pleading.

"I don't care who you think you are. You're grounded."

My mind went white, a searing-hot white, and I shut my eyes to push back the tears. *Don't cry again, don't cry again.* "But they'll lose without me."

Grandma snorted. "I'm glad to see your confidence is intact, but your principal has an attendance policy on game days, doesn't he? Do I need to remind you that you're cutting class right now?"

Panic tightened the muscles in my chest. I was cutting class. I, Amelia Mercer, the girl who'd never missed a day of school for a nonmedical reason, had just walked out the front doors in the middle of the day, like I was allowed to. Blackburn's no-exception attendance policy for school sports—*full day or no play*—hadn't even occurred to me. I'd been too busy freaking out over Charly, the crumpled Jeep, her mangled body. Nothing else had mattered.

Coach Hershey was going to kill me. If she didn't, my teammates would. I felt a sob coming and swallowed it.

"Now, I would hate to ruin your father's trip with

this." Grandma raised her eyebrows and everything was understood.

Her anger stung, but Dad's disappointment would be so much worse. There were expectations. He loved Charly because she was sweet and me because I was good. He didn't need to know that his adorable darling had been out all night boozing, and I, the one he could count on, had lied and lied and lied.

Charly nodded. I nodded.

"Don't make me regret that decision," she said.

We listened to the click of her heels on hardwood, down the hall, down the stairs, and to her bedroom.

Now I could cry, but the sob I'd swallowed was gone. *No game. No homecoming.*

Charlie crawled onto her bed and collapsed, not even caring about her wet hair on the pillow, or that the towel had slipped and she was more than half-naked.

"So tired," she mumbled.

"I can't believe you did this to me," I hissed. *"I hate you."*

She didn't even open her eyes.

Being ignored hurt even more. So I said it. "Mom would be so ashamed of you."

No response.

Chapter 5

We lost the game by one goal. One goal. That meant that for several weeks it was hard to find a single person in Tremonton who wasn't pissed at me. Coach Hershey, the girls on the team, their families, friends, boyfriends, cousins, dog walkers—it was like I'd personally insulted all of them, which in Tremonton meant I was getting my change in pennies at the gas station and having my burgers spit into at DQ. At least I'm pretty sure they were being spit into.

The real problem was that the guys lost the football game, so there was anger in the air. I was just a convenient target. Never mind that the average idiot thought field hockey was a nonevent, just a bunch of girls running around in short skirts, glorified cheerleaders with sticks and mouth guards. No, suddenly my "shocking lack of dedication to Primrose High" was to blame for the entire homecoming humiliation.

Those were Coach Hershey's words. *Shocking lack of dedication.*

She had every right to be mad, and she was. First thing Friday morning she informed me that she'd decided to reevaluate team leadership, and that Nadia Pinsky would be finishing out the season as captain. Nadia freaking Pinsky.

Savannah and Sebastian were ticked too. Not about the game, but about the dance. When I'd called Nick and explained, he'd sounded relieved more than anything, but Savannah was annoyed I wasn't going to the dance to see her crowned Homecoming Princess or whatever, and Sebastian was annoyed that I'd annoyed Savannah.

Who else? Oh yeah, Grandma. She followed up my week of grounding with a double helping of passive aggression. The silent treatment.

Dad was the exception. He wasn't angry, but only because he didn't know what I'd done, and he was too out of it to feel the tension in the air. He'd caught a cold on the airplane coming home, and colds always knock him flat for a few weeks. Something about his unusually small sinus cavity, he claimed.

Three weeks after homecoming, Charly and I still weren't talking. At first I'd been too angry to keep it civil, so when Dad was around it was smart just not to speak to each other. And at some point, the silence between us had hardened into something solid. The few words we did exchange were meaningless.

"Pass the milk," I mumbled one evening over reheated casserole. We were eating dinner alone. Grandma was at her Bible study group and Dad was at the Tremonton Horticulture Center for a citrus presentation (he was determined to force the lime tree to produce an actual lime this year).

She didn't even look up.

"I said, pass me the freaking milk!"

"Wow, freaking? Listen to you." She nudged the jug about an inch toward me. "Amelia the rebel."

I stood up, walked to her end of the table, and jerked the jug fast enough to slosh milk onto her open *People* magazine.

"Come on! Really?" She picked up the magazine, shook it, then put it back down. "Did you seriously just do that?"

Pour it on her.

My heart was racing. She deserved it. I was so sick of the sullen and wounded act, just because she didn't get to try out for the play, like it wasn't her own fault. She wiped the milk droplets from the page with her sleeve and scowled at me.

Pour it on her.

She more than deserved it—she needed it. Charly had spent the last three weeks shrinking into something that wasn't Charly at all. She didn't even look like herself. Her hair was beyond greasy and she was breaking out, like she was too busy moping to keep up with basic hygiene? Give me a break. And at school, when she should have been getting her social fill for the day, she'd been cranky with Dean and downright mean to Liam and Asha since play rehearsals had started. I don't know why they were all still following her around. A good milk bath might shock her back into herself, or at least force her to take a shower and wash her face.

Pour it on her.

But even with my brain screaming at me, I couldn't do it. Retaliation would be certain, and our method of hating was pretty stable. This was war, and there were rules. The first week had been crazy fighting—screaming till my throat burned, two actual shoving matches, no punches or hair pulling, though books and shoes were thrown—but that was over. We weren't screaming at each other, we weren't pulling each other's hair, and we weren't pouring milk on each other.

I poured the milk into my glass instead and screwed the cap back on. Less temptation.

If she would just snap out of it, we could go back to the way things were. Maybe not immediately, but eventually. I was still mad, but three weeks was a long time.

"So are you coming over tonight?" Savannah asked.

I shifted the phone to my other ear so I could reach for the colander.

"Can't. The choir concert is tonight, remember?"

"Oh yeah. Sorry. I probably should've known that. You want me to come?"

I thought about it for a second. It would be nice if she came, but it didn't really sound like she wanted to. Besides, Dad and Grandma would be there. "No. It's not like I'm going to be singing a solo."

"Not intentionally, anyway."

"Ha." She was right, though. Not being heard was my goal for the night. Dr. Kinzer's constant advice was *Blend, Amelia, blend!* but what she meant was *Lip-sync, Amelia, lip-sync!* She'd probably breathe a sigh of relief if I didn't show.

"We'll miss you," she said. "No slasher movie marathon is complete without the Mercer sisters. Hey, does Charly still want to come or is she going to hear you sing?"

I forced a laugh. Charly was not going to my concert. Her grounding had ended two weeks ago, but nothing had changed. We still weren't talking, or at least not civilly.

Six weeks. It wasn't supposed to last this long.

"You know how much Charly hates scary movies," I said, and grabbed a wooden spoon to break up the browning chunks of hamburger. "If I'm not dragging her, she won't go."

"But who's going to scream their head off and eat all the brownies?"

"I guess you." Since successfully cramming herself into her homecoming dress, Savannah had replaced the carrots in her diet with chocolate. She looked the same size to me, but less orange. "I'd better get off the phone. I'm cooking dinner and my grandma's going to be home any minute."

"Yikes."

Savannah had been afraid of Grandma since we were eleven and Grandma had yelled at us during a sleepover for playing teddy bear taster and destroying the kitchen. In Grandma's defense, it was three a.m., but that had scarred their relationship for life. I'd spent six years trying to convince Savannah that Grandma wasn't that scary, but she wasn't buying it.

"See ya," I said.

"Bye."

I put the phone down and pulled the marinara sauce out of the fridge.

The doorbell rang. I glanced out the front window and saw the brown of the UPS truck.

"Get the door," I yelled.

No answer, just the sound of TV laughter. *America's Funniest Home Videos* again. She couldn't get enough of it, even though every single episode was identical, not to mention geared toward pubescent boys. Really, how many times could she watch the same set of crotch shots and still find them hysterical?

"Get the door!" I yelled louder. "It's UPS. They might need a signature."

"Get it yourself," she called back.

"Excuse me?"

"You're closer."

I dropped the wooden spoon into the sink, splattering droplets of marinara all over, and stomped to the front door. I glared at the dorky guy in his dorky brown get-up, signed for the package, then marched over to where Charly was sprawled on the couch.

"How about getting off your butt and helping for once? I'm making *your* dinner."

"Not my dinner," she said, digging around in the bottom of a bag of barbecue chips. She pulled out a handful of orange crumbs. "Whatever you're cooking smells like vomit."

"It does not. It's hamburger."

"Hamburger you puked into? It's making me want to throw up just smelling it," she said, then licked the salty seasoning off her fingers. Her tongue was stained orange too.

"So don't eat it. Go up to your room like you do every night and leave me to eat alone with the old people."

"Thanks for the permission. You can go back to cooking your vomit-burger." Her eyes were back on the screen.

"No, I've had it with this. Snap out of it! You aren't grounded anymore. Listen, I'm sorry I said Mom would be ashamed of you. It was six weeks ago. Get over it!"

She rolled her eyes. The whites would've been visible from fifty feet.

I took a deep breath through my nose and tried to calm myself down without looking like I was trying to calm myself down. It didn't matter. She was still staring at the TV.

"That's right, Amelia. Take deep breaths. Maybe that'll help you control the universe."

"Why are you acting like this?" I asked.

"Because I don't want to miss my show playing butler."

"You know what I mean."

Her face was a wall. She grabbed the remote and made deliberate jabs at the TV as she turned up the volume three bars.

Without thinking, I crossed the room, grabbed the remote, and chucked it. It bounced across the wooden floor and slid underneath Dad's recliner just as the smoke alarm started to shriek. She yelled a string of words that definitely called for Grandma's bar of soap, while I sprinted to the kitchen and yanked the pan off the stove.

It didn't matter. The hamburger was already burned.

I didn't have time to dump it before Grandma came home, so we had to eat it anyway. Scorched, rubbery meat in watery sauce over spaghetti clumps.

Dad alone was spared the food and the bad dinner table vibe. He called to say someone came by the church and really needed to talk. That was the difficult part of pastoring, he always said, being willing to give himself to anyone's life crisis.

The choir concert went well by Dr. Kinzer's standards: We didn't forget our words or mix up our entrances, and nobody (meaning me) made a fool of themselves singing loudly and out of tune.

From the top left section of the riser where she'd placed me, I could see Will. He was in the second row, looking kind of dorky in a black shirt and blue tie combo, with a big grin. I'd always made sure he didn't wear crap like that. Luciana had a solo in one of the songs, so he, no doubt, wanted to be able to see and hear her.

I could see Grandma too, with an empty chair next to her for Dad. No Charly, of course. Grandma smiled. For a moment, I forgot how mad I was at her and smiled back. Charly could ruin dinner and keep on hating me, and Dad could get held up saving someone's soul, but nothing changed Grandma.

That night I lay in bed and stared at my computer monitor, too tired to get up and turn it off. My screen saver was set to slideshow, so I watched the last two years (since I'd gotten my own camera) flicker by. There was one of Dad and Charly hunting for shells at Santa Rosa Beach. Then one of Grandma braiding Charly's hair last Halloween. She'd gone as a Viking, complete with horn hat and sword.

The next one made me laugh. I couldn't help it. It caught me off guard. It was of just Charly, from the beginning of last summer, and she had a powdered donut hole wedged in her mouth, the sugar all over her face. She was wearing a tank top and frayed jean cutoffs, and stood beside her bike, with her right arm poised like she was about to hurl the donut hole in her hand at the camera.

The picture was from before the golf course tan and the losers from Baldwin, when we had nothing better to do than putz around and ride bikes to Dunkin' Donuts. Seconds after the picture was taken she'd decided to start chucking holes off Tremonton's one and only overpass. I'd pulled the box away from her and sped off before she could get us both arrested.

I didn't even recognize that girl.

The picture changed to a close-up of Will and me before a youth dance at the church. He hated dancing, but he always took me to the dances anyway, just because he knew I loved them. He would only dance the slow ones, and spent most of those whispering stupid jokes in my ear. I loved those stupid jokes.

I got up and turned off the monitor.

"Are you awake?"

I blinked. Charly's voice had reached into my dreams like a hand and yanked me out.

The moonlight from the window was just enough to see her outline as she made her way across the room.

"No."

She crawled clumsily over me and flopped down between my body and the wall. The bed bounced like a trampoline, springs squealing. I was still too much asleep to be properly confused by her wandering into my room and crawling into bed to talk like she used to.

"What do you want?" I asked. I sounded more annoyed than I wanted to. This was something, wasn't it? Her coming to talk.

"I don't know."

We lay there, just listening to ourselves breathe, staring at the star stickers on the ceiling. They'd been there for seven years. We'd put them up together, before

Charly had moved across the hall, but we'd run out of stickers so they were mostly clustered above my bed.

A minute passed. Maybe two. It felt like twenty.

"I want to tell you something," she said finally, "but I need you to guess so I can just say yes or no."

"Why?"

"Just because."

"Not an answer."

"Because I don't want to say it out loud."

"But how am I supposed to guess it?"

She paused. I felt her cross her arms beside me. "Something's wrong with me."

"As in you're sick?"

"Yes. No."

"Pick one."

"Not officially."

"But you think you have a disease or something?"

"I wish."

"Good to know your inner drama queen is still intact."

I looked over at her. Even in the dark I could see she was pale, almost greyish, and her skin looked like it was draped over her cheeks, making shadows beneath them. Gaunt, that was the word. Maybe she was doing drugs. Liam and Asha smoked pot, and I wouldn't be surprised if those idiots from Baldwin did meth. Except Charly hadn't even seen them in forever. She hadn't seen anyone.

It was my job to ask. I knew it. And she'd asked me to, but I didn't want to say the words, because she just might answer.

"Charly, are you on drugs?" I closed my eyes tight.

"No."

"Are you lying?"

"No."

Thank you, God. "Then why do you look so pale?"

"Because I've thrown up every day for the last two weeks."

Bulimia. The word exploded in my brain like fireworks. I hadn't seen anything—how had I not seen *anything*? She didn't look any skinnier, and she ate crap, but that wasn't new. Skittles, Little Debbie cupcakes, onion rings—she'd always been proud of her junk food addiction. How'd I miss the purging?

It didn't make sense. She'd never been one of those girls who cared, the ones like Savannah, who ordered salad with no dressing and Diet Coke and knew exactly how many calories thirty minutes on the elliptical trainer burned. Charly was just thin.

I was the worst sister in the entire world.

Thalia French came to mind. She was PHS's poster child for eating disorders. Thalia stood down a row and to my left in choir, close enough for me to see her knobby arms, like flamingo legs, and her buggy eyes when she turned to the side. Her jaw looked too big for her face, and the skin hung loose around her mouth.

I turned back to Charly, who was still staring at the ceiling. She looked nothing like Thalia. Yet. I wanted to yell at her, grab her arms and shake her hard, but I stopped myself. She'd come to me for help, not a freak-out. Besides, an eating disorder wasn't something I could shake out of her.

"Why would you do that to yourself?" I asked. "You need to stop it. *Now*."

"It's not like I can just stop it."

"You have to. Sticking your finger down your throat every day is crazy and dangerous. Look at Thalia. She's like a skin-wrapped skeleton. People die of bulimia, Charly."

"*What?* I'm not sticking my finger down my throat. That's disgusting."

I paused, taking in the change in her tone. She'd gone from tragic to outraged in a second. "I know it's disgusting. You're the one who just said you were puking every day."

"Because I have *morning sickness*."

The stars above me, the ones that hadn't moved in seven years, suddenly quivered and slid across my view. I blinked. Back in place.

"Morning sickness," she said again, "but not really in the morning."

I wanted to reach out and put my hand over her mouth, but it was heavy and numb by my side. My whole body was paralyzed.

"It's all day," she said. "It's every time I'm not stuffing food down my throat, but the food doesn't even taste good and I think I want it, but then once I'm eating it I realize it isn't what I wanted at all, and I just want to puke it up. . . ." She trailed off weakly.

I followed the melody of her voice, listening but not listening, twirling around inside her words and keeping my eyes on the stars, holding them in place with my gaze so they wouldn't slide again. The air-conditioning was turned up too high, and the sweat dripping down my sides into the small of my back had turned cold. Shivering, I pulled the sheet up around my shoulders.

"Aren't you going to say anything?" she asked. I could hear a shimmer of panic in her voice.

I didn't want to say anything. As long as I didn't take her words and assign them meaning, I wouldn't have to see the cataclysmically stupid thing she'd done.

"What am I supposed to say?" My voice was hollow. "I don't even understand what you're saying."

"Yes, you do."

Morning sickness.

I wasn't going to say it for her. She couldn't just hint and suggest around it, so that I was the one who had to say it and make it real.

Morning sickness.

My heart and my stomach dropped down down down

through my body and the bed and the floor, leaving me empty. *Charly. You idiot.*

"Say it." My voice sounded flat and hard in my own ears, but I couldn't infuse life into it. Everything had already drained out of me.

"I can't."

"Yes, you can. Say it, or I won't help you."

"I'm pregnant."

I felt nothing. I rolled onto my side and looked at her. She was chewing her bottom lip, staring at the same fake stars. And she was wearing the silver hoops Savannah had bought me for my birthday. Not that she'd asked if she could borrow them.

That's when the flood of sadness fell on me, forcing the air out of my lungs, crushing every bone in my body. And that casing of anger I'd built around myself, I could feel the brittle shell crack and six weeks of hating just shatter and fall like broken glass.

Pregnant. That wasn't even physically possible. It's not like I was totally naive, despite Dad's refusal to sign the sex ed waivers every year. I'd been sent to the library to do projects on careers in the arts or money management, but I'd gotten all the info from Savannah later on, and I'd made sure Charly knew.

But it was impossible for a virgin to be pregnant, and Charly was a virgin. Like me. Like Dad and Grandma and

God expected us to be. She didn't even have a boyfriend, and that wasn't something she could've hidden from me. I would have known. She'd told me every single detail of her relationship with Finn Grier last winter, from first glance and first kiss to final fight. She would've told me if she was seeing someone, and even if she hadn't, I would have seen.

"I'm pregnant," she said again.

"No, you're not. That's not funny. You've never even had sex."

She shuddered, brought her knees to her chest and hugged them, eyes closed.

"Right?"

She didn't answer. She started to cry. I watched her, forcing myself not to close my eyes or plug my ears. I kept watching, even when it got ugly, when the crying became gasps and sobs and gulps, and I was dying to pull her to me and squeeze her until it wasn't true. Or roll out of bed and run away from her and this feeling.

I'm pregnant. Those words ended everything.

"Dean?" I asked.

"What? No. Of course not." She wiped her face on the sleeve of her shirt and hiccupped. "He's nobody. It doesn't matter. He doesn't know about it, and I'm not going to tell him."

"*What?*"

She shook her head, and wrapped her arms back around her knees. "Trust me, he doesn't want to know."

I looked away so she wouldn't see the disgust in my eyes. I couldn't help it. I was just so . . . disappointed. Except that word didn't hold half of what I felt. She wasn't who I thought she was. Definitely not who Dad thought she was.

Anger flickered somewhere inside of me.

"Since when . . . ," I started, feeling the flame spread. "I mean, why didn't you tell me you were having sex, and what . . . I mean, I just can't believe you've been doing this behind my back. Dad is . . . and Grandma . . ."

"I know."

"You *know*? No, you don't! You don't know anything! If you'd thought for one second about what you were doing, if you'd even once considered what it would do to Dad and to Grandma, *then* you'd know. And you wouldn't have done it."

She had no response.

"But you did do it, because the only thing you really *know* is that you're the center of the universe."

It was true, and I wasn't going to feel bad about saying it just because she was all curled up and wounded and crying. "You know what you are now? A statistic. Another pregnant sixteen-year-old. You should give MTV a call and see if they'll take you. Oh, and not just any pregnant sixteen-year-old, but a pastor's daughter—an *abstinence*-preaching pastor's daughter."

"I know, but—"

"The entire world already points their fingers at us and thinks we're religious freaks, and now you're fuel for their fire. You're making us all look pathetic and ignorant."

"You think I don't know that?"

"I have no *clue* what goes on inside your head. This'll kill Dad. I'm assuming you at least get that, right? And Grandma will be too humiliated to leave the house for the next decade. Have you even thought about the gossip? The entire congregation—no, all of Tremonton—is going to be talking about this forever. You can't just ride this out. The pastor's daughter isn't allowed to get knocked up."

I paused to breathe. My voice had gotten loud without me noticing and the silence burned my ears. No answer from Charly, but the crying had stopped. I almost wished it hadn't. I needed to feel her hurting, for what she was doing to all of us.

"A *baby*, Charly," I whispered. "That's forever. Your life is over."

"I know."

"So what are you going to do?"

Silence. Then finally, "I don't know. Whatever you tell me to do."

Of course. It was on me, because it always is. A thousand scenes flew by, of strawberries and sugar in the black walnut tree, of painting our legs with mud after rain, of tanning on the dock by the lake in matching summer bikinis. They kept on coming, swirling together like a spinning pinwheel until they weren't separate anymore.

Chapter 6

We had to tell Grandma. Unless we weren't going to tell Grandma. Because as soon as Grandma knew, we'd lose an option. The option we weren't saying out loud.

"Are you sure?" I asked.

"Of course I'm sure." She was chewing her raw lower lip.

"Stop doing that. It's going to start bleeding again."

She stopped.

We were standing in the bathroom, pretending to get ready for school. I was already done, and Charly was looking bad regardless.

"Because that's the only way that nobody would know," I added.

"I know that. But it's still . . . you know."

I nodded. Murder. We weren't saying that word either. It'd been three days and we weren't even saying pregnant anymore. Amazing the things we could talk about without saying.

"Yeah," I said, wishing I could disagree. I just wished I didn't. I kept hoping that if I reasoned it through, I would be able to come to a different moral conclusion, that there was a loophole no one had thought to mention. One that made abortion for immature idiots permissible.

"So why do you keep bringing it up?" she asked.

"I just want you to think through every possibility."

"That's not what it feels like to me."

I rubbed the back of my neck, but my tension headache ignored the effort. "Then what does it feel like to you, Charly?"

"It feels like you just want this all to go away, and that it doesn't matter that it's all on me. But it's, you know . . . my *soul*, right?"

"All on you? Of course it is. You're the one who got herself pregnant."

She grimaced at the word.

"Yeah. I said it."

That shut her up for a minute. She stared at herself

in the mirror, grumbled and pulled her hair elastic out again. She'd been trying to put her wet hair up in a ponytail for the last five minutes, but kept ending up with bubbles.

Tears welled in her eyes. This was the third time today, or at least the third time I'd seen. I took a pick from the drawer and fished some detangler out from under the sink. "Kneel," I said. She obeyed and I started spritzing.

I took a section of wet curls and tugged through it with the pick. Right and wrong were so much clearer from a distance, or in a sermon, or in somebody else's life. But this was so muddy, I couldn't even see Charly in it, and she was right in front of me.

I used to know exactly what kind of girl got pregnant, and exactly what kind of girl got an abortion, and Charly wasn't either. Except Charly *was* pregnant. So either I didn't know who she was at all, or she was an exception to the rule—accidentally shuffled into the teenage slut category.

"Dad would never forgive me if he found out."

"Probably not." Not to mention God. "But that's the point. Dad and Grandma and everyone else wouldn't have to find out."

"Yeah, but I'd go to hell. Right?"

"How am I supposed to know?"

"I don't know. You think you know everything else.

And you're the one who keeps bringing it up."

"So now I'm trying to lead you down to hell? Maybe if you'd been a little more concerned about your soul's destination in the first place we wouldn't be here."

Charly ignored me. I yanked through a knot.

"Ouch."

"Did you even use conditioner?"

"No. My hair has been so greasy lately, I thought it would help."

Greasy hair. Another symptom to add to the nauseating list of complaints. There was the vomiting, the dizziness, the sore boobs, the crazy dreams, the crying, the exhaustion, the hot flashes, the freaky veins, and they just kept right on coming. I'd been in the know for three days, and already it was getting old. Buying her a diary was number one on my list of things to do, just so she could have somewhere else to park her symptoms.

"And my skin," she muttered at the mirror.

"Your skin looks fine." Her face was a pimply mess, but I couldn't handle more tears.

She took a deep breath and met my eyes in the mirror. "I don't know how God ranks sins, but I'm pretty sure fornication and murder aren't equal. I mean, I'm in trouble, but I'm not . . ."

She reached up and grabbed the pick in my hand. I had no choice but to let go.

"Of course not. You know that's not what I meant."
I didn't think it was what I meant, that she was beyond
forgiveness or redemption or whatever. She couldn't be
damned.

She put the pick on the counter, accepting defeat. "Do
I have time to shower again?"

"No. Pass me that clip," I said, pointing to a big
tortoiseshell claw on the counter. She did and I wrapped
her hair into a lumpy twist.

She inspected it in the mirror. It looked less bad.
"Good enough."

"So. Grandma, then?"

She raised her eyebrows. "You're telling her for me,
right?"

"Hilarious."

She cracked a smile. I saw it and realized—she hadn't
smiled in forever. "I just thought, seeing as she doesn't
already hate you, it might be easier for her to hear it from
you. Ya know?"

"Nice try. The whole easiest-on-Grandma angle is
very clever."

"I thought so too. But you'll be there, though, right?"

I smiled back, but it made my insides hurt. Being angry
was easier. "Of course."

"Okay. Tonight, then."

"Tonight."

• • •

"You're never going to believe who broke up!" Savannah squealed when she found me by my locker.

"Wrong."

"What?"

"I believe ninety-nine percent of these idiots will break up." I glanced around me at the throng of couples, almost-couples, wanting-to-be couples, just-over-being couples. Nobody had staying power. "And the one percent that stay together will wish they hadn't."

She ignored me. "Will and Luciana! And get this: *He* dumped *her*."

I kept rifling through my bag, refusing to give her the satisfaction of seeing my jaw drop. "I swear that lip gloss is in here somewhere." I found it, looked up at her.

She was wide-eyed and grinning, and I resisted the urge to grab her by the shoulders and shake her. Even if Will and Luciana had some huge, mortifying public breakup, it wouldn't change the real reason Will and I couldn't be together. The real reason was . . .

My brain stalled. The real reason was pregnant. Irresistible Charly. Will was way too wholesome and traditional to see *knocked up* Charly the same way. Once he knew, once the world knew, Charly wasn't going to seem so irresistible anymore.

I stopped myself. I had some self-respect—*I'd* refused

to be with Will, *I'd* dumped him because I'd known he would always love Charly.

But that was back before I'd ever dreamed that Charly would be making herself unlovable.

I couldn't help it. I had to imagine what it would be like to have him waiting for me by my locker again, feel his hands on my waist, hear him talk about cross-country like it was a matter of life and death. I could be a much better girlfriend this time. More demonstrative, like he wanted. This time I could hold his hand in the hall without cringing. Maybe even kiss him in public.

"So, you're ignoring me?"

I shrugged. "No. It just doesn't matter."

Savannah shook her head. "Who do you think you're fooling?"

"Everyone."

"Everyone else," she corrected.

"Fine. Everyone else."

"I'm going to be late to World History. See you at lunch?"

"Can't," I said. "I'm helping Dr. Kinzer stock the choir folders. Extra credit."

"You have got to be the only tone deaf person in history to be forcing an A out of Kinzer."

"Yeah." I wasn't listening. *Will and Luciana are over.* "Wait, I'm not tone deaf."

"Sure you aren't. See you later."

A snappy comeback was in order, but I couldn't pull one out. My brain was too strained with Charly and her irreversible mess, and single Will. Too complicated. If I relied on feelings I'd feel . . . who knows.

I slammed my locker and went to class.

We found Grandma that night at the kitchen table doing her crossword puzzle. For some reason, she felt like reading a novel was a frivolous use of her time, but the almighty *NYT* Sunday Crossword was not. By the time she worked her way through a book of puzzles, it was nearly as well worn as her Bible.

Head bowed, immersed in her clues, she could never have seen it coming.

Still, Charly should have set it up better. Not that *how's it going, Grandma?* would have softened the blow anyway. But she was on the verge of chickening out, her hands all jerking and jittery like they get when she's nervous, when suddenly she just folded her arms and smacked Grandma in the face with "I'm pregnant."

I closed my eyes. It was cowardly, but I couldn't make myself watch what was bound to be a mixture of righteous indignation and pure rage. Because Grandma is a fortress, a mighty pillar of strength, a beacon guiding people in their quests for salvation. And also, Grandma gets mad.

But when I opened my eyes, what I saw was steel crumpling like tinfoil.

Her face puckered. She placed her pencil in the spine of her crossword book, removed her glasses, and dropped her head to her arms. Her whole body bounced and shook with silent sobs.

I wanted to sit down beside her and put my arm around her, but I couldn't. She wouldn't want me to acknowledge that this convulsing wreck was (a) her, and (b) in need of my help.

It was Charly—a terrified, wide-eyed version of Charly—who made me. She elbowed me and mouthed *go hug her*.

I shook my head.

She shook her head.

So I slid into the chair beside Grandma and put my arm around her shoulders. She let me, for a few seconds, before she filled her lungs with as much air as she possibly could, sat up straight, and put her glasses back on. My arm fell limply to my side.

"Charlotte, we'll talk about this in the morning. Neither of you are to tell your father."

She stood and walked out of the kitchen, spine straighter than a steeple.

Neither of you are to tell your father. Did she think either of us told him anything? Ever?

I left Charly in the kitchen, walked to the hall, and

looked down to where a sliver of light glowed beneath the den door. I could hear his voice. He was talking to himself.

The next morning I had an early practice (Saturday practices were Coach Hershey's answer to the blitzkrieg launched by Baldwin's Teutonic coach), and when I got back, Charly and Grandma were sitting at the kitchen table, just staring. Grandma was staring at Charly, and Charly was staring at her Froot Loops.

"Good morning, Amelia," Grandma said, voice flat, eyes swollen. "We were just discussing prenatal care. Your sister seems to think babies thrive on high-fructose corn syrup and food dye."

Charly took another bite of cereal.

"You'll be seeing an obstetrician in Tallahassee next week," Grandma said, nodding at Charly, "and we'll buy you some prenatal vitamins while we're there."

"Not Dr. Reed?" I asked, pouring a glass of orange juice and leaning against the counter a safe distance from both of them.

Doctor Reed was Tremonton's only OB. He'd delivered both Charly and me and pretty much every other baby born in Tremonton in the last thirty years.

"No, not Dr. Reed."

Grandma took a rag from the sink and wiped down the already clean countertop.

"They sell prenatal vitamins at the Walgreens," I offered. Will worked at the Walgreens, so I used to spend way too much time wandering the aisles waiting for his shift to end.

"We aren't buying prenatal anything from Walgreens," Grandma said. She sounded tired. "Do you want the entire town to know?"

"No, but . . ." Grandma had to know where this whole thing was going. Charly was going to slowly expand until she was the size of a whale. I'd seen enough *16 and Pregnant* episodes to know it was the skinny girls whose bellies ended up looking like skin-wrapped basketballs.

I shuddered involuntarily.

Grandma looked up at me suddenly, panic lines creasing her forehead. "Where did you buy the pregnancy test from?"

"Me? *I* didn't buy it. I didn't even know she was pregnant until four days ago."

Grandma looked down at Charly, clearly more than a little skeptical of her ability to diagnose herself.

Charly refused to look up from her bowl. She was the only person I knew who ate an entire bowl of Froot Loops by color. A glance over her shoulder revealed a bowl of greens and yellows. She was going to be a mother. This had to stop.

"I bought it in Baldwin," she said, "but I peed on it in Tremonton. Should I not have done that? Do you think maybe people could sense that a pregnancy stick was being peed on somewhere in town and just assumed it was me?"

"This isn't a joke," Grandma said quietly, wiping down the table now, even though it was spotless.

Charly put the spoon down and looked up. The Grandma I knew would have chewed her out.

"Are you ready to be serious?" Grandma asked. She moved to wiping the fronts of the cupboards.

Charly nodded.

"You are not having this baby here. I won't let you break your father's heart, not to mention his credibility as the moral compass of this community. I won't let you become the next Marnie Croll, or Serena Torello." She paused, letting those names sink in.

Marnie was four years older than me, but I used to be friends with her little sister Paula. Once Marnie was pregnant though, Paula and her family stopped going to church regularly so we saw each other a lot less. Marnie had done the "right thing" and married the dad, or at least it was the right thing according to all the conversations I overheard. She didn't graduate with her class, but she did get her GED, so when her eighteen-year-old husband ran off a year later she didn't have to start at minimum wage. She went straight to night manager at the Texaco station, which was not a bad gig, she claimed, when you had a toddler and your mom worked full time and couldn't babysit for you during the day. We talked sometimes when I filled up the Jeep. Grandma didn't like Charly and me hanging out at Paula's anymore.

Serena didn't have it nearly as good. She was my age, but she hadn't seen the inside of PHS since she got pregnant when we were freshmen. Since then she'd had one of those on-again/off-again things with the baby's father that provided the whole town with entertainment. Screaming fights in the Dairy Queen parking lot, the Dollar Store parking lot, the post office parking lot. Grandma's bridge group loved talking about her with sad faces, shaking their heads, because she'd been such a sweet little girl and had done pageants and everything. Now Serena wore sunglasses that covered half her face to work at Winn-Dixie, and her boyfriend stayed home with the baby.

Marnie and Serena weren't like the lepers cast out of cities in the Bible, though. People were subtle. It wasn't as obvious as rooms going quiet when they entered, at least, not for more than a second or two. And people still did their Christian duty and smiled, but eye contact was optional and not sustained. Nobody wanted to be seen condoning teenage pregnancy, or aligning themselves with girls who were flaunting it. Or just being it.

It was just a feeling in the air. Disappointment. And pity.

I didn't want Charly to be pitied.

"I don't understand. I've got nowhere to go," Charly said, tears glimmering in her eyes.

I didn't understand either. Unless Grandma was sending her to a convent. Except we weren't Catholic, and it didn't seem like pregnant girls were still getting sent to convents.

"How late is your period?"

"I don't know. Three weeks."

"Good. You won't show for a while. Four or five months with looser clothing. I expect you to hold it in until Christmas."

Hold it in? Under other circumstances I would have laughed, but Grandma wasn't kidding, and Charly was nodding like holding it in was something she thought she could manage with willpower, never mind that *it* was a rapidly expanding human being in her abdomen.

"After Christmas," Grandma continued, "you'll go to Canada."

Canada. A stream of references came flying at me, none of them possibly relevant to this situation. Cold. Bacon. Maple syrup. Avril Lavigne. Justin Bieber. Bacon. Cold.

And of course, Mom.

"I don't suppose you remember meeting your Aunt Bree at the funeral," Grandma said.

The graveside photo appeared in my mind. It was in an album in Dad's den, and I'd looked at it a million times to stare at the sixteen-years-younger versions of the people I knew. In it, a rounder, brown-haired Grandma is holding a fat baby on her hip and a scowling toddler by the hand. Us. Grandpa stands on the far left and Dad is alone in the center, looking like he might float away if someone doesn't step on his foot to anchor him.

On his other side are the rest: Mom's family. Strangers. An over-glitzed woman I'd been told is my other grand-mother, wearing a boxy fur coat and a theatrical sad face, clutching the arm of a tall man who's been caught midblink. Her third husband, according to Grandma. Then come two tall, bored-looking teenage boys, obviously belonging to the man, and the nanny they forgot to push out of the shot before the picture was taken.

At the photo's edge, a ten-year-old girl with shiny platinum hair and a pointy chin has the only smile. Bree. It's her half sister's funeral, but she obviously doesn't know you're not always supposed to smile for the camera. She's wearing wire-rimmed glasses, which for years made me think she was a child genius. She would have to be twenty-six now.

Relief trickled down my spine. *Canada. Why didn't I think of that? Charly can live with Aunt Bree and Dad will never find out.*

"I spoke to Bree last night and she said you could stay with her in Banff until you have the baby. The adoption will take place up there."

"But . . . ," Charly stammered. "But she doesn't even know me. I don't even know her."

It was as if she hadn't spoken. Grandma was brokering a business transaction. Deals had been made. Goods would be exchanged.

"You already called her? What if I want to stay here? What if . . ."

Grandma glared at Charly, and for a moment I thought the dam was going to burst. I could see Charly bracing for it too. There had to be a world of anger bubbling behind that somber front, but Grandma shook her head and spoke just as calmly as before.

"Charlotte, you're confused. You use the words *I want* like they still mean something. You're pregnant. You made that choice, thinking only about what you wanted at the moment. Now what *you want* is irrelevant."

Charly shrank into her chair. The last few green Froot Loops bobbed around in the milk, looking spongy and anemic.

"You're acting like I'm about to explode," Grandma said evenly as Charly cowered. "Relax. I'm not going to yell at you. It's too late. Discipline has failed."

I poured the last of my orange juice down the sink. I didn't want to be here for this anymore.

"Sending you to Canada is the only way we can survive this without your father finding out."

"He'd never forgive me," Charly said, still staring into her milk.

She was right, but I wasn't so sure she deserved forgiveness.

"I'll go," she said.

"But what are you going to tell him?" I asked Grandma.

"That you girls are flying up north to get better acquainted with your aunt. That it's important for teenage girls to connect with their mother, even if it can only be through her relatives. That you'll attend an excellent school up there."

I didn't hear a word after *you girls*. "Charly, you mean."

"No. I mean you girls. You'll go with your sister."

"*What?*" Panic twisted every muscle in my body. "*Why?*"

"Stop shouting."

"*I'm not shouting!*" I shouted.

"Calm down." Grandma pointed to the chair next to Charly, but I shook my head.

"I'm not the pregnant one! I don't need to sit!" I thought I'd been exhausted from practice, but I suddenly had an urgent desire to run.

"Fine, then. Stand there and listen. You need to go to Canada too or this story will have no credibility. A girl going to visit a relative for half a year means one thing and one thing only to some people."

"Maybe in the 1960s," I argued, realizing as I said it

that Tremonton was probably at least fifty years behind the rest of America.

"People will wonder, then gossip, then assume it as truth—all of it, if Charly goes alone. If you both go, *you* especially, if you go, nobody will think that."

She meant it as a compliment, but it didn't feel that way. Nobody in this town would imagine I could possibly get pregnant. Probably not even if I was still with Will. "And this is my reward for being good, then? Being sent away just in case people start to wonder about Charly?"

"Your dad would never let Charly go on her own."

I exhaled, feeling every ounce of breath leave me. "But he . . ." *But he* nothing. She was right. I met Grandma's eyes and saw a faint softness behind them.

"Amelia. You have to take care of her."

"But it's my senior year," I said, still not really believing this conversation was happening. She couldn't be asking me to do this. I had Savannah, and field hockey, then soccer after that, and graduation.

And just maybe, I might have Will.

I looked to Charly, but she was staring out the window. Of course, anything to avoid being mentally present.

"When do I stop getting punished for her mistakes?" I asked, gripping the countertop behind me with both hands. "She is and will always be a complete disaster. Does that mean I have to be collateral damage for the rest of my life?"

"That sounds eerily similar to what Cain told God when He came looking for Abel," Grandma said.

"Are you kidding me?" I yelled.

"Am I my brother's keeper?" she quoted calmly.

"I haven't murdered my sibling yet!"

Grandma raised her eyebrows, as if *I* was the one committing blasphemy. Could she not hear herself?

"Do you have a better solution?" she asked.

"Yes! Send her by herself!"

Charly pulled her eyes from whatever it was outside that was so captivating and turned to me. "Please."

"Has the whole world gone insane? You want to be exiled to Canada? Seriously?"

"It doesn't matter what I want, right?" She glanced in Grandma's direction, then back at me. "I need for Dad to not find out, which means I need to leave, which means I need you."

There was too much pleading in her eyes. It made me want to drive my fist through the microwave.

I left the kitchen without saying another word.

Chapter 7

n the weeks and months that followed, I went through the
motions of my normal life, of school and of friends and
of making everything fine. I played along. I hid Charly's
secret. I sold Grandma's semester-in-Canada charade to
Dad, ignoring the possibility of Will, ignoring everything
that was supposed to be happening next semester, just
holding on and waiting waiting waiting for one thing.

December 15. Acceptance day.

Also, ten days after Dad's birthday and ten days before
Jesus's birthday. That had to mean something.

I'd never been idealistic enough to force symbolism
onto real life before, but AP English had clearly warped

my brain because I'd started seeing metaphors in much less—Charly's sudden aversion to eggs, the untimely death of Grandma's magnolia bush (bacterial blight), Dad losing his bifocals again. Life just seemed so literary now.

I woke up early on December 15 floating. I'd decided in advance that for one whole day I wasn't thinking about Charly or Canada or the wreckage of my immediate future. Today was mine.

Because even if Charly had destroyed her life, and even if I was being punished for it, there would be an after. Yes, the next six months would suck, but I would survive Canada, and then I'd have my new beginning in New York in the fall.

Maybe Charly would get another chance too. If Dad didn't find out, if Tremonton didn't find out, if she gave the baby away and started taking school and life seriously for once, maybe her after would be okay.

I found the email waiting for me when I got home from school.

Dear Ms. Mercer,

Your application to Columbia has been carefully considered by the Committee on Admissions, and we are sorry to advise you that we are unable to offer you a place in the class entering this fall.

The Committee regrets that the large number of highly qualified applicants makes it impossible for all of them to be

accepted. We appreciate your interest in Columbia and wish
you the best in your pursuit of higher education.
    Sincerely,
    Donald P. Crowley
    Dean of Admissions

Well.

That was it.

I felt nothing, so I read it again, slower this time. Still nothing. I wasn't crazy or desperate enough to think something was hidden between the words, but the message was so wholly unbelievable—no acceptance, no waiting list, no suggestions—I had to read it one last time.

No. I understood. My after was not going to be any better than Charly's.

I deleted it.

Barefoot and aching from the inside, I made my way downstairs, past Grandma at the sink, past Charly at the table, and out the back door.

"Did it come?" I heard Charly ask, just before the door clattered shut behind me.

Please don't follow me.

I stared straight ahead. Winter had come, and everything had decided to die—the grass, the citrus, the hibiscus, the maple. The black walnut's skeleton stood naked against the grey sky.

A thousand blades of dry grass stabbed the soles of my feet as I crossed the lawn, but there was no way in hell I was going back for shoes. I walked, passing Dad's ailing lime trees, cringing with each step.

When I reached the black walnut, I let my fingers run along the rough bark for just a moment before I gripped the lowest branch and hoisted myself up. Behind me, the back door creaked and banged shut again, but I kept climbing.

"Hey," Charly called from below.

I didn't answer, didn't look down, just climbed limb by limb until the branches were too thin to hold me and I had no choice but to sit.

"So, the email . . . ," she started, then stopped. Hesitation was so rare for the queen of speaking without thinking. "It came?"

"Go away."

"Not good news?"

"I said go away, Charly." I plucked a rotting walnut husk from the branch and rubbed the oily black pod between my palms. Grandma had made us gather the walnuts over a month ago, but somehow this one clinging hull had escaped.

"I'm coming up," she said.

I looked down, just in time to see her fingers reach up and curl around the lowest branch.

Did she actually think she could comfort me? I squeezed the walnut in one hand, rolled it between my palms, then squeezed it again. The impulse was too strong. I had to throw it.

It hit her forehead with a satisfying *clunk* and dropped to the ground. *"Ouch!"* she cried, more surprised than mad.

I gripped the branch and braced myself for her fury, ready to spew every nasty thing I could think of saying. But she dropped back down to the ground, and just stood there. Slowly, she leaned forward, pressing her forehead into the bark where our names were carved, almost as if she was praying to the tree.

I held my breath. Anger pumped blood through my veins, but I waited.

Wordless, she pulled back and walked away. I watched, heard the grass crunch beneath her feet, and felt relief pour through me as she made her way up the steps and into the house.

She'd left me alone. Now I could cry.

Chapter 8

Are you nervous?"

"Don't talk to me."

"In general, or just right now?"

I didn't answer.

"Because I won't talk to you at all if you don't want me to, but we don't actually know anybody in Canada, so it might not be the worst thing in the world if we were at least on speaking terms with each other. You know?"

"Stop talking."

"Okay. But first can you pass me that magazine? Somebody already did the Sudoku in this one."

I passed her the magazine.

"Umm, pencil?"

I slammed my pen down onto her tray, then reclined my seat and closed my eyes. Sleep was my only hope, the only escape from the suckage of reality. Charly, meanwhile, was acting like she had drunk a jug of coffee. Obviously this—leaving Tremonton—meant something entirely different to her, and I got that. For her it was deliverance. She'd been sullen—no, worse—downright hostile for the last eight weeks, and now here she was so giddy I wanted to slap her.

But her deliverance was my banishment. Staying up all night packing hadn't helped me much either. I thought I'd had everything ready in advance, but then at midnight I'd looked in my closet and seen all the stuff I was leaving and freaked out. Repacking took forever, but I ended up stuffing another ten pounds worth of clothing into both my suitcases. Six months, two suitcases. Ridiculous.

"Amelia," Charly whispered, close enough to my ear that I could feel her breath.

I pretended to be asleep.

"Amelia, I have to pee."

"Are you five?" I snapped, louder than I'd meant to. The man in front of us turned around, frowned, then sank back into his seat.

"I'm *sorry!*" she muttered. "I would've climbed over you, but I thought you might wake up and punch me or something."

"You just went twenty minutes ago," I hissed.

"That's what I just told my bladder. It said it doesn't care."

"Hold it."

"So, if I pee my pants do you have an extra pair in your carry-on, or do we get to smell like urine for the next few hours?"

"Go."

Charly climbed over me and I glared at the lady across the aisle and up a row who was watching us like we were a live episode of daytime trash. She looked away.

Pregnant Charly was a beast. Cranky, impatient, and practically incontinent. Basically, she'd turned into livestock. Livestock that wouldn't shut up.

Once she was gone I switched our carry-ons and slid into her seat. She'd whine about it since I'd had the window for the first flight, but we had another three hours on this plane, which meant several more bathroom trips. I couldn't promise I wasn't going to lose it on her the next time she crawled over me.

At least she wasn't puking anymore. She hadn't thrown up since Christmas Eve (which I thought was a lovely way to celebrate the birth of baby Jesus), and that was over a week ago.

Out the window was nothing but blinding white, so I closed the shade and thought about Savannah's New Year's

Eve party. She'd made it a going away party for Charly and me. In typical Savannah style, it'd been fancy—twinkling lights and fresh flowers scattered all around her huge veranda and backyard, candles floating in glass dishes in the fountain. She'd sent out real invitations too. The party hadn't been huge, maybe thirty people, but everyone had dressed up, and we'd eaten bite-sized cheesecakes and sausage balls and cream puffs. It'd been warm, and Savannah let me wear the green dress that never made it to homecoming.

I should've felt like the princess of the party. Charly had certainly looked like she was having fun, and she'd just found out she'd flunked algebra. I should've at least felt nostalgic, because it really was the last time we would all be together like this, and because it seemed like everybody else was.

But I'd spent the night looking around for the guest who wasn't coming. Savannah had invited Will, only to find out that he was visiting cousins in Nashville for the holidays. I couldn't stop thinking, though, if he hadn't been, if he'd come to the party and seen me one last time, maybe we'd have had a moment. To talk. Or more.

Was that so bad, wanting just one last memory to savor? If he'd come, maybe I'd have more than a last memory. Maybe I'd have something to come back for.

It didn't matter. He hadn't.

I'd walked around my own party feeling buffered, like I was gliding through it all in the bubble of our secret. People couldn't stop telling me how much they were going to miss me, how cool it was that we were getting to go meet our mom's family, how fun it was going to be to play in the snow. I'd smiled and responded appropriately. *Yeah, I'll miss you all too, and it will be cool to meet them, and I'm going to love being miserably cold.* Another thing to thank Charly for: turning me into a liar.

Not telling Savannah felt wrong in every way. I'd slid this glass wall between us, and now we only looked like we were side by side. If I'd reached out to touch my best friend I'd have found the cold pane.

I should've at least told her about not getting accepted to Columbia. I just couldn't. And with Charly's mess already separating us, it didn't seem like the worst thing in the world to hold back. I'd tell her eventually. Besides, she hadn't even remembered to ask me about it.

After the party, Savannah had cried and cried, to the point where I'd had to cry just so I didn't look totally heartless. But truthfully, I wasn't sad. Since finding out about Columbia, I'd felt nothing. Except when I thought about Charly. Then I felt rage.

"Nice," Charly grumbled, sitting down in the aisle seat. "If I wasn't worried about getting kicked off the plane, I'd totally fight you for that seat right now."

"Bring it."

"You think you're so tough, but I don't need biceps to scratch and pull hair," she said, taking out her *Us Weekly* to read. "And by the way, every time the drink cart or a flight attendant bumps into me, I'm going to be accidentally elbowing you."

I closed my eyes again. No matter what, I wasn't opening them again until we got there.

The plane jerked downward and Charly gasped.

"It's okay," I said. "It's just turbulence."

She looked around at the other passengers and tightened her seat belt. She'd only flown once before. When she was eight and I was nine, we'd all gone to Louisville to visit Dad's crazy aunt Yvette. I'd flown twice since then, both times with Savannah's family up to their cabin in New Hampshire during the summer.

"How do you know? It felt like an engine just blew up or something."

"It happens all the time." I'd never actually felt turbulence before. "Trust me." The plane bounced again.

"I don't want to die on this plane."

"You're not going to die on this plane," I reassured her. "You may freeze to death in the Canadian wilderness, or die from the agony of pushing out a baby, but you aren't going to die on this plane. You haven't made me suffer enough yet."

"Promise?"

"Promise."

"Amelia?"

"Yeah."

"When we get to Canada, are you still going to hate me?"

"I don't hate you. I'm just . . . I just . . ."

An announcement from the pilot about the turbulence, first in English then in French, bought me enough time to think of something better to say than *I just really strongly dislike you*, which was the direction I was heading.

"I've lost a lot, and I don't feel like anybody cares. It's hard not to be mad about it."

"I know." Her voice sounded thin.

I wanted to say something kinder, but I wasn't going to lie. She'd wrecked everything.

We sat in blessed silence, except now I couldn't sleep. I wasn't thinking about all the things I was losing, but the one thing I'd already lost. Even if he wasn't really mine to lose, the possibility of him was.

After Will and Luciana had broken up, he hadn't gone out and gotten himself a new girlfriend like I'd thought he would, and on more than one occasion, Savannah had sworn she'd seen him looking at me. But Savannah would say anything.

My stomach grumbled. There was one protein bar left

in my backpack, but I had no idea when I'd see real food next. Better to save it.

"*Mesdames et messieurs, s'il vous plait . . .*" The pilot's voice came over the intercom again, and I strained to decipher the rush of words. Jibberish. Three semesters of French, perfect grades in all of them, and all I had to show was *ladies and gentlemen, if you please blah blah blah . . .*

"Why is he yammering in French?" Charly asked, the sad voice gone, the annoying one back. "I thought they only spoke French in Quebec."

"Two national languages. Everything has to be repeated in both."

"Everything? As in, hi my name is Charly, *bonjour je m'appelle Charly*?"

"I hate it when I can't tell if you're joking or not. Everything official."

"Good. 'Cause *bonjour je m'appelle Charly* is all I know." She paused. "I'm not feeling so great about leaving America, you know?"

"We'll still be in North America. Canada isn't the Congo."

"Yeah, but . . ."

I knew. It made me nervous too, and I couldn't even really say why.

A mother across the aisle pulled out a portable DVD

player for her toddler to watch, and I cursed myself for not thinking of it earlier. Diversion. That would work.

"Do you want to watch a show on my iPod?" I asked.

"Do I ever." Charly held out her hand and waited for it while I found it in my carry-on bag. She'd lost her own iPod two weeks after getting it, which is why I generally refused to let her touch mine. This, however, was a special occasion.

Charly spent the rest of the flight watching some Drew Barrymore movie, and I finally fell asleep.

I didn't wake up until I was being told to please bring my seat to an upright position. I lifted the shade. The city of Calgary glowed below, a million lights glittering like pinned-down stars. The sky was hopelessly black. I checked my watch. Local time was 5:34, but it may as well have been midnight.

I pressed my forehead to the window and watched, waiting for the snow to appear as we descended. It didn't. The ground was bone white, but not a flake was falling.

"It's kind of beautiful," Charly whispered.

"I guess." It may as well have been the moon.

"It looks nothing like SeaWorld."

"What are you talking about?"

"The Antarctica thing, remember?"

I did. Last spring break we'd driven down to Orlando and done Disney World and SeaWorld. She was talking about the Polar Expedition, a simulated trip to Antarctica, which was actually just an overly air-conditioned warehouse with polar bears and fake snow and eerie music.

"You do know Canada is *north*. So not the South Pole."

"Whatever."

We disembarked from the plane and dragged ourselves through customs, where we had our brand-new Canadian passports examined. We hadn't even known we were Canadians until Grandma had done a little research and found that a Canadian parent was enough. It seemed sketchy. We'd never even set foot in the country, but maybe they were desperate. Maybe nobody actually wanted to be Canadian anymore.

"Welcome home," the customs official said, as he stamped both our passports.

I mumbled something back, and motioned for Charly to follow along. I managed to heft all four of our fifty-pound bags off the conveyer belt while Charly sat on the baggage cart with her head between her knees.

"Move," I ordered. "Please."

She groaned.

"Are you going to pass out?" I asked.

"I need something to eat," she whimpered.

I sighed, dropped the suitcases, and pulled the last protein bar out of my carry-on. "Enjoy," I said.

"Crap. More healthy food?"

"Then don't eat it," I snapped. "I'm hungry too, by the way."

Normal Charly would have split the bar with me, but the savage pregnant beast before me didn't even look up. She ripped open the package and inhaled it.

Finally, we passed through the last customs checkpoint, me pushing the two-hundred-pound cart and Charly practically wilting under her six-pound backpack.

"You have no idea how much my feet hurt," she moaned.

"Your fourteen-week-old fetus is how big—half a pound?"

"What's your point?"

"Just checking."

"It's not about how big it is. It's *everything*. My skin itches, my back hurts, my nose is plugged up, I feel like I'm going to puke, my joints kill, I have heartburn and the hiccups, and when I stand too long my vision starts to look carbonated around the edges. I think even my blood hurts. My body is being taken over by aliens."

"Congratulations. You've convinced me to never have children."

The last set of glass doors *whooshed* open, and Charly and I were met by a crowd of loved ones. Other people's loved ones.

Chapter 9

Wow," Charly whispered. "Canada does not mess around."

No, it did not. We were surrounded by parkas, ski hats, big clunky boots—all the basic gear for tackling Everest.

"It's like we've stumbled onto a movie set," she continued, "and everyone's been through wardrobe except us."

I scanned the sea of Gore-Tex for Bree. No clue what I was looking for, so by default I found myself searching for the face of the grinning ten-year-old from the picture on a grown-up body. I'd tried to find her on Facebook, but she was either the only person in the world under thirty without a profile, or Bree was short for something weird.

I pushed the cart to the side and watched the other passengers be claimed. Kisses, long hugs, a few squeals, one guy even had flowers—everybody got something. It was impossible not to watch, or for me, at least. Charly sat down on the floor with her cheek pushed up against one of the suitcases and fell asleep.

"Excuse me, are you Charly?"

I turned around to see a guy about my age with a crooked nose, a cherry-red ski jacket, and a brutal case of bed head. Dark sweaty hair was plastered to one side of his head and winged out on the other.

"No. Who are you?"

"Oh, sorry," he said, stepping away. "I'm picking up some girls for a friend."

"Wait a second," I said. "Who's your friend?"

He frowned. His eyes were dark, almost black. "So you *are* Charly?"

"No. But who are you?"

"Ezra."

"Amelia," Charly called groggily from over my shoulder. "I need to go to the bathroom."

"*Amelia.*" Ezra snapped his fingers. "How did I forget that one?"

The irony.

"Washrooms are over there," he said to Charly, nodding to the right, and she went off to find them.

"So that's your stuff?" He moved toward our baggage mountain, hand outstretched. "How'd you push all that?"

"I'm stronger than I look." I put my hand on the cart first. "No offense, but I don't know who you are. Nobody said anything about you picking us up."

He looked confused. But it looked natural on his face, like maybe it was a permanent state for him.

Or maybe he was a human trafficker. Had either of us said Bree's name? No. He hadn't even known my name, and if he was just standing around, he may have heard me say Charly's. There was no reason to assume he wasn't a sex predator wandering the airport looking for vulnerable girls, like on that *Dateline* I'd seen.

"Oh, sorry. Richard asked me to come get you."

I narrowed my eyes. "I don't know a Richard."

"Bree's boyfriend?"

I sniffed, the air so dry the insides of my nostrils felt raw. So he knew Bree. "You're Bree's boyfriend's chauffeur?"

Ezra ran a hand through the hair, which made it worse. "No. Richard's a friend of the family. I do odd jobs for him sometimes."

"Odd jobs. Good to know we're top priority."

He ignored that. "Bree works nights and Richard had

something come up. He didn't have the time to drive you all the way out to Banff tonight."

"Maybe I should call her. Can I borrow your phone?"

Grandma had investigated international cell phone plans and determined one of us would have to sell a kidney to pay for it. I'd suggested we put Charly's uterus up for sale, but Grandma didn't think that was funny. She didn't seem to understand how tragic life without a cell was going to be.

"You can borrow it, but I know Bree turns her phone off while she's working. The bar is really loud."

"The *bar*?" Bree had told Grandma she worked at a restaurant. Grandma had seemed to think she was a manager or something.

"Yeah, or I guess technically McSorley's is a pub. She bartends there."

Bree the bartender. Grandma was going to freak. I tried to recalculate my mental picture of Bree with this new tidbit factored in, but couldn't. The problem was three different Brees: the towheaded ten-year-old, the Bree I'd talked to on the phone, with a Canadian accent so thick I could hear the plaid flannel shirt and overalls, and now Bree the bartender.

Charly reappeared, looking closer to awake. "Hey," she said to Ezra.

"Hey. So you're Charly?"

"Yeah. And you're . . ."

"Ezra."

She nodded like that made sense to her. "You have crazy hair, Ezra."

"It's been in a toque all day. Do you want me to take your backpack?" he asked her.

"I have no clue what a toque is, but you can definitely take my backpack."

She handed it over and he fished a knit ski cap out of his pocket. "Behold a toque."

"Got it," she said.

I fiddled with the zipper of my hoodie and stared at the big weird cowboy statue in front of me. Ezra hadn't offered to take my bag. What was it about Charly that made everybody want to jump in and help?

Then a thought hit me like a shove from behind: Bree had told him that Charly was pregnant. I felt sick. The idea that he could know, that *anybody* could know, just because Bree had decided to blab, made my heart race. The last three months had been torture, gripping that secret, using every particle of energy my body had to hold Charly upright and myself together, faking and smiling and outright lying to Dad and Savannah and the whole world. It wasn't Bree's secret to tell.

"So are we ready to go?" Ezra asked.

I hesitated, but it was just for show. He knew Bree's

name, and Charly's too, and there was something innocent about his features. Like you could insult him and he might not get it. "I guess so," I said, and took my hand off the cart so he could push it.

"I think I missed something," Charly said. "Are you a friend of Bree's?"

"Sort of. Banff is small and mostly tourists, but the locals all know each other."

"Small," I said. "Super."

"Calgary's big, though, right?" Charly asked.

"About a million," Ezra said. "But more than an hour away from Banff."

"Good thing small towns are our specialty, right, Amelia?"

"I think you mean our fate," I answered.

We walked in silence for a few seconds before Ezra stopped the cart, a good thirty feet before the automatic doors. He pulled a pair of gloves out of his pocket and started putting them on, then he gestured at my shirt. "Coats?"

"Um, yeah. I just have to remember which suitcase they're in." I unzipped the bag on the top of the heap. Grandma had taken us to Tallahassee last week for a winter-wear shopping spree, but we hadn't really known what we would need. We'd bought a few basics from Old Navy—coats, a few pairs of socks, sweaters—and then decided to get the rest in Canada.

I found Charly's first. It was lime green and potentially cute, but two sizes too big. Grandma had refused to take her to a maternity store, telling her to "Size up and wipe that scowl off your face."

I tossed Charly her huge coat, and then found mine, a navy peacoat that Savannah insisted made me look like Kate Middleton.

"You guys are going to freeze to death," Ezra commented.

"Wow. Blunt," I muttered. I looked at the people coming through the doors. They were bundled up like astronauts. Gender was not discernible.

"You bought those in Florida?"

Yes, genius.

Charly answered. "Yeah. Aren't they going to be warm enough?"

"We're kind of having a cold snap here. It's really bad out there." He ran another hand through the crazy hair, then pulled on his ski cap. "Yeah, you guys are going to freeze to death in those."

I sighed. Loudly. I was way too tired for the tough guy warnings.

"Do you have gloves and hats and stuff?" he asked.

"We figured we'd buy them here," I explained. "What do you mean by cold snap?"

"It's minus thirty out there. Without the windchill."

"I don't speak Celsius," I said.

"Doesn't matter. Fahrenheit and Celsius meet at minus forty, so minus thirty Fahrenheit is pretty close to the same thing. It doesn't feel much different either. You just have less time—like thirty seconds—until skin freezes." He pulled off his gloves and tried to hand them to me.

"Give them to her," I said, pointing to Charly. My brain was still trying to process *thirty seconds until skin freezes*.

He held the gloves out for Charly, and she took them. "Here, take the toque too," he said, handing her his ski cap.

"I'll go get the car," he said. "When you see me pull up, just leave the bags and run out. I'll come back in for them."

"I can push our bags. What do you drive?"

"A red Pathfinder. Ski rack on top. Deer-sized dent in the side." He zipped up his coat and pulled his bare head down into his body like a turtle. Then he stuck his hands in his pockets and took off. I watched him go, bowlegs running before the door had even closed behind him.

Charly and I waited in silence.

Person after person came through the doors, hunched over, faces pinched, shaking out their arms and rubbing their cheeks, but we were too far from the entrance to feel more than a breath of cold air each time the doors opened and shut.

"This is different," Charly said finally, the exhaustion in her voice outweighing the attempt at optimism.

"Only if by 'different' you mean 'horrific.' They look like they're in pain." A couple rushed through the doors pushing suitcases and dragging two bundled, crying children.

"Maybe it's not that bad," she said.

"Of course it is. Look at those poor people."

"It's human nature to exaggerate pain."

"Really?" I asked. "Like with pregnancy?"

"Very funny."

"Seriously, though." I paused, not sure if I wanted to go the direction I was already going. "It's not like you're the only person in the world to ever go through this. There are worse things."

"I know. Like actually pushing the baby out."

"Gross," I said.

"You know I actually have to do that, right?"

"I don't want to talk about that. I just thought I should mention you might want to tone down the whining."

It really did make me sick to my stomach to think about. The birthing video was the one part of sex ed I hadn't let Savannah describe to me. Every time I thought about it, I had a whole-body reaction: My throat tightened, my stomach fell, and I swear my uterus shuddered.

Charly sniffled.

"I know, I know, you feel like crap. Just don't start bawling right now."

She sniffled again, then put her thumb and her index

finger over her eyelids, like she could push the tears back.

"Good," I said. "You've got to hold it in, at least until we get to Bree's. You're going to totally freak this guy out if you start sobbing in his car."

She nodded. "I'm just tired."

"I know. I'm tired too."

"I can't believe we left home thirteen hours ago," she said. "Feels like thirteen *days*."

I took Ezra's ski cap out of her hand and put it on her head. "Careful. The crazy hair might be contagious."

She laughed. Mission accomplished.

A muddy SUV with skis strapped to the roof and a sizable dent in the passenger door rolled into view. From the driver's seat, Ezra motioned for us to come.

I pushed the cart through the first set of doors, and when the second set slid open, the cold rushed in at us.

Pain. Not cold. Just pain, from that first second. My lungs stung with the first breath, the moment the cold reached down my throat and touched them. It was like acid burning my face and hands and wrists. My entire body tensed and shrank inward, but somehow I kept on moving, too shocked to think, or speak, or do anything but keep pushing the cart toward the car. *Just a couple more feet.*

"Oowwwww," Charly whined behind me.

"Get in," Ezra called, his voice angry.

I pretended not to hear him over the sound of taxis and

shuttles, instead trying to lift the top suitcase off the stack myself as he came around the back of the car. The suitcase wouldn't budge. It was either heavier than when I'd hefted it up there, or my muscles had shrunk. I growled at it as Charly climbed into the backseat.

"I said get in!" Ezra shouted, beside me now, and I let go of the handle just as my feet began sliding out from beneath me. My brain and stomach registered that I was falling for only a second before pain shot through my shoulder like a bolt of lightning. I felt Ezra's grip on my arm, holding me, no, dangling me, my face scraping against a tag on the front of his coat.

"You okay?" his voice thundered in my ear.

My feet found solid ground and I stood, my shoulder screaming from being yanked, Ezra's hand still squeezing my arm.

"I . . ." Why was the world still spinning? Why was my face on fire?

"*Get in.*" This time Ezra dragged me to the passenger door, pushed me up into the front seat, and slammed the door.

I was too cold to breathe. I brought my arms to my chest. Hot air roared from the vents into my face, but I couldn't feel the heat. I couldn't feel anything. The car bounced as Ezra tossed in the bags, and I squeezed my eyes shut and prayed: *Shut the door, shut the door, shut the door.*

Finally, he slammed it, and I leaned forward, pushing my face right up to the vent.

"Holy crap," Charly muttered through chattering teeth. "Holy crap, holy crap, holy crap."

And then Ezra was there beside me in the driver's seat, his face splotchy red, his eyelashes glittery with ice crystals. "You girls don't pack light, do you?" He was shaking his hands like he was trying to knock the life back into them.

"Two bags each *is* light," I said. "We're going to be here for six months."

He didn't answer.

"Tell me it isn't this cold all the time," I said.

"It isn't." He made his hands into fists and blew into the end of each. I tried it too, and it worked, at least for a second. The skin on my palms ached under my hot breath.

"It only gets this cold a couple of times a year. Yesterday it was all the way up around zero."

Zero. It took a moment to register that he was talking in Celsius, and another moment to translate. Thirty-two Fahrenheit. "That's *warm*?"

"For January, yeah."

"So it got this cold just for us."

"Think of it as a welcome gift."

I shivered and tucked my chin to my chest. This was hell. *Hell.* Why hadn't we brought scarves and hats, and how long until the car warmed up?

I don't belong here.

The weight of the thought was crushing. It was too late. I was here. I was stuck. I felt hollow, like my insides had been scraped out, leaving just a shell of skin. An empty walnut husk. I unclenched my fists and stared at my white, bloodless fingers.

"I wish it was snowing," Charly said from the backseat.

"Of course you do," I mumbled.

Ezra put the car into drive and pulled away from the curb. "It's too cold to snow. But there's plenty already on the ground."

Too cold to snow? What did that even mean? Up ahead, where the covered drop-off lane ended, I could see it, a thick grey crust edging the road, hip high and rising into dirty-white mounds easily taller than me. We were walled in by snowbanks.

"Is it always grey like that?" Charly asked.

"No, it's just muddy from the road. Wait, you've never seen snow before?"

"Only on TV," I said.

"And from a window at the Chicago airport," Charly added.

Ezra laughed, then realized we weren't joking. "Seriously?"

"You'd be surprised how infrequently it snows in Florida."

"Yeah, but . . ." He rubbed his hands together, then blew into his fists again while he steered the car with his knees. I knew what he was thinking. We were a couple of hicks who'd never been more than ten miles from home. And if he knew about Charly's *condition*, then he thought we were a couple of trashy hicks who'd never been more than ten miles from home. At least we weren't the ones with homeless-man hair.

"Do you need help steering?" I asked. Freezing to death while I waited for an ambulance seemed like a bad way to go.

"No. The wheel feels like ice, but it'll warm up in a few minutes."

"Charly, give the guy his gloves back."

She tossed them up and he put them on. "Thanks," he said. "Hey, is it okay with you guys if we do a drive-thru for some food before we leave the city?"

"Yes!" Charly called. "Yes, it is definitely okay with us!" Apparently the protein bar had not been enough.

I shrugged. Last year Coach Hershey had sat us down and forced us to watch a disturbing documentary on fast food to scare us away from it, but all that seemed pointless now. It wasn't like I was in training for anything anymore.

We pulled up to an A&W and ordered three burgers. I fumbled with the zipper on my backpack, but Ezra was faster. He found two purple bills that looked more like

Monopoly money than legal tender, and paid before I could even find my wallet.

"Thanks."

"Yeah, thanks," Charly echoed.

Charly scarfed hers, but the meat didn't taste right to me. Too much like cow. I wrapped mine up and shoved it back in the bag. It was better as a lap warmer anyway.

"So you guys are starting at BPH?" Ezra asked.

It took a moment for the acronym to register. Banff Public High.

"I am," I said. "Charly's doing classes by correspondence."

I stole a sideways glance, but Ezra's face was expressionless.

"I went to BPH," he said.

Went. So he wasn't in high school anymore. Dropout or graduate?

"Don't miss it," he added.

"That bad?"

"No. Just cramped my style, you know?"

"I guess."

Ezra looked like the kind of guy whose *style* was sleeping till noon and playing Xbox for the rest of the day.

"It's my last semester," I said, "so it's not like my classes matter. I'm just here to be crowned prom queen."

"Good luck with that. There's no prom here."

"Oh." So the prom queen sarcasm must've been lost in translation. Mars. I'd landed on Mars. "Do you even know what prom is?"

"Yeah. American TV."

I took a deep breath and told myself it didn't matter. If I was at home, Savannah would've had to drag me to PHS's prom anyway. It's not like I would've gone with Will. Probably not, anyway. It would have been extremely unlikely.

Ezra's voice interrupted my thoughts. "The Southern drawl should win you some points at school. Or at least some laughs."

Clearly he had no idea he sounded slightly Scottish, slightly Minnesotan, and slightly idiotic.

"I hadn't thought about it," I said, listening to my words, trying to hear what he heard. "I've never had an accent before."

"Trust me, you've had a Southern accent since the day you started talking."

"Yeah, thanks, I get it. I just mean I've never lived anywhere else. I've never been, you know, out of context."

"Welcome to out of context."

I stared out the window in silence, and felt the minutes roll by. The city lights were behind us now, leaving just the outline of bleached hills glowing under a heavy black sky. It was eerie. Or magical.

"That's the color snow is supposed to be," Ezra said.

I nodded. It was beautiful.

We sank back into silence. It should have been awkward, sitting beside a stranger with nothing to say, but it wasn't. Maybe because I didn't care what he thought.

After another few minutes, Ezra spoke again. "We've got a Chinook coming."

"Am I supposed to know what that is?"

"Oh. I guess not. Warm wind from the mountains. Temps are probably up in Banff already. At least I hope they are. I froze at work today."

"You work outside?" That seemed impossible. Or if not impossible, then incredibly stupid.

"I'm on ski patrol at Lake Louise. The slopes were practically empty today."

"Any theories why?"

He either didn't hear my sarcasm, or he ignored it. "Only diehards ski in this kind of cold, but they still have to have people out there clearing for avalanches and on patrol, eh?"

I glanced over my shoulder at Charly, but she was asleep. How was I supposed to make fun of my first "eh"? "And you didn't get frostbite or hypothermia or anything?"

"No. When it's this cold I wear a lot of gear. Balaclava, goggles, the whole deal, you know?"

Clearly, I didn't know. "I hope they're paying you well."

"It's a volunteer thing."

"You spend all day outside in this and you don't get a paycheck?"

"I get a free season's pass for Lake Louise. And the jacket."

I must've looked unimpressed because he shrugged and said, "It's better than going to university."

That explained everything. He was a cold-weather Baldwin boy, going nowhere and not caring.

Our next bout of silence lasted longer.

"Have you ever skied?" he asked after a while.

"No, that would have required me to have seen snow, right?"

"Oh. Yeah."

Charly snored softly in the backseat.

"She didn't last long, did she?" Ezra asked.

I paused. "She gets tired quickly these days." There. If he knew she was pregnant, that made sense. And if he didn't know, he now thought she was terminally ill, which was probably preferable.

Outside, the hills swelled and grew steeper. I stared at my reflection, pale and angular in the glass, and wished I was different. Softer. Less harsh. Ezra was good-looking, even if he was completely devoid of ambition and intelligence. Other girls would've at least been friendly, but I couldn't seem to manage even that. He probably thought I was a total brat.

Except he didn't know me. He didn't know how drained I felt, or how horrible the last few months had been. I just didn't have any pretending left in me. Small talk, making a good impression, being nice, being *cute*—it all took too much energy. It wasn't like I was going to see him again anyway.

"You don't want to be here, do you?"

His voice startled me. Of course I didn't want to be here. "I'm just tired. Long day."

"You can go to sleep if you want," he said.

Tears pooled in my eyes and I felt my throat thicken. Why was he being so nice to me? I couldn't say thank you. He'd hear the tears if I spoke, and think I was crazy. Instead I reclined my seat and closed my eyes.

Like sleep was going to happen. I teetered on the edge of it instead. But everything—hurtling down an icy highway into the mountains of a foreign country, lying in a stranger's car, closing my eyes—felt wrong.

So I thought about camping with Will. It'd been the single most rebellious act of my life, telling Grandma I'd be spending the night at Savannah's and then sneaking off to sleep under the stars with him. But worth the guilt. The memory was all warmth, lying in his sleeping bag with his arms around me, feeling completely safe.

Chapter 10

We met Bree's apartment before we met Bree. It was a huge, high-ceilinged loft, with dark hardwood floors, white suede couches, and red candles and throw pillows.

"So swanky," Charly whispered, rubbing a red flower petal between her thumb and finger. It was a poppy. "I'm guessing this didn't grow outside."

"Don't touch that," I said, my teeth still chattering from the ten seconds we'd spent sprinting from Ezra's car to the stairwell. "That vase looks expensive."

"Hmm. Crystal or something?" she asked, letting go of the petal and tapping the vase.

"I said, *don't* touch it. As in, the opposite of what you're doing right now."

"Pardon me," Ezra said. I stepped out of his way and he rolled the first two suitcases across the main room to the far corner where a spiral staircase twisted upward.

Pardon me? Charly mouthed to me, then, "You are pardoned, kind sir."

I gave her the *shut up* head shake. I was all for mocking the Canadians, but not to their faces and not while they were doing our heavy lifting.

Ezra hoisted a suitcase and started up the stairs. "Bree said to take your stuff up to the loft."

"I thought this was a loft." We were on top of an art gallery, in a building facing Banff Avenue. I looked up. There was, in fact, a loft. A waist-high wall hid most of the room from this angle, but I could see eggshell-blue walls and the rounded edge of a mirror, then Ezra's head and shoulders.

"A loft-let," Charly said. "Cute."

"Adorable."

The apartment was warm, thank goodness, so I slipped off my coat while I glanced around, taking inventory. The room was a giant cube, with one brick wall to my left and an open kitchen to my right. The far wall had two doors: bedroom and bathroom?

I wandered through the kitchen, eyeing the marble

countertops, stifling the urge to examine the contents of the shiny stainless steel fridge. This was the kind of kitchen that would have capers and Camembert cheese and weird condiments in it. An array of copper-bottom pots hung from a suspended metal rectangle. I could almost hear Grandma's voice: *How many saucepans could one woman need?*

Svelte barstools along an island separated the kitchen from the living space. Charly was already sitting on the couch with her feet on a glass coffee table beside another vase of poppies.

"I feel like I'm in a magazine," she said.

I walked to the other side of the room, past the accordion screen with a geisha girl fanning herself on it, past the massive flat-screen TV, over to the window. According to Ezra, Banff Avenue was the main drag, but the restaurants and gift shops looked closed for the night. "Wild West ghost town meets Siberia," I whispered.

Ezra was on his way up the stairs with the second bag. "Yeah, Richard has a decorator for all his places. I think this one actually was photographed for a magazine last—"

"Wait, what?" I interrupted. "This is Richard's apartment?"

"Well, no. Yeah. I don't know."

He disappeared into our room again. I waited for him

to come back, my mind cartwheeling. Were we moving into Bree and her boyfriend's little love nest? Grandma was going to freak.

"He doesn't actually live here," Ezra said, coming back down the stairs. "He lives in Calgary, but he has a lot of real estate here in Banff, so he's here on the weekends to ski and to see Bree, I guess."

A lot of real estate. People who had *a lot of real estate* had butlers and Bentleys and half-empty tubes of Aspercreme in their medicine cabinets. "How old is Richard?"

"Mid-forties, I think." He paused. "Yeah, he went to high school with my mom."

"That's a twenty-year age difference!"

"You might not want to point that out to Bree."

"She doesn't realize her boyfriend is old enough to be her father?"

"Yeah, but you know what she's like."

"Actually, we don't," Charly said.

I sent her a death glare, but she was too busy making the lights flicker with the remote control in her hand to catch it.

"I've been imagining her as a skinny version of my first grade teacher, Ms. Paulson," Charly continued, dropping the remote and picking up the coffee table book. "Not sure why."

Ezra squinted at Charly. "You don't know her?"

"It's complicated," I said before Charly could say something else stupid.

He didn't smirk, but it was in his eyes. They were dark, brimming with things he was too polite to say.

"What about you. How do you know Bree?" I asked.

"Bree and my brother used to be, you know . . . together."

"Oh." I tried to construct a mental diagram of the relationships, but having no faces made it hard. Bree had dated Ezra's brother, but was now with Richard, who went to school with Ezra's mom?

"It's complicated," he added.

"Speaking of complicated, modern art hurts my head," Charly said, yawning. She chucked the book onto the coffee table, then flopped over onto her side. "Amelia, I'll give you a million bucks to pick me up and carry me to bed. A million more if you brush my teeth and put my retainer in for me."

Ezra looked from Charly to me. "I should go get the other two suitcases." He left.

"Have you considered saving the weirdness until people know you?" I asked, staring out the window. It was dead out there. Dead cold. Dead dark. Dead quiet.

Ezra clearly thought we were freaks, but so what? Charly *was* a freak. And the two of us flying across the continent to move in with a complete stranger like we were

part of the witness protection program or something—
that was freakish.

"He's kind of cute," Charly said. She was still sideways
on the couch, face-planted in throw pillows. "You should
go for him. He has that same serious, never-say-what-I'm-
thinking thing as you. You guys would be perfect together.
You could just sit around being broody together."

"Not funny."

"Oh, come on. I'm sure he wouldn't mind if you followed him out to the car and—"

"*Shut up!*"

"Jeez. Cranky."

I wandered over to the tight spiral staircase and
started up.

"Dibs on the better bed," she called after me.

"Dibs on somebody else's life."

The "loft-let" was the size of a closet. The furniture
consisted of a double bed, a tall, skinny dresser pushed up
next to it, and a card table masquerading as a desk in the
corner. There was a tiny window, so it wasn't quite the
same as a prison cell. But close.

Ezra had wedged the two suitcases in the space between
the foot of the bed and the overlook, which was just tall
enough to hide me from view unless I was standing right
next to it.

I dropped my backpack on the bed and leaned over the

wall. "Hey," I called down to Charly. "Good news. We're sharing a bed."

Charly didn't look up. She'd picked up another book of artwork and was busy thumbing through. "My bladder wants to sleep closest to the stairs."

I pulled off my sweater and fell backward onto the white duvet. At least the mattress was soft.

"Are these okay here?"

Ezra's voice brought me to a sitting position. I hadn't even heard him come in, but he was at the foot of the bed, piling the suitcases next to the other two.

"Fine. Whatever." Where else were they going to fit?

"Well, I should be going, then."

"Okay. Thanks."

He nodded, then stared at me for a second too long.

"Good-bye," I said, lifting my eyebrows.

Ezra turned and went back downstairs. I listened to him say good night to Charly and leave before I let myself fall back into the bed.

Alone. I'd been dying to be by myself all day, and now that Charly and I were sharing a room, not just a room but a bed, this was as close to it as I was going to get. I was just starting to float away when Charly's voice from below startled me awake.

"Why were you such a jerk to him?"

"I wasn't," I called back. "And why do you care, anyway?"

"It's embarrassing when you do that."

"Embarrassing? *I* embarrass *you?*"

Silence.

"Because last time I checked, you were the one who was knocked up with a complete stranger's baby."

Dead silence.

Hands shaking, I pulled off my jeans and socks, wriggled out of my bra, and climbed into bed in just my shirt and underwear. My heart thumped against my rib cage and my throat ached. This air was too thin and too dry for my lungs to hold on to.

I was supposed to call Grandma. She'd be worried if I didn't let her know we'd gotten here safely, but I was too tired to get out of bed and I couldn't be in the same room as Charly right now. Besides, I couldn't just call from Bree's home phone without asking her first. Grandma deserved to worry a little.

And I deserved a good cry, but now that I was actually alone, the tears wouldn't come. Instead I hugged my knees to my chest and felt the blood pulse through me. I closed my eyes and pictured the lights at Savannah's party, muggy nights in the black walnut tree, Dad's warm hand on my shoulder, Will's deep-set blue eyes. The last noise I remembered was the refrigerator door opening and closing. Of course Charly would be helping herself to Bree's food, uninvited.

Then sleep pulled me down.

. . .

I woke up to the *Wicked* soundtrack and the smell of sizzling pork fat. It wasn't the CD (that I'd heard a million times, thank you, Charly), but a live duet of *What Is This Feeling?* accompanied by pot clanging. Ah yes, the song about roommates hating each other. Appropriate.

I opened my eyes and a beam of white sunlight drilled a hole into my eyeball. I groaned and rolled over. One tiny window, what were the chances?

I pulled the duvet over my head, which blocked the light but only muffled their voices. Decision time. I could go downstairs, or fake sleep until Broadway musical hour was over. On the one hand, the singing was too loud to sleep through and could go on forever, but on the other hand, I had no place down there. Bonding with the lost aunt over bacon and show tunes—that was Charly's scene.

Except I was starving.

I swung my legs out of bed and looked around me. My jeans were on the floor, so I grabbed them and put them on. The left side of the bed was still tucked in. Charly must have slept on the couch.

The singing broke off below. "Pass me your plate, babe."

Babe? Bree's voice was husky—not low, but just scratchy enough to be grating.

I glanced at my reflection in the oval mirror over the dresser. Pale skin, colorless lips, dull brown hair, mascara wells under my eyes—this was going to be a great first impression. I looked like a junkie.

"Can I have that syrup?" Charly sounded awfully chipper for someone who hated mornings, someone pissed off enough to sleep on the couch rather than share a bed with me.

"This is the real deal," Bree said. "Canadian maple syrup. One taste and you'll never go back to Aunt Jemima."

I took the double-helix staircase slowly, looking up only when I got to the bottom. Both had their backs to me, Charly at the island stuffing her face and Bree at the stove, still nattering about syrup. She had white-blond hair cut pixie-short, and a black rose tattoo on the nape of her neck. From behind I could see she had one of those dainty cartoon frames: curvy hips, tiny waist, and mysteriously, no shoulders. I could probably bench-press her.

Neither noticed me until I reached the bottom and Bree turned around, pancake on a spatula.

"Amelia!" she squealed, and tossed the pancake onto Charly's plate. She was instantly across the room and on me, squeezing the air out of me. "You're *beautiful*!"

"Thank you." That was maybe arguable on a good day, and definitely not true as of one minute ago when I'd looked in the mirror. I returned the hug and waited for her to let go. She took her time. Awkward. It didn't help that she was short enough for me to rest my chin on top of her head. Her hair product smelled like coconut.

"No, really, you're gorgeous!" she said, pulling back.

Again, awkward. I tried to smile.

"Your hair is so dark—nothing like your mom's. I don't really remember your dad, but you must look like him."

"That's what people say."

She kept examining my face from close up, so my only option was staring right back. She had round eyes spaced just a little too far apart, a tiny diamond stud in her nose, and a silver lip ring. It's hard enough not to stare at people's piercings from a normal distance, but from six inches? Impossible. The nose stud was incredibly sparkly.

She put her hands on her hips. "You're too skinny. Do you eat?"

What was that supposed to mean? She was the one who was the size of a twelve-year-old. "Of course I eat."

"Good, have some pancakes. And bacon."

I took the stool beside Charly. Bree shoveled a full piglet's worth of bacon onto my plate. "Um. Sure."

"So Charly and I were just having a little *Wicked* sing-along."

"I heard."

"You've got some pipes, girl," she said, dumping more

pancakes onto Charly's plate, then mine. "Do you sing too?"

"No." Whatever I was doing in choir, I was pretty sure it didn't count as singing. Credit earned, transcript diversified, rejected anyway. "Charly got the singing genes."

"Me too. I sing in a band, actually. It's punk. We mostly do covers of 80s music, but sometimes we do show tunes too. Wild mix, eh?"

I chewed on my bacon.

"What's your band's name?" Charly asked.

"The Pedestrians. We play at McSorley's about once a week, on a night when I'm not behind the bar. Usually Thursdays. Hey, I know." Bree turned to Charly and waved the spatula at her. "You should sing with us sometime."

Charly's eyes grew to golf ball size. "Really?" she whispered.

"Of course!"

I pictured Charly on stage in an acid-washed jean miniskirt with pink hair, a giant pregnant belly hanging out under a halter top. Classy.

Bree poured coffee into two mugs and brought them over to us. "So you didn't call your grandma last night."

She wasn't looking at me, but it felt like she was. "Yeah," I said. "I was just so tired, I totally forgot. And I don't think Charly is supposed to drink coffee. What with . . . you know."

"Oh. My bad." She pulled the mug away from Charly, who glared at me. I didn't actually know if it was bad for the baby, but I really didn't need her any peppier.

"She called this morning at five to make sure you guys were alive. She must've forgot about the two-hour time difference."

"Yeah," I said. Probably not. "Sorry."

"I told her you guys would call her when you got up." Bree took the phone off the counter and held it out to Charly.

"Nope," Charly said, hands up, staring at the phone like it was a gun. "That's Amelia's job."

"Why is that my job?"

"Because Grandma doesn't want to talk to me."

It was hard to disagree with that.

"Well, just as long as one of you calls her," Bree said, sweetly but not that sweetly.

"After breakfast," I said.

She put the phone beside my mug. It felt like a threat.

"So Ezra stopped by McSorley's after he dropped you guys off last night," she said. "That boy is such a sweetheart."

Sweetheart? He'd seemed more like a big, domesticated primate.

"He said you guys might need some winter gear, and

that you could stop by and dig through the lost and found at Lake Louise if you want. That stuff can be really expensive, and you only need it for one season."

"Nice," Charly said.

I wasn't going to argue. I didn't know exactly what *really expensive* meant, but I did know that money was tight at home. Grandma's lecture about interest rates and responsible spending had been completely unnecessary. Did she really think I was going to run out and buy a two-thousand-dollar pair of moccasins with her credit card? Charly maybe, me no. The thought of blowing a ton of money on ugly snow gear made me cringe.

I'd just assumed that we could get by on the bare minimum. But the shock of last night, of how the cold had felt like a thousand teeth taking a thousand bites out of my skin—that changed things.

"His older brother, Quinn, and I used to, you know . . ." Bree swirled the bottle of syrup around high up in the air, drizzling a squiggly crosshatch pattern onto her own pancakes. It was all very bartender-ly. Charly looked completely mesmerized, like she'd never realized syrup could be so beautiful.

"But that was forever ago," Bree said.

I waited, hoping talk about boyfriends past would lead to talk of boyfriends present, specifically, who Richard was, and whether or not he was going to show up and walk around like he owned the place. But Bree transitioned to clothes instead.

"I'm guessing you'll need more than you can scrape together from the lost and found, though."

"We did bring clothes," I said, hearing the defensive edge to my voice after it was too late.

"Oh, of course! I didn't mean you didn't have clothes. I just thought I could help you get a few things you might not already have. Like some good boots, and a few pairs of long johns. I found these silk ones at Mountain Equipment Co-op last winter that have seriously changed my life."

I nibbled on a piece of bacon, wishing it wasn't so chewy. She wanted to *help* us get a few things? "Help" was a little ambiguous. Was she talking about buying us stuff, or was she talking about dragging us to the store and maxing out Grandma's credit card?

"Sounds good to me," Charly said, mopping up the syrup with her last bite of pancake. "We nearly froze to death last night."

"It'll be my little welcome gift to you guys." Bree smiled and the lip ring gleamed. "What do you say?" she asked, putting a hand on my arm.

I say you're trying too hard. "Sure. Thanks."

She squealed and Charly squealed and I almost squealed for solidarity.

"How about you guys get ready and then we head into Calgary to shop? That way you'll be all set for starting school on Monday. We can stop by the Alberta Healthcare Office to get your ID numbers so we can make an appointment for Charly. Are you guys going to need school supplies too?"

"Charly's not going to school," I said. "She's got her stuff for the online classes she's doing, and I brought school supplies."

"Well . . ." Bree's voice trailed off. When she picked up again, her voice was bright and shiny like cheap fabric. "Actually, I thought maybe we should talk about that."

I turned to face her, but she wasn't looking at me. She was looking at Charly. "I mean, I know your grandma wants you to do the correspondence class thing, but it doesn't make a lot of sense to me. It just seems like you're going to miss out on the whole semester."

Charly stared at Bree, eyes wide and innocent.

"So I enrolled you both."

"*What?*" I sputtered.

"You don't have to go if you don't want to," she said, ignoring me. "I just thought I'd give you the option. They don't make pregnant girls stay at home here."

"They don't *make* pregnant girls stay at home in Florida either," I said. "She's choosing to do online classes for one semester."

Finally, Bree turned to me. "I just want to make sure that's what *Charly* is choosing to do."

So I was the bad guy.

I put my fork down, so gently it only made the softest *clink*. She wasn't getting the satisfaction of seeing me mad. I looked at the floor and waited for Charly to jump in and defend me. She owed me that. She knew I hadn't bullied her into staying home.

"I guess," Charly started slowly, "well, I guess I assumed I'd do what Grandma told me to do. But now I don't know. Maybe I *do* want to go."

Traitor.

"Can I think about it?" she asked.

"Of course," Bree said. "It's a big decision. You *should* think about it. I just thought you might get lonely, being cooped up in the apartment alone. It would be pretty isolating, you know, not knowing anybody."

"Aren't you here during the day?" Charly asked. "I mean, you work at night, right?"

"Yeah, but I have class during the day," she said. "I'm in nursing school."

"Oh," Charly said. "That sucks."

Bree laughed. "You sound like Richard. Oh, you guys have to meet Richard still. He's my, you know . . ." She twirled her fork in the air, like that was the universal sign for sugar daddy. "He wants me to drop out and come hang out in Calgary with him during the week. I keep telling him no way. The classes are hard, but I love it, and it took me forever just to get in. I totally screwed around in high school and then I dropped out, so I had to get my GED first and then my nursing prereqs to get into the program. Anyway, so just think about the school thing."

"She's not dropping out," I said. "It's one semester."

"But do you want to?" Bree asked Charly, her voice dramatically somber.

Charly stared at her plate, opened her mouth, and waited. "I want . . ."

Want? Who cared what Charly wanted? Nobody was getting what they wanted anymore—not her and not me.

I still had half a pancake and several pieces of under-cooked bacon to go, but I wasn't hungry anymore. "Sorry. I can't finish this."

"That's okay," Bree said, all sweetness again.

Charly pulled my plate toward her and started trans-ferring the bacon onto hers.

"Shopping, then?" Bree chirped.

Shopping, then.

I showered and dressed first, then forced myself to call Grandma while Charly and Bree took turns in the bathroom.

She was mad, but curious enough to calm herself down and interrogate me.

"So what's it like?"

"Colder than you could even imagine. So cold I want to die."

"I'm not talking about the weather, Amelia. What's your aunt like?"

"I don't know. We've only talked for a couple of minutes so far." That was both true and false. We *had* only talked for a couple of minutes, but I was pretty sure I knew what she was like: She was a bartender with at least one tattoo and several piercings, she sang in a band and had screwed around in high school and lived in an apartment owned by a boyfriend who wanted her to quit nursing school. Oh, and she was trying way too hard. "Charly loves her."

"That doesn't tell me much. What's her apartment like?"

"It's beautiful," I said truthfully, looking around me. "All modern and fancy with real art on the walls. But our room is really small and we have to share a bed."

That calmed Grandma right down. Real art translated into a stable, conservative atmosphere. She made me promise to read my Bible and to make sure Charly got plenty of rest before saying she had to go. There were bridge ladies waiting.

"Wait, wait," I said, before she hung up. "What about Dad?"

"Clueless. Thank the Lord."

My rib cage felt hollow, my entire body empty. How

had he not seen through it? Not that it was his fault, since I'd lied my little heart out. We all had. But still, he should've connected the logical dots. Dad figuring things out would have been the worst and best case scenario—the end of the world for Charly, and deliverance for me.

"Good. Okay. Bye."

"What's the matter, Amelia?"

"Nothing." I'd made myself invisible. I couldn't hate him for not seeing me.

"I'll call on Monday to see how school went, then."

"Okay." I took a deep breath and considered whether to tell her about Bree's campaign to get Charly to go to school with me. But what was the point? Charly just had to think it through for a minute and then she'd remember that she'd hated school since fifth grade. A semester at home was the only thing about being pregnant that didn't totally suck for her. "Bye, Grandma."

Grandma hung up.

"Does she seem like Mom?" Charly whispered.

I glanced toward the closed bathroom, then shook my head at Charly. "Why would you even ask that? You know I don't remember Mom."

"Yeah, but I thought maybe meeting Bree would remind you of something, you know? Jog your memory."

"I was *two*."

Charly didn't respond, just turned away.

. . .

"Mind if I smoke?" Bree asked as we left the apartment.

"No, go ahead," Charly said.

Great. I wondered how long it would take for my pink lungs to turn tar black from secondhand smoke.

"Thanks. Richard would freak if I smoked in the apartment. He kind of thinks I quit last year. I *did* quit last year, I just still occasionally need a cigarette. Like a few times a day."

Charly nodded sympathetically.

I cleared my throat. "Sorry, but I'm pretty sure secondhand smoke is bad for the baby."

"Oh." Bree looked at the cigarette in her hand like this was the first time she'd been told it was toxic.

"It's okay," Charly said. "Just stand downwind."

"Are you sure?"

"Yeah. No biggie."

Bree looked to Charly, then at the cigarette, then to me. "No, it's okay. I'll have one later. You know, I should probably just quit for real. Yeah, I'll quit for real."

Denial to quasi-resolve in seconds. Impressive.

I turned away from both of them and started down the stairwell to the sidewalk, gripping the ice-cold railing on both sides. The steps were steep and a beautiful thought bubbled up from my subconscious: Grandma would let me come home if I broke my leg. Maybe. But maybe not. A broken back definitely, but that was a little extreme.

Behind me, Charly started whistling the theme song from *Moulin Rouge*. Bree joined in with the harmony. I sped up.

Banff Avenue was different by day. The air was so blindingly bright it stung my eyes. I stepped out onto the sidewalk and turned a slow circle. The street was wide. So were the sidewalks, and glimmering snowbanks edged them both. Everything was white-crusted, like gingerbread house icing had been piped over every surface and into every crack.

"It's warmer," Charly said, and I realized she was right. I was cold, not in pain.

Charly reached down to dig her fingers into the snow.

"It'll chinook for the next couple of days," Bree said. "Enjoy it while it lasts. I'm parked just around the corner." She pointed up the street and started walking.

"It's like the North Pole," Charly whispered behind me. "Minus Santa and the elves and the toys."

And the joy.

The sky, for all its brightness, was too small. Huge mountains surrounded us, jagged walls of rock and ice, clawing at the sky. I'd never seen a real mountain before. It was disorienting, being enclosed by them, like being trapped inside that print Señora Lopez had hanging on her wall, the Salvador Dali maze, with stairs twisting and changing directions, floors becoming ceilings, doors opening up into nothingness.

"Amelia, touch it," Charly begged.

Snow. It was everywhere. Packed hard beneath me, piled in mini-mountains along both sides of the street, hanging on store awnings, blanketing cars. In movies it floated around like heavy pollen, or like manna fluttering down from heaven for Moses. But the snow wasn't falling.

I reached down and trailed my fingers over the bank to my right. "It feels like ice."

"That *is* ice," Bree said. She scooped up a handful of powder, then held it out to me. "I give you snow."

I put out my hand and she dropped the snow into my palm. It was cold. And surprisingly wet. "Thanks."

"Banff is your typical ski town," Bree said. "Gift shop, restaurant, gift shop, restaurant, ski shop, restaurant. Or at least Banff Ave is that way. Off the side streets you get more residential."

I glanced up the street of tourists shops, not yet open for business, except for what looked like a coffee shop. "Where's school?"

"About a kilometer that way." She pointed behind her.

A kilometer. I was pretty sure that was less than a mile, so probably walking distance, which was good since we had no car.

Bree let out a sigh. "Warm weather! I've been outside for two minutes and I can still feel my face."

I shivered and pulled my hood up. It was still colder than Florida on our coldest day.

We turned the corner and I looked up at the church to the left. It was tall and white with a steep black roof and sharp angles. Anglican, according to the sign. Nothing like the sprawling brown brick of First Southern Methodist. Tomorrow Dad would be up at the pulpit and everybody else would be in their usual pews. Savannah's family. Will's family. Grandma would be sitting alone, but I couldn't feel sorry for her. Nobody forced her to exile me to Siberia.

Dad always made a point of smiling at our row a couple of times per sermon. Maybe he'd do it tomorrow, out of habit. Or maybe just so everyone could see that he was thinking of his family. As usual.

"Ready to shop?" Bree called from up ahead. She was scraping frost off the windows of a sporty-looking silver Audi. Charly had already climbed into shotgun.

I stopped. My hand hurt. I opened my fist and let the slush and ice drip through my fingers.

"Hurry up and get in already!" Charly yelled.

I obeyed.

Chapter 11

Shopping was a success, but only if success is defined by number of purchases made. If the definition has anything to do with enjoyment, or self-esteem, or bonding, shopping was a complete failure.

Bree had insisted on buying us two pairs of boots each.

Back at the apartment with boot boxes spread all over the floor, Charly was modeling a different boot on each foot.

"I think we should return a pair each," I said.

"What?" Bree said. "You got some good deals. You're just not used to the exchange rate."

"But we don't need two pairs."

"You need at *least* two pairs. See, these ones you'll want for when you're going to actually be in the snow," she said flipping the lid off the first pair I'd bought, some trendy-but-utilitarian fur-lined boots with pom-pom tassels.

"Oh yeah," Charly said, "I love those ones on you."

"Me too," Bree continued, picking up the wedge-heel knee-highs. "And these ones won't be quite as warm, but you can wear them with a skirt or pants, to school or wherever. And plus, they're really sexy."

They were. I'd never have picked them out on my own. "But it's too much money. I mean, aren't you saving up for school? Isn't that why you're bartending?"

I knew as I heard it come out of my mouth that I was crossing the boundary into none-of-my-business land, but Bree just laughed.

"First of all, this is Richard's credit card, and he doesn't care if I go out and blow five hundred dollars. It makes him feel like a man to buy me stuff to keep me happy. He's weird like that. He'd pay for nursing school too if I let him."

My mind spun like a fan, receipts blowing in every direction. Richard had funded our spree? Now we *had* to return the boots. It was bad enough when I'd thought it was Bree's money. "These are going back," I said, closing the lid on the wedge heels.

"No, they're not. You'll offend Richard."

"He wants to pay for nursing school and you won't let

him?" Charly had stopped prancing around in the boots and was standing sideways, hands on hips, facing Bree. Still no baby bump. "Why not?"

"It's complicated," Bree said, leaning back into the pile of throw pillows on the couch and folding her arms. "It's just important to me to pay for school by myself."

"But . . ." I stopped myself. He was already paying for everything—apartment, clothes, food, and who knew what else. Either way, she was what Grandma would call a kept woman.

"So when do we get to meet Richard?" Charly asked, unzipping her boots and reaching for one of my boxes.

"Don't even. You know they're too big for you," I said, pulling it away from her.

"He's got business in Victoria all this next week," Bree said, "but he said he'll probably make it back by next weekend."

"He'll stay here, then?" I asked.

"Well . . . he's got some rental property a couple of blocks away that's vacant right now. He could stay there if you guys are, you know, uncomfortable with him staying here."

"This is his place though, right?" I asked. "Doesn't he mind that we're here?"

"No." She looked away from me, over to Charly. "He knows this is a big deal."

"We're not uncomfortable if he stays here," Charly said.

Bree smiled and Charly looked like a stroked cat.

"Amelia?" Bree asked, as if it mattered.

"No, of course. It's fine."

Theoretically, it was. What did I care if Bree was living in sin? Technically, though, it was one more person to share the bathroom, and an old man at that. He'd better not wander around in his underwear.

Charly finished sifting through the bags of stuff Bree—no, *Richard*—had bought for us: silk long johns, lip balm, wool knee socks, and cable-knit sweaters. She stood, wandered over to the kitchen, and opened the fridge like she owned it. Bree, sprawled out on the couch, didn't even seem to notice.

"So, is he hot?" Charly asked.

"Richard? No."

I gave Bree a glance. She had a sort of delicate-punk look I'm sure plenty of guys went for. And she seemed like the kind of girl to fall for the beautiful bad boys. The ones who flirt with everything female.

"You'll like him," she continued. "He's really sweet."

"I hope you don't mind me just helping myself," Charly called from inside the fridge.

"Of course not," Bree said, and turned on the TV to *CSI*.

"Oh, I've seen this one," Bree said. "It's the one with the

guy with the horse fetish who murders jockeys. You seen it?" she asked me.

I shook my head. "Would I be able to use your computer? I just want to check my email."

"Go ahead. We should leave in about an hour, but you're welcome to use it until then."

"Leave? Where are we going?"

"Lake Louise. Ezra said he's off work at eight thirty, so if we stop by then he can take us through the lost and found."

"Oh. I forgot."

I sat down at the writing desk in the corner and turned on Bree's computer. Or Richard's computer. My inbox was exactly what it had been a couple of days ago: American Eagle coupons, an iTunes receipt, a Sports Authority sale notice. My old retail world had no clue what'd happened to me. It was just piling up like nothing had changed.

There were only two real emails, one from Dad and one from Savannah. I clicked on Savannah's and read the first line.

Hey Girlie ☺☺☺ U okay??? Miss ya
soooooo bad!!!

Crap. I'd forgotten she emails like she texts. Communicating solely like this for the next six months was going to be brutal.

I skimmed the rest. Sebastian got a job bagging groceries at Winn-Dixie, her mom fired their housekeeper for stealing Vicodin, somebody plowed over the Thompsons' mailbox in the middle of the night, yada yada. No mention of Will.

I leaned back in the chair and the words became fuzzy. In Tremonton time was ticking steadily onward without me. It hurt. And for whatever reason, Savannah's gratuitous emoticons felt like salt in the wound.

The email from Dad was to both of us. He missed us already, he was proud of us, and he hoped we were being the well-behaved young ladies he knew we were. It moved from generic praise to generic advice—this email wasn't for me and it certainly wasn't for Charly. It was for the stereotypical daughters in his head. It ended with the address and phone number of a Methodist pastor in Canmore, a Pastor Frank Header. He was expecting us to call.

I stared at the screen. If there was just a single sentence that sounded like he'd been thinking of me when he wrote it, I'd have kept it. I'd have called Pastor Frank Header and introduced myself as instructed, borrowed Bree's car, and dragged Charly to church with me in the morning. I reread it. There wasn't. *Delete.*

It took us forty-five minutes to get to Lake Louise. Unfortunately, that was long enough to hear The Pedestrians' punk rendition of the *Evita* soundtrack twice.

"This is incredible," Charly shouted over "Don't Cry for Me Argentina" being screamed, double-time. "I love it!"

I loved when it was over, but then they just moved on to the next song. Unfamiliar but equally painful.

Charly sat shotgun again, which was perfect—I didn't have to lie about how amazing Bree's vocals sounded since they couldn't hear me anyway. Instead, I fogged up the glass with my breath, then rubbed it clear with my fist, over and over. Still there. That jagged line where white mountains met indigo sky couldn't be rubbed away. It looked like fractured glass, sharp enough to draw blood if I slid my finger over it.

Sharp. That was a good word for Canada. The cold, Bree, the mountains. It was a miracle I wasn't bleeding yet.

"Did you hear that, Amelia?" Charly shouted from the front seat.

I shook my head.

Bree turned down the volume at the same time as Charly turned around and yelled, *"I said I've decided I'm going to school!"*

I blinked. Bree was watching me in the rearview mirror. I could feel her big round eyes on my face.

"On Monday," Charly continued at normal volume. "With you."

I was stone. No emotion here. "Okay."

"You think Grandma is going to freak out?"

"Yes."

"Tell her for me?"

I raised an eyebrow.

"Just kidding." She turned back around.

Bree reached out and put her hand on Charly's shoulder. "It'll be tough, but I know you can do it."

I didn't know whether Bree was talking about doing high school pregnant, or telling Grandma, but she sounded like she was playing a part in a movie. Either the sympathetic guidance counselor or the all-knowing big sister.

Grandma was going to prune the life out of her rosebushes when she found out. Defiance from a whole country away—that would drive her nuts. She thought Charly should be locked up to marinate in her own shame. Flaunting her sluttiness in public, and at a school of all places, was disgraceful.

I didn't want to agree. But I didn't feel like being reduced to *the pregnant chick's sister* either, which was all I'd ever be if Charly walked into Banff Public High beside me. I'd already given up on the possibility of real friends—I was a foreign, last-semester senior in a small-town school. A snowball in hell would have as much chance for social fulfillment. I just didn't want to be a pariah.

The song changed. "Do you recognize this one?" Bree asked Charly.

Charly gave a nod, then grinned like she didn't have a care in the world and turned up the music.

• • •

We took the turnoff for Lake Louise, and drove and drove and drove up the mountain, then parked in a loading zone at the base of the lodge.

"He said he'd be coming in from his shift at about eight thirty, so he should already be there," Bree explained, and led us into a side entrance marked Employees Only.

She stamped the snow off her boots onto a mat by the door. I did the same, then nudged Charly till she did it too.

"Hey, Taylor," Bree called down the long hallway.

"Bree! Long time no see!" A girl with two French braids and suspendered snow pants waved and started toward us. She was eating a banana. "Where've you been, girl?"

"Studying."

"Oh, that's right, I forgot. How's nursing school?" She took a swig from the bottle of orange Gatorade in her other hand. "Sorry to be rude. I've gotta refuel."

"No problem. School's hard. Really hard. I'm still working at McSorley's, though. You should come by sometime."

"I will." She glanced at Charly and me for the first time, her eyes catlike and deep green. "I'm assuming you guys aren't here to ski?"

"No," Bree said. "Oh, these are my nieces, by the way. They're from Florida but they're living with me till summer. Is Ezra here?"

Taylor shook her head and the auburn braids swung

too. "He's pulling someone in. I don't know when he'll be back."

So we'd come all this way for nothing.

"Shoot," Bree said. "Ezra picked these guys up from the airport for me last night and said if we came by he'd let them look through the lost and found."

Taylor looked us up and down, her gaze suddenly critical. She stuffed the last bit of banana into her mouth and chucked the peel in the garbage. "Seriously, it's like that boy is trying to get himself fired."

Fired from a volunteer position? Scary.

Bree wrinkled her forehead. "Should we not be here?"

"Oh, no, you're fine." Taylor said. "Ezra can do no wrong in Jake's eyes. Now if *I* dipped into the lost and found before the end-of-the-season sale, there'd be hell to pay, but Ezra . . ."

"That's right. I'd forgotten Jake was running things down here." I tuned out as Bree nattered on about people I didn't know or care about.

I glanced at Charly, who shrugged. Did Ezra even remember telling us to come by? I couldn't say I was surprised he'd flaked. He had too-spacey-to-be-trusted written all over him. Probably smoked a lot of pot.

And as for Taylor, she seemed about as interested in making friends with Charly and me as I was in building an igloo.

"Why don't you guys come with me," Taylor said, bringing me back into the conversation with an earnest nod. Apparently the conversation with Bree had softened her up.

"I don't want to get you in trouble," Bree said.

"Friends of Ezra? Not possible. Boy Wonder's got special status."

"Are you two still together?" Bree asked.

Taylor rolled her eyes. "Depends who you ask. Not really."

Charly poked me with her elbow and I considered hip checking her into the wall.

I gave Taylor a closer look. Her features were either unusual or stunning, depending on the angle. Wide cheekbones, creamy skin, guarded eyes.

"I missed your names," Taylor said as we passed open doors on the left and right.

"Oh, sorry," Bree said. "I should have introduced everyone. This is Amelia and this is Charly."

"Amelia and Charly. You guys know you've got it backward, eh? People go south for the winter."

"Yeah," I said, and paused. Was it worth even giving her the tidy version? Telling her that we were here to get to know our dead mother's sister seemed like more than we owed a complete stranger, but maybe we'd be seeing her around occasionally. It was hard to tell.

"Charly's pregnant," Bree said without warning.

It felt like a kick to the gut. I wasn't breathing, my heart may not have been pumping, but somehow I was still walking—we were all still walking down the hall like Bree had updated us on the weather and not the status of Charly's uterus.

"They came here to, you know"—Bree waved her hand in the air—"get some space."

Any reservations I'd had about hating Bree evaporated instantly. She was pure evil.

Charly kept her chin tucked into her coat so I couldn't even see her face.

Taylor turned around and walked backward, looking back and forth between us. Then it hit me: She couldn't remember which of us was Charly. I jerked my thumb in Charly's direction.

Taylor gave her a weak smile. "Um, congratulations?"

"Yeah, thanks," Charly said, still looking down.

Taylor turned back around. *Swish-swish, swish-swish, swish-swish.* The sound of her snow pants did nothing for the awkwardness. It was like one of those horrific dreams where you're at church and you suddenly realize you're naked at the same time as everyone around you does. Except we weren't going to wake up. Charly was just going to get fatter.

I concentrated on Bree's feet in front of me. She was

close enough to trip. If I had a field hockey stick, I could just snake it between her legs, hook the ankle, and yank. Did she have Tourette's syndrome? What next, screaming obscenities? There'd been no reason for that little outburst. It was like we were a tragedy arranged especially for her to show off.

We reached the end of the interminably long hall, then followed Taylor down an echoey stairwell to another hallway. Bree had gushed about how gorgeous the Lake Louise Lodge was, but the grey cement floors and cinderblock walls looked less than impressive.

Taylor opened a closed door and flicked the lights on. "Welcome to the treasure box."

Several rows of overflowing wooden shelves stretched out before us, cluttered with huge plastic bins. Someone had gone nuts with a label maker: GLOVES/MITTENS, TOQUES, GOGGLES, NECK WARMERS, JACKETS.

"This isn't what I pictured," Charly whispered. "At all."

I was still too mad at Bree to speak. Charly was right, though. What I'd pictured was a box of mismatched socks and ratty scarves that smelled like bad breath.

"It's amazing the things people leave behind, isn't it?" Taylor said. "Most of it's expensive too, and barely worn. What are you guys looking for?"

"Everything," Bree answered for us.

A half hour later we were outfitted for nuclear winter. Mittens, gloves, scarves, neck warmers, ear bands, break-and-enter style face masks Taylor called balaclavas, toques, heavy jackets, and snow pants.

"Are you sure this is okay?" I asked. The mountain of clothes combined with the mountain of new clothes at home was too much. We must just scream charity case.

"Do you guys need ski gear?" Taylor asked, as if she hadn't heard me at all, holding up a pair of goggles.

"I don't ski," I said.

"What about you, Charly?"

Awkward silence.

"Are you kidding me?" I asked, the words coming out harsher than I'd meant them to. But how many pregnant women could she possibly encounter on the slopes?

"Oh yeah. Sorry." Then she turned to me again. "Are you sure you don't want to learn? I'm an instructor here too. I could teach you." She put the goggles over my head and the world turned orange.

I pulled them off and stared at her. I didn't want to hate her. She was probably very nice. She had one of those big sincere smiles and the look of someone who had a dog, something lovable like a Lab. Under different circumstances, I was sure we could have all eaten cookie dough and watched *Top Model* marathons together.

"No, thank you," I said.

. . .

"That was so humiliating," Charly hissed.

I sighed and rolled onto my back, then scooted back over to my side of the bed. She'd been downstairs talking with Bree for the last hour. The least she could've done was get in bed quietly.

"I know," I said. Thanks to Bree and her fat mouth, the entire experience had been every shade of awkward. We'd left the lodge with a duffel bag of winter wear and zero dignity, actually relieved to get outside into the cold. And Ezra hadn't even showed up.

"What is the matter with you?"

I sat up. "*Me?* Bree puts you on display like you're a traveling freak show and you're pissed at *me?*"

"*Shhh!*" She pointed over the edge of the loft, like I'd forgotten we only had three-and-a-half walls.

"She closed her door," I muttered. But the last thing I wanted was Bree worming her way into a fight between Charly and me. I lay back down. "You're seriously mad at me?"

"Why do you have to treat everyone like you can barely stand them?" She was whispering, but her proximity to my ear canal made it sound more like really quiet screaming. "You think you're so much better than everyone else! Bree bought us all that stuff, and you treat her like crap, and then Taylor, who doesn't even know us, was super nice and you treat her like crap too! You're like some crazy rabid dog, just waiting to bite somebody's arm off."

"Nice. Thanks." I turned away so she could continue griping at my back.

"I know, you're miserable here. Your life is over and it's not even your fault, so fine, go ahead and feel sorry for yourself, but would it kill you to consider that it could be worse? Because it could. You could be me." Her voice cracked. I refused to turn and confirm tears. "So just stop being so obnoxious to the people who are actually trying to help me. They aren't the reason your life sucks."

"I know that. You are."

"Whatever."

"No, *not* whatever," I said, bringing my legs up to my chest and hugging them to me so I wouldn't turn and start pulling her hair. "You caused this! You want me to feel sorry for you because you screwed up? How about taking a little personal responsibility for once in your life?"

"I am! That's why I'm going to school Monday."

"That has nothing to do with taking personal responsibility. That's just getting bossed around by Bree." I wanted to growl just thinking about the look on Bree's face when she'd asked me if it was what Charly really wanted. Like that was relevant. Like I was the worst kind of sister rather than the one who was trying to protect her. "Think about it, Charly. In a few months you're going to be a whale, no offense. People are going to treat you like you're contagious. Do you really want that?"

"Oh, I get it now!" she said. "*You're* embarrassed. You'd rather go to a new school completely alone than with me."

"Exactly!"

I stared hard into her face. She didn't look grey like she had for the last few months, the sunken skin below her eyes had filled out, and the acne had cleared. After three months of looking terrible, she'd morphed from sickly to beautiful again. Her yellow hair shone gold in the moonlight.

Maybe Charly wouldn't be an embarrassment at all. Maybe she'd be adorable, lovable, effervescent Charly again. Maybe that would be worse.

"What did Bree do to earn your undying love?" I asked.

She didn't answer.

"She's not our mother."

"I know that."

"She didn't even know her," I continued. "She's nothing like her."

"But you *don't* know that!"

I sucked in two lungs' worth of air, ready to fire back, before realizing I had no rebuttal. I did know that. Deep in my gut I knew my mother would've been the one person in

the universe to care about me right now. And Bree didn't.
When I looked at Bree, talked to Bree, thought about Bree,
I just knew my mother was nothing like her.

"Bree was ten when she died," I said. "Five when Mom
moved away. They're only half sis—"

"*I know!*"

But I could hear the lie in the way her voice shook.
Knowing and feeling aren't the same thing.

Chapter 12

t snowed all Sunday, fat, wet flakes, so thick the world beyond the window was just a curtain of lace.

My first blizzard. That was a pretty good excuse for not going to church. According to Bree, the roads would be slippery. Grandma wouldn't want us dying at the expense of one Sunday's worth of worship. Bree did say I could borrow her car, but I didn't want to owe her anything.

Instead, Charly dragged me out to explore Banff in the afternoon while Bree was at the library studying. We wandered around in the snowstorm until I couldn't feel my fingers or toes or face. It was misery, not that Charly would admit it. Admitting it would have required her to say more than two words to me, which she wasn't doing. We spent most of our time in gift shops, pretending to be fascinated with stuffed animals dressed up like Royal Canadian Mounted Police and maple leaf coasters, just so we didn't have to be outside.

At an ice cream shop around the corner from Bree's, we actually pretended to deliberate over flavors just so we could be inside. "How does this place stay open?" I asked through chattering teeth. The shop was warm, but I still couldn't stop shivering. "This is like selling hot chocolate on the beach."

Charly shrugged and tossed her mini sample spoon in the garbage.

"Your lips are blue," I said. "We're going home."

She didn't argue.

"Banff one, Mercer sisters zero," I said as the bell over the door jingled.

"Thanks for coming!" called the lady behind the counter.

"Will there still be school tomorrow?" I asked Bree when she reappeared at seven with pad thai and spring rolls.

"What do you mean?"

"I just thought there might be a snow day or something."

She laughed. "Snow day. That's cute. So American."

"That smells so good! Pad thai is my favorite," Charly said, taking the stool beside me, suddenly alive after her day of sulking. She'd had Thai food once before in Tallahassee. Once.

"Eat up." Bree put bowls in front of us and started scooping spoonfuls of oily noodles into them.

The pad thai smelled like man sweat. "I just had a bowl of cereal. I'm tired. I think I'm going to go to bed."

Nobody objected.

I lay in bed and stared out into the star-studded blackness beyond the window. The noise was impossible to ignore—not loud but grating. The giggling. The *shh*-ing. The trying to be quiet, then forgetting midway through a story and erupting into hyena cackles. For all her cute-as-a-button-ness, Bree had a laugh that reminded me of the noise Charly had made that time she shredded her fingertips on the cheese grater.

Tonight Charly's laugh was worse, though. She'd spent the entire day refusing to talk to me, but now she was sunshine personified. Apparently cute-as-a-button Bree brought out the sweet-as-pie Charly. They were perfect for each other.

I closed my eyes and pictured Banff Public High. Bree had pointed it out from the car on our way back from Calgary yesterday. It looked small and stark and unforgiving.

I'd already had thirteen first days of school, and I'd

choreographed every detail of all of them: wardrobe down to hair accessories and underwear; backpack contents from backup calculator to emergency tampon; color-coded schedule for the whole day, including time allotted for a longer-than-usual hair conditioning treatment, a slower-than-usual walk from the parking lot to my first class, and an extended post-lunch makeup check.

Charly mocked, but I ignored her. Uncomfortable underwear, a broken calculator, or frizzy hair could put a serious damper on a first day, and first days meant something. Or at least they used to.

What mattered about tomorrow? Not my classes. I just had to pass. I'd wasted far too many years earning perfect grades to get into Columbia, and the thought of that huge chunk of my life squandered stung. *A thousand paper cuts and a thousand lemons.* That was one of Savannah's favorite phrases. I'd never had a first day without Savannah.

I wasn't too late to apply other places—University of Miami, Florida State, University of Central Florida—but even starting to fill out the applications turned out to be acute torture, so I gave up. I'd get to it later.

I didn't belong at any of those schools. The one place I thought I belonged had already decided I was wrong.

As for tomorrow, friends didn't matter either. My real friends were a thousand miles away and I wasn't fooling myself about anybody I would meet tomorrow.

Last-semester seniors didn't waste time on new girls, and I didn't really feel like wasting my time on them.

New girl. I'd never been that before, but I'd spent the last few weeks stewing over it. In Tremonton new girls got ignored unless they were gorgeous like Luciana, in which case they were drooled over by the guys and hated by the girls. They were mostly just alone. I'd accepted the fact that that'd be me: walking alone, studying alone, eating alone. But now Charly would be there.

A wave of something sweet and rancid rolled through me. Relief and dread weren't supposed to combine like this. Maybe I was getting the stomach flu.

The synthesized *American Idol* theme blared from below.

Then, "She sucked," from Bree.

"Agreed," Charly said.

"We should be on that show."

"I know."

I put a pillow over my head. I had no clue what I was going to wear tomorrow and my backpack wasn't packed. I didn't even know what time we had to leave to get to school on time. And it didn't matter.

It was still snowing in the morning.

We sat in Bree's car, shivering, watching flakes fall as she scraped the ice off her windows. White flakes on a black sky, like chalk on a brand-new chalkboard. It would've been beautiful if it wasn't so horrifically cold, and if my body didn't ache from clenching.

It was still snowing as I trudged up the icy steps of Banff Public High School behind Charly and Bree, still snowing as I stood in the principal's office, staring out her window. Still dark too. I could barely see the row of town houses across the street, and I couldn't see the mountains at all, but I could feel them pushing in on the air around me.

The principal walked in. Dr. Ashton was a leathery woman in a white pantsuit. Apparently the tanning booth industry was alive and well in Canada. She greeted us with a cigarette-stained smile and sour breath.

"How are you doing, dear?" she asked, giving Bree a hug. Then she pointed to chairs. "Sit," she commanded.

We sat.

"Sorry I'm late. There is a whole gaggle of brats out there wanting to talk to me about something or other. Diploma exam grievances, schedule grievances, missing rugby equipment grievances, premenstrual grievances, who knows." She put a pair of cat-eye bifocals on her nose, then pulled two pieces of paper from a binder. "Behold, your schedules," she said, handing one to each of us. "Don't worry about being able to find your classes. This building is too small to get lost in. Trust me, I've tried."

I pictured her hiding in a stairwell, chain-smoking,

shuddering at the thought of being found by teenagers. I hadn't planned on liking this woman.

"If you'd like, I can have one of the students show you where each room is, but to be honest, unless you're complete idiots, you shouldn't have a hard time."

"No," I said quickly, picturing the social misfits who volunteered for the tour guide assignment back at Primrose. "No, thank you."

She looked from me to Charly, then back to me again.

"Good choice. We're having a short assembly this morning, and from there you'll go straight to your first classes."

I looked at my schedule. First period was photography, followed by something called CALM. That'd better be an acronym for something and not some New Agey meditation class being shouted at me by my schedule. "What's CALM?"

"Career and Life Management. It's a required course for an Alberta high school diploma. Don't even try to wriggle out of it. Many have tried, none have succeeded. And you," she said, turning to Charly, "you're the pregnant one?"

Out of the corner of my eye I saw Charly flinch. She'd never had to say yes to that question aloud. She didn't have time to before Dr. Ashton barreled on. "You're meeting with Ms. Lee, the guidance counselor, after lunch."

"Um," Charly said, picking at a little rip in the upholstery of her chair with her index finger. "Why? I mean, too late for the safe sex lecture, right?"

Dr. Ashton raised one eyebrow. "I'll say."

"I don't do well with guidance in general."

"You'll be seeing Ms. Lee regularly," Dr. Ashton continued, "on the off chance that pregnancy is more than just a physical condition."

Charly's finger was digging into the stuffing of the chair now. I resisted the urge to pull her hand away.

"Stop destroying my piece-of-crap furniture," Dr. Ashton said, squinting over her bifocals at Charly's hand. "Have you thought about when you want to tell the other students?"

Charly put her hands in her lap. Of course not.

"You don't look pregnant yet, and you're . . . three months?"

She just sat there.

"Four," I said.

Dr. Ashton swiveled her head to me, blinked, then swiveled back to Charly. "Theoretically, you could keep it a secret for another couple of months under baggy clothes, but I'm not so sure that's a good idea. From what Bree's told me, you've been playing that game for too long."

I stared at Charly's face, willing her to look at me. If she'd just look, she'd see my eyes screaming, *Bail, Charly!*

Go home! Curl up on the couch and hide until this is over! But she wouldn't.

"It's not my decision, but I'd recommend you tell people why you're here," Dr. Ashton continued, wiggling a pencil between her two fingers like she wished it was a noxious, tar-packed cancer stick. "It'll be a relief, and it'll take the pressure off later. You won't be wondering how and when to explain, you won't be wondering if people suspect why you look like you swallowed a basketball."

I turned my glare to her. Did she honestly think *Hello, my name is Charly, and I'm knocked up* was a good opener? Why not just make her wear a scarlet letter? And while she's at it, a T-shirt for me saying *I'm with preggers.*

Dr. Ashton was tapping the pencil on the rim of her mug now. Maybe she wasn't just hopped up on coffee and nicotine. Maybe it was crack.

"Either way," Dr. Ashton said, "you'll need someone to talk about things with, which is why you've got a standing appointment with Ms. Lee."

"She *has* people to talk about things with," I blurted out.

Dr. Ashton did the swivel-head-and-blink again. Bree gave me a subtle shake of her head.

"I realize that," Dr. Ashton continued slowly, like I was mentally disabled or something. "And she's lucky to have a support system." Then back at Charly, "But you might need someone besides your sister and your aunt."

Bree. She'd done this. I looked at her but she was gazing at Dr. Ashton, nodding like an audience member on those TV evangelist shows. Any moment now she'd shout *Amen!*

Charly, meanwhile, looked like she was about to become roadkill, and it was hard to feel sorry for her. Why hadn't she thought about what going to school here meant? Obviously, she had issues with thinking things through, but I'd *told* her she didn't want to do this.

She'd been caught up imagining meeting cool people on her great Canadian adventure. Just a little push in the wrong direction from surrogate-mother-of-the-year Bree, and now here Charly was with her bugged-out eyes and sinking shoulders, realizing this wasn't going to be summer camp or even winter camp. This was going to be hell.

Something glittered in the window and I looked up. Crystal daggers framed the top edge. Real icicles. They looked just like the plastic ones Grandma strung up every Christmas. The sky had lightened to an inky blue. At this rate we'd see daylight by noon.

"Okay," Charly said.

"Okay, you'll talk to the guidance counselor?" Bree asked.

"Okay, I'll tell people."

I kept my eyes on the icicles. No need to look at Dr. Ashton or Bree; the smugness rolling off them reeked almost as much as the nicotine seeping from Dr. Ashton's pores. But they *could* be smug. Neither of them would be cleaning up the devastation when Charly was completely humiliated and ostracized. For them this was just stadium seating at a really depressing movie.

Bree left after the meeting. Charly and I followed Dr. Ashton into the empty gymnasium.

"Brace yourselves for impact," Dr. Ashton said, and motioned to a couple of chairs.

We sat and watched as the BPHS student body, all 163 of them, filed in.

They didn't look like Primrose students, but I couldn't say exactly why that was. I wanted there to be one salient reason, some kind of generalization to guide my future generalizations, but all my observations just contradicted each other.

At first the girls seemed more glam—jewelry, heeled boots, runway outfits—but then a big group of granolas settled in the left-middle section. They looked like they'd rather eat makeup than wear it.

Maybe it was their hair. It was just *less* in every way: shorter, less teased, less bleached, less curled. I was suddenly aware of how long mine was. I had to be the only person with hair that went past my shoulder blades, although a few of those granolas had messy buns hiding hair of indeterminable length.

Where were the cheerleader types? I thought of Savannah, with her perfectly hot-rolled ponytail and hair bows, and felt a pang of homesickness.

"Is it just me, or is everyone wearing black?" Charly whispered in my ear.

"It's just you," I whispered back. But maybe there was less color.

As for the guys, they weren't so foreign. The universal high school guy prototype: all dorks, some just more so than others.

A handful of teachers clumped together in the back, where they could nurse their coffee mugs and glance warily at Dr. Ashton from a safe distance.

Nobody pretended to be friendly. Nobody smiled. Some of them stared at us with lukewarm curiosity as they walked in—*hmm, new people, I almost care, except I don't*—then turned back to their friends.

It didn't really matter, though. These people could've been exact copies of the students at Primrose, and it wouldn't have made me more permanent or Charly's pregnancy less defining.

Dr. Ashton stood up front and spoke into a completely unnecessary microphone for a crowd this small.

"Welcome back," she said, panning the audience, waiting for the talking to die down. "I can't tell you how much I missed you kids over the break. Longest two weeks of my life, as usual. You all look thrilled to see me too."

Somebody coughed. The apathy in the room was too thick for groans.

Dr. Ashton launched into a halfhearted motivational speech, covering a bunch of totally unrelated topics: New Year's resolutions, how to access results of something called diploma exams online, less skipping school to go skiing, carbon footprint awareness. And then at the end she threw Charly and me into the mix.

"As you all probably noticed walking in, we have two new students." She gave us a wave and the sea of heads turned our direction. I kept my eyes on Dr. Ashton. "They're from the States, so keep the anti-American tirades to a minimum when they're around. Amelia is in grade twelve—Amelia, stand up—"

I stood, silently cursing her.

"—and Charly is in grade eleven."

Charly stood too.

"They'll be here for the rest of the year, so please try to make them feel welcome. Or at least resist the urge to make fun of their adorable little accents. Girls, sit."

We sat. Up until that point I had respected the sarcasm, the deadpan humor, the unwillingness to pretend the students liked her and vice versa, but that was over. Now I had to hate her.

The rest of our day unfolded with a predictable degree

of doom. I found my classes, none of which had assigned seats, which meant I was surrounded by people who actually liked each other and wished they'd arrived sooner so they didn't have to pretend I wasn't right there in their midst.

Everyone was polite, and a couple of people were even friendly, but in a brittle way. Like their Canadian consciences were forcing them to be welcoming, but they were secretly wishing I'd never been born.

"This is purgatory," Charly said over lunch. We were sitting just the two of us at one end of the table closest to the exit, eating the roast beef sandwiches Bree had surprised us with this morning. I'd have to find a way to tell her how much I hated mayo.

"Purgatory? I wish."

"Well, it isn't hell."

"What makes this better than hell?" I asked, scraping the mayo off my bread with a plastic fork. Charly hadn't thrown this many words in my direction in days.

"Me. Hell would be you sitting alone at this table. You'd be the sad, lonely mayo girl."

"Wow. Thanks for making my life worth living, Charly. Where would I be without you?"

"You're welcome."

We sat in our own thick silence, conversations and laughter pushing in on us from all directions.

"So I told a few people."

I put the sandwich down and wiped my fingers on a napkin. My mouth felt sticky from the mayo I'd missed. "Wow. I . . ." I needed a minute before I opened my mouth and said something too mean to take back. "You didn't waste any time."

She shrugged. "It wasn't as hard as I thought it would be. This guy in my English class asked me why I was here and I just said because I'm pregnant and I wanted to stay with my aunt until I had the baby."

I glanced around me. The bubble around us seemed suddenly larger, more impenetrable, and the people on the outside were staring. Even the ones not looking at us. How long did it take for a tidbit of gossip to become common knowledge?

"And then this girl in Chem asked me the same thing, and I gave her the same answer."

The stares intensified. All morning, I'd been floating from class to class feeling invisible, but now I realized that was all wrong. Charly and I weren't invisible. We were the focal point. They all knew.

"You couldn't have given me," I sputtered, "I don't know, a week, to meet a few people before turning us into sideshow freaks?"

She crumpled her brown bag and tossed it into the garbage can beside the table. "It doesn't have anything to do with you."

"Like hell it doesn't."

"Are you going to finish that?" she asked, pointing to my half-eaten sandwich.

"No." Before she could take it, I picked it up and threw it in the garbage.

As arranged, we met after school at the front doors.

We walked home in silence, daylight fading around us. It had finally stopped snowing and the air felt eerily still.

I didn't want to find out how her appointment with the guidance counselor was. And I didn't need to tell her how the rest of my day went, how there had been polite smiles, pitying glances, and a couple of timid hi's from people already far enough on the fringe to not have to worry about their social status getting any worse—freaks and geeks.

It was cold, but I was bundled up enough, and mad enough, that I didn't notice until my thighs were on fire. Silk long johns. Mine were still at home in the package. How was I supposed to know that frozen denim scraping skin felt like sandpaper?

By the time we reached Bree's apartment it was nearly dark and my hands were shaking from the cold. It took me a good minute to get the key in the keyhole, and I suddenly remembered that Jack London short story we'd read last year in English where the guy freezes to death because his hands are too cold to light a match.

Bree was still at school, but she'd left a note on the table.

Hey Girlies,

I'll be back at 4:30, but I have to leave again for McSorley's at 6:00. Help yourselves to the leftovers in the fridge (shepherd's pie.)

Bree

Almost forgot—Charly, I called and made your appointment with Dr. Young for next Tuesday at noon.

"Girlies," I muttered. "Super awesome."

Charly was already dishing the leftover pub food into a bowl.

"So your doctor's appointment," I said. "Am I supposed to cut class for that?"

"No."

"Since when do you go to the doctor's by yourself? I have to hold your hand for the flu shot." I took a bite of the cold shepherd's pie. Too salty.

"Bree will take me."

Of course. I chucked the container back in the fridge. From the corner of my eye I could see Charly watching me, chewing like a cow.

"You aren't going to heat that up?" I asked.

"What do you care?"

"Good point." I left her, lugging my backpack up to our room. I had a surprising amount of homework, considering the pointlessness of my classes.

The wobbly card table in the corner was littered with Charly's makeup and candy wrappers and *People* magazines, so I sat cross-legged on the bed and took out my CALM textbook. We were starting with personality testing and then moving on to career testing. Apparently I needed a textbook to tell me I didn't want to work at McDonald's.

Downstairs, the TV went on.

She'd chosen Bree.

The textbook sat on my lap, open to the wrong page, its corners digging into my thighs. I didn't even try to find the personality test. I was pretty sure it couldn't tell me why my own sister hated me, or motivate me to apply for a college I didn't want to go to. The weight of the day pushed down on me. I leaned back into the pillows and closed my eyes. This was a different kind of exhaustion. Every inch of my body felt weary from cold and frustration, but I was too agitated to sleep.

I needed the old Charly. Or maybe Savannah.

I closed my textbook and went back downstairs to the computer, ignoring Charly and the booing fans on *Montel* in the background. And there it was, a single miraculous email from Savannah. It was like she'd known. Despite the entire continent and the curtain of lies that separated us, she could tell I needed her. I opened it.

Call me

I wasn't supposed to do that. Grandma had assured Bree that we wouldn't be racking up international call charges unless it was an emergency. I'd told Savannah that. My stomach churned. *Call me.* Something was wrong.

I dialed her cell, then tapped jittery fingers on the desk and imagined catastrophes. Maybe her parents were finally getting a divorce. Maybe she and Sebastian broke up. Maybe she'd broken her neck at cheerleading practice and was lying in a hospital bed hooked up to a ventilator. She picked up after the second ring.

"Amelia."

The sound of her voice made me so happy I wanted to cry. "Are you okay?"

"I'm fine." She didn't sound fine. She sounded nervous. "Fine."

"Yeah. I mean, I miss you. Calculus sucks and I wish you were here to do my homework for me. I don't know why I didn't take it with you last semester. And Sebastian works 24/7, which means I'm spending way too much time with the squad girls. They're driving me a little nuts."

I exhaled warily. This was not emergency material, but her voice was guarded.

"So how is Canada?" she asked. "Are you loving it?"

I'd almost forgotten. Talking to Savannah meant suffocating in lies. "Yeah, it's great."

"Real convincing."

"No, it is," I said. "I'm just tired."

"And is your aunt cool?"

"So, when you said *call me* . . ."

She sighed. "Still just as anal as usual, I see."

"I'm not anal. This isn't my phone and you know I'm not supposed to call the States just to chat. I assumed *call me* meant there was some kind of emergency."

"Fine, it's not an emergency. I just needed to talk to you about something." Her voice broke over *something* and all her oddness, the banal chatter, the twinge of hurt in her voice over my questioning her became clear.

She knew.

I felt cold, momentarily drained of blood and thoughts. Words wouldn't come. I sank into a seat at the island, put my forehead on the marble, and waited.

She couldn't know. There was no way.

"I heard something today at school," she said. "At first I couldn't even believe it was true, it was just so . . ."

School. If someone at school knew, the whole town

knew, which meant Dad was about to know. I felt sick to my stomach. Maybe he already knew. Or maybe he was finding out right now.

". . . I don't know. I tried to write you an email, but it just felt wrong. Are you still there?"

"Yeah."

"I thought it'd be better to really talk, you know?"

I wasn't sure. Hearing about our scandal seeping through Tremonton like poison—how would that be any less sickening than reading it?

"Why aren't you saying anything?" she asked.

"Because you're freaking me out."

"Don't freak out."

I waited for a reason not to freak out, but she didn't give me one. She wanted me to ask what she was talking about, I could tell, and was most likely pissed that I'd lied to her—like that was even close to the worst part of all this. But I was too sapped to play along.

"It's Will," she said finally.

"Will." His name, coming from my own mouth, sounded ridiculous. So short and dull and insignificant.

"He got back together with Luciana."

"Will," I said again. It sounded different this time. That single lame syllable stung. My whole body felt singed, and my lips ached with the effort, but I had to say his name once more. "Will did."

"Yeah. But it's more than that. They're *engaged*. As in, going to get married. I keep thinking she's got to be pregnant or something, but the rumor mill says she's not and that they're just total idiots. I mean, seriously, they're seventeen. Supposedly his parents are freaking out."

She waited for a few long seconds that I should have been filling with something dismissive, like *surprise, surprise* or *give it up for this year's prom king and queen*, but I couldn't. I might break if I tried to speak.

"I'm so sorry, Amelia. Maybe I shouldn't have told you. I feel terrible for, you know, making you think he might still be into you."

Oh, that. She *had* done that. But this sensation of my heart being squeezed and crushed had nothing to do with anything Savannah put into my mind. I'd pretended my own way into this pain.

"I really did think he was going to try to get back together with you. Are you okay? I know you were kind of hopeful about things."

Kind of hopeful. That was an interesting way of saying it. Humiliatingly and inexcusably *kind of hopeful*.

"Hey, crazy," Charly muttered, "what's with the pacing? I'm trying to watch TV here."

I stared at her. She was on the couch, wrapped in a black crumb-covered throw, shoving the last cookie of an entire sleeve of Oreos into her mouth. I'd forgotten she was even in the room. And I *was* pacing—circling the couch, then the island, then the couch again, then the island again—but I didn't even remember getting out of the chair.

I shook my head at her and turned the next corner of my figure eight. She had no idea. The devastation was so painful my chest might explode if I stopped moving.

Charly shook her head in disgust and turned back to the TV. "And I'm the one who has to go to counseling."

Teenagers screamed out from the television. Montel was doing some my-kid-is-out-of-control intervention, and the delinquents were all getting sent to boot camp for a couple of days, wailing and kicking like it was death row.

"Amelia, are you okay?" Savannah repeated.

Will was engaged to Luciana. Was I okay? I didn't own him. I'd never owned him, or if I had, it'd only been for a short while, before I'd been eclipsed by Charly. We'd been together for so long—eighteen months?— but how much of that had he spent falling out of love with me?

"Amelia?"

"Yeah. Sorry. I'm okay."

Tears burned behind my eyes, so I squeezed them shut. It was all so screwed up. I'd wanted him, and I thought he'd wanted me, but then he'd wanted Charly, and then he was with Luciana, and I was with nobody, and Charly was with child, and that made me think he'd want me all over again? So stupid.

But if she hadn't been so *Charly* in the first place, he would never have stopped wanting me. That I knew.

"You're way too good for him," Savannah said.

"No, I'm not." I sunk down on the couch beside Charly. She glared at me and turned up the volume. Apparently my pacing the room was preferable to being this close to her.

Savannah moved on to vilifying Luciana, but the chanting audience members were louder. I couldn't focus. I ripped a hangnail off with my teeth and watching a single drop of blood spring to the surface.

"—supposedly she called him every night sobbing for the entire time they were broken up, but—"

I should have been loving her for this. This was what best friends were supposed to do, and she was good at it, so emphatic and blindly supportive. So why couldn't I stomach it? I just didn't want to be cheered up or lied to anymore. I closed my eyes and willed her to understand that I was finished pretending that Will was ever going to come back to me. But of course she couldn't really know me anymore—there were too many layers of lies between us. It wasn't her fault. My secrets, my deceit, my isolation. All for Charly.

"—and everybody knows that while they were broken up she hooked up with half of the—"

"*Enough!*" The anger in my own voice startled me.

A sharp intake of breath on the end of the line made my stomach lurch. Regret washed through me.

"I'm sorry," I said. "It's okay. I'm okay. I didn't mean to yell."

"*Go somewhere else,*" Charly hissed in my ear.

"What was that?" Savannah asked. "It sounds like you're in a movie theater or something."

"Nothing. Just Charly."

Charly scowled and turned up the volume three more bars.

Savannah sighed, and pretended I hadn't just yelled at her. "I feel like you need me. I hate that I can't be with you right now."

"Yeah, me too." It was the right thing to say, and I wanted to mean it. I'd thought I did need her, up until a moment ago. But now I felt like metal, hard and cold, like I was beyond needing anyone at all.

"You know he wasn't right for you, don't you?" she asked.

"Whatever. It doesn't matter anymo—"

"*Go. Somewhere. Else!*" Charly screamed without warning, her face so close spittle sprayed my cheek.

I turned and stared into her eyes. Huge pupils, bared

teeth, she was practically vibrating with rage. She looked like a wild animal.

"I'm watching TV!"

I'd lost Will to this beast.

"Amelia, are you okay?" Savannah asked. Too much. The concern was thicker and sweeter than I could stand. "Is that the TV or Charly? Are you sure you—"

"I have to go," I said. "I'll call you later," and hung up before she could say another word.

In a single second my blood surged from cold to boiling, pumping too fast to control how hard I slammed the phone down on the coffee table. The back flew off. The battery clattered to the floor.

No Will. No friends. No life. No Columbia. No future. My chest felt raw, like claws had ripped me open and scraped my heart.

"Hey psycho, you broke her phone!" Charly pointed to the piece that had spun to a stop in front of her. Montel hugged a blubbering reformed teen.

"Her phone? *Her phone?*" I was yelling now, louder than Charly, louder than the TV, louder than the screaming in my brain. "You broke my life, Charly! And if you weren't such a *slut* I'd be at home right now. Instead I'm stuck here, watching both of our lives end."

"Oh, poor you!"

"I wish you'd never been born!" I screamed, and paused

long enough to suck in air for the death blow. "And if mom was alive she'd feel the same way."

"*So leave!*" she yelled.

Suddenly I was watching, not acting or feeling, but watching myself get up off the couch, fumble with my boots, rip the door open, and slam it behind me.

Chapter 13

Outside.

It took a moment to grasp what I'd done. At first it was all pain and heat and blood screaming through my veins as I ran down the stairs and onto the sidewalk.

But then I realized. *Outside.* Still in Canada, still winter, without a coat, I was *outside* and I couldn't turn around. There could be no slinking back in for my coat and wallet.

My cheeks burned. I put my hand to my face and felt tears. Were they freezing to my skin? I wiped them with my sleeve as a gust of wind blew right through my sweater, wrapping cold fingers around my rib cage.

I stumbled forward. I had no choice. I walked. A gift shop, a bank, a church, the post office, a Sushi bar, another gift shop—I didn't want to go into any of them. They were all too small and well manned to hide in. I needed somewhere big and warm and impersonal that didn't want me to spend money, where nobody would come and ask me if I was interested in buying maple candies or how the weather at Lake Louise was. And preferably not somewhere with a CANADIAN GIRLS DO IT BETTER T-shirt in the window.

I closed my mind, and let the wind push me forward, farther away from Bree's apartment, the opposite direction of school and McSorley's and the roads I'd already explored. I couldn't go back. I zigzagged, right on Caribou Street, left on Beaver, right on Bear, and then right again on Wolf, around and around until I had no clue which way I'd come.

Will didn't want me. Columbia didn't want me. Had Dad ever wanted *anybody*? And after everything I'd done for her, Charly didn't want me either. Grandma only wanted me to be the Amelia she required me to be, and she clearly didn't want me *with* her. Or if she did, she wanted her dignity and the Mercers' tidy Christian image more.

My skin stung and my ears ached, but the pain felt deserved.

Block after block, I wandered on, the blur of garish ski jackets all around me, everyone moving forward, pushing toward the warm places they were heading.

Why was I trying to live in this godforsaken ice tomb when all I had to do was call Dad and tell him everything? I'd known that all along, hadn't I? That I could just pick up the phone and this whole stupid thing would be over. But what if I did? Grandma would never forgive me and Dad would never forgive Charly. We'd be permanently broken.

Suddenly, the anger wasn't enough to keep the cold out. When had I started shaking? I had my hands curled into balls, the sleeves of my sweater wrapped over my fists, but it hadn't helped. I couldn't feel my fingers at all. I had to get inside.

It was dark now, and the sidewalks were even busier with people still bundled from the slopes, the post-ski glow on their chapped cheeks. Out here in nothing more than a flimsy sweater and jeans, and surrounded by mountain-bundled diehards, I was practically naked. But invisible too.

My thoughts were fuzzy and the muscles in my legs felt weak. I just needed to sit down for a minute, but a snowbank seemed like a bad idea.

I hit Bison Street and saw a group of girls across the way who looked vaguely familiar. Had I seen them in school? I had. They were standing in a cluster under a streetlamp, laughing. I ducked left so they wouldn't see me, turned the corner, and saw my sanctuary: the Banff Public Library. Warm and free and perfect. My body shuddered in anticipation of relief, and I forced my feet to move faster.

I hurried across the street, ignoring traffic and ice patches, ignoring numbness, letting the glowing windows pull me in by my eyes. I was a mosquito charging toward a bug zapper. A flight of stairs led from the sidewalk down to the entrance of the wood building, as if the library had sunk a full story into the ground over time. I ran down the stairs, nearly tripping over the uneven steps, catching myself on the railing. It took me three tries to curl my fingers around the door handle and pull it open, but when I finally did, the heat rushed out and sucked me in.

Warmth! The door clattered shut behind me. I felt the heat, but I didn't. I'd imagined it just pouring into me and filling me up, but I was encased in too many layers of cold. I stood perfectly still, body clenched, eyes closed, my muscles like strings tightened to near snapping.

Then finally, my face started to burn. Pain and relief—who'd have thought they'd be such a horrifically beautiful mix? It meant I was warming up, didn't it?

I hobbled forward, my legs feeling like somebody else's, then glanced around. The library was almost empty and blurry around the edges, like an antique photograph. An old man sat on the far side of the room reading a newspaper at a table. And off to my left a middle-aged woman was twirling the romance novel spinny thing. What was that word? "Merry-go-round," but books didn't ride merry-go-rounds.

I tried to sigh but my chattering teeth stifled it. No tourists, no canned retail music, no cozy ski-town aura. Just quiet. Books. Heat. A tacky maroon chair at the end of one bookshelf sat empty. It looked velvety. Maybe I could curl up in it and sleep forever.

"What are you doing here?"

I turned toward the sound and the room spun. When it stopped, there behind the circulation desk was a guy. A guy I knew? Yeah, *that* guy, the cute one from the airport. Why couldn't I think of his name? Ezra. Yeah, Ezra, except he looked different.

"What are *you* doing here?" I tried to ask, but the words slurred together. Why did I sound drunk? He looked good. And annoyed.

"I work here."

"*Here?*" But wasn't he a ski guy, a skier, a patroller guy whatever? Ski guys didn't work in libraries. Librarians had master's degrees and bifocals and hot flashes. Hot flashes. Was that what was happening to me, or was I still cold?

"I work part-time here. My mom's the librarian. Are you okay?"

"Okay?" My whole body was burning and I was shivering. No. I wasn't okay. Charly and Will and Savannah and Columbia and Dad. No. Nothing was okay, or would ever be okay. I thought about nodding, but instead I just stared at the chest of his mustard-colored shirt where the words FREE TIBET floated over a setting sun. Or maybe a rising sun. Yeah, rising.

"Did you walk here?"

This time I managed to nod and the sun on his shirt left streaks behind it. Sunshiny sunbeam trails.

"In *that*?"

I looked down at my sweater. Old Navy. $29.99.

He put down the books. Large print. "You can't do that here."

"W-w-w-what?"

"You can't go wandering around outside in just a shirt and jeans. You'll kill yourself. Look at you: You're shivering uncontrollably, your lips are blue, and"—he leaned over the counter and squinted at me—"your pupils are dilated. You've got mild hypothermia. How long have you been outside?"

Hypothermia. Savannah was going to be so impressed. Way cooler than when I had mono. "Uhhh . . ."

"Judgment is obviously impaired," he muttered, "although I think that may have been an issue before."

"M-m-my judgment is awesome." Except, why couldn't

I remember how long I'd been outside? And how had I gotten here?

"And you're hard to understand, but that may just be the accent."

That was mean. I wanted to be mad, but mad felt like a lot of work. Curling up into a ball in that velvety maroon chair seemed like a better idea.

Ezra came around the desk. He looked different than I'd remembered him. Maybe it was because he was in jeans and a T-shirt instead of ski pants and parka. Or the hair. Yeah. His hair was longer and shinier. It fell almost down to his jaw. How did he make his hair grow so fast? I wanted to reach out and touch it, but my arms wouldn't move. He took a step closer. He smelled like candy. "You smell like c-c-candy." Had I thought that, or said that?

He was trying not to smile, arms folded. A tattoo of some kind of animal with fangs stretched over the muscle in his forearm.

"B-b-but the tattoo is kind of scary."

"You're a lot nicer when you're delusional," he said, then reached out and touched my cheek. I couldn't feel it, but I saw his thumb brushing the skin beneath my eye. It tingled, then stung. "Probably not frostbite, but it's hard to tell. You're lucky it isn't that cold out there today. We need to warm you up. Your shirt isn't wet, is it?"

"Um, no?"

"Good thing it isn't snowing. Let me get you my coat." He disappeared into a room behind the circulation desk and I stared at the fluorescent light panels. They looked warm. Ezra came out with a different parka from the red one I'd seen the other day. It was brown and looked like an entire grizzly bear encased in Gore-Tex. "I'd offer body heat, but I'm pretty sure you'd turn it down."

I squinted at him. What was he saying?

He shook his head. "Don't worry. I'll just wait until you pass out for the emergency life-saving treatment."

He slid the coat across the desk and I tried to pick it up, but my hands wouldn't grip. It fell to the floor. *Bend down.* My brain sent the message, but I was sure I couldn't, that I'd stumble if I tried.

"You're worse off than you look," Ezra said. He was back on my side of the desk picking up the jacket, holding it out in front of me and guiding my arms into the holes.

"My fingers are stinging."

"That's because your body cools your hands to keep your vital organs warm and it hurts when normal blood flow resumes. Why didn't you go inside somewhere sooner? Are you suicidal? There are about a hundred shops you could've hung out in if you were lost."

"N-n-no wallet."

"Nobody would turn you out to freeze to death. And where's your coat?" He was zipping up the jacket while

I stared at the FREE TIBET sun on his chest again.

"Bree's. I like the D-d-dalai Lama." He'd been in that old Brad Pitt movie about Tibet, hadn't he?

"I'm sure you do. Come sit by the heat vent back here." He dragged me by the sleeve back behind the counter and pointed to a rectangular grate in the floor. "Sit beside it, not on it. You'll burn your butt before you can feel it. I'm going to go heat up some water bottles in the back room for you."

I sat. The vent. The vent was heavenly. Beautiful. I was never leaving the vent. I closed my eyes and tried to will the shivering to stop. I couldn't. Why *hadn't* I gone in somewhere sooner? I wasn't really suicidal. Not having a reason to live wasn't the same as wanting to die.

Ezra reappeared with two pink hot water bottles, the same kind that Grandma used to put in our beds on January nights, nights when Dad draped sheets around his citrus trees and people brought their dogs inside. Forty-degree nights.

"Put one in each armpit," he instructed.

I did as I was told. Angels sang. Heat—no, liquid gold—seeped through my body, and I shuddered.

"Feels good, eh?"

I couldn't even answer.

The front door opened and Ezra left me. I could hear voices, something to do with picture books about recycling, but all I could think about were beautiful water bottles and beautiful heat vents and what a beautiful world it was where they both existed together. And suddenly it didn't matter that I was on the floor behind the circulation desk and semivisible to the public. I had to close my eyes. Then I had to lie down.

Dreaming or thinking, or something in between, warm waves pulsed through my brain, thoughts of Will with his arm around me, Charly laughing, Savannah brushing my hair.

When I opened my eyes Ezra was sitting on a stool staring down at me. "Good. You're still alive."

I blinked. "How long have I been here?"

"An hour-ish."

My tongue felt fat and dry. "Can I have something to drink?"

"I've got coffee in the back room. You want that?"

"Please."

He disappeared and reappeared with a steaming mug. "Here."

I took a sip. It was black and bitter and too hot. I took another sip.

"You had me kind of scared when you started waxing poetic about the Dalai Lama."

"What?" I'd said something about the Dalai Lama? "Oh. Yeah." I took another sip of coffee and let the realization that I'd been totally blathering on without a filter sink in. So this was what hangover regret felt like.

He was staring at me. I forced myself to hold his gaze for a minute, then let my eyes fall to his folded arms and the tattoo, dark blue ink sprawling over the right forearm. It was a bear.

"So what were you doing out there?"

I took another sip. Did I owe him answers? Maybe, what with the vent, the coat, the coffee. Or maybe I was just sick of lying. "I had a fight with my sister."

"Must've been some fight to make you try to kill yourself."

"I wasn't trying to kill myself. I just forgot my jacket and didn't want to go back."

"Does Bree know where you are?"

"Bree's not my mother."

Ezra raised an eyebrow. My bitterness hung in the air between us for a few seconds before I spoke again. "Bree's at work. Nobody's out there looking for me, if that's what you meant."

He eyed the giant clock over the photocopy machine. It said 7:10. "I'm here until we close at nine. I can take you home then."

I nodded. Two more hours away from the apartment. I could do that. I closed my eyes and tipped my head back against the wall.

"You really hate it here, don't you," he said.

It wasn't a question. I didn't answer.

The library door opened and two men entered with a blast of cold air. Ezra knew them. They chatted about ice fishing, while I stayed hidden behind the desk. It wasn't a bad place to be. He went off to find them fishing guides or something or other.

I unzipped the parka and pulled the water bottles out of my armpits. My fingers felt stiff, so I curled and straightened them over and over. They weren't cold anymore, but they were still white and achy. The ache felt better than no feeling at all. It meant I'd thawed. My body had actually frozen and unfrozen.

Ezra was right and wrong. I did hate it here, but it would be so much easier if it were just that, if my problems were just geographical. If things weren't broken everywhere.

Ezra came back around the counter, talking with the men as he scanned their books. They laughed at something he said, but I didn't hear what. I was too busy watching him handle the books, run their spines over the black surface beside the scanner, slide a glossy bookmark between them from a stack below the counter. The bear on his arm wasn't realistic, wasn't meant to be. The swirling patterns on its body reminded me of pictures of totem poles I'd seen. It was hard not to stare.

The men didn't notice me on the floor beside the vent.

The taller one asked about Ezra's brother or maybe his mother and Ezra smiled and shrugged and nodded. Then they left and an old woman in an Elmer Fudd hat came in and asked for help using the computer.

It went on like that for a while, Ezra helping a steady trickle of locals. He either forgot I was there or actively ignored me, which was fine.

When there was a lull, he pulled a box of books from under the counter. I watched him take each book, put a barcode sticker on its spine, scan it, and enter something into the computer.

Finally, he glanced over at me. "Skittle?" He pulled an open bag out of a drawer.

"Yes, please." I leaned forward and took the bag from him.

"Careful. They may make you smell like candy."

Oh. Crap. I'd actually said that. It was hazy, but definitely real, not some hypothermic hallucination, but an actual memory.

I looked up. He was staring at the computer screen, trying not to grin.

I poured myself a handful, then reached up and put the bag on the counter, something between fatigue and pain shooting up my arm. Apparently I only felt better if I didn't move.

"Why the tattoo?" I asked.

"You don't like tattoos?"

"I didn't say that. I meant why the bear?"

"My dad's mom was Shuswap."

"Sorry, I . . ." I wasn't sure whether to feel like an idiot, or be annoyed that he was making me feel like an idiot. But was I supposed to know what that meant?

"Native. It's tribal."

I waited for more, some Indian legend or birthright tale, but he was silent. "When did you get it?"

"Last summer after graduation. Gift from my brother."

"What's the story with your brother and Bree?"

He put down the book he was holding and started rifling through the open drawer. Eventually, he gave up looking for whatever it was he was looking for and went back to rubbing stickers onto book spines. "They used to go out."

"What happened?"

"They don't anymore."

"Does he live in Banff?"

"Not really. So you started school today?"

"Yeah."

"How was it?"

"It was . . . fine." I'd spent all day telling myself it was hell, but it wasn't. I'd wanted it to be horrific. Being able to hate every person and teacher and class as much as I felt like would've been nice. But truthfully, the school day was only long and vaguely lonely. Nobody had been mean.

Indifferent was all. After lunch, after Charly had started telling people, I'd been waiting for comments and whispers, but none of it had happened. We weren't important enough to gossip about.

"My sister told people she's pregnant." The words tumbled out like someone else was saying them. But it was me. I'd said it. I stared at the blinking red light on the copy machine and waited for the world around me to explode.

Ezra didn't flinch, just poured a few more Skittles into his palm and passed me the bag. "Is that what you guys fought about?"

"No. Yes. Not directly. It's complicated."

He didn't fish, just waited. Or maybe he wasn't waiting. Maybe he was just sitting and eating Skittles and scanning books into the computer.

"She can't think outside of herself. She doesn't see what the pregnancy is doing to other people."

"Like you."

"Like me."

"And the rest of your family?"

I snorted, watching him closely for any type of judgment, still not believing we were actually talking about this. "My dad doesn't know."

His face was like stone. He took the stack of books and placed them on a wheeled sorting shelf, then went back to the computer.

"My grandma sent us here so he wouldn't find out. So nobody would find out."

"Drastic measures."

"My dad is a pastor and our town is small. Small and Southern and judgmental."

"Still. Not telling him?"

"It would . . . I don't know. Kill him, maybe." I stuck my hand on the vent. The metal was hot, but I held it there. Lots of things could kill you. Fire. Ice. Why not sadness?

"But nobody made you come, right?"

"What do you mean?"

"I'm guessing you weren't forced onto the plane at gunpoint. You must've come because you wanted to."

I pulled my hand off the grate. "I came for my sister. Everything is about her." It was true. I knew it was, but Ezra's total lack of expression almost made me doubt it. "It's complicated," I added.

"Yeah, you said that. What about the dad?"

"I already told you. We aren't telling my dad."

"No, the baby's dad."

I put my hand back on the grate. Him. After all this time, I'd almost forgotten there even was a him. But there had been one—somebody so meaningless, he wasn't even worth tracking down, just some loser. "There is no dad."

"You do know that's impossible, right?"

I shook my head. I'd already aired enough dirty laundry. No way I was telling him it was a one-night stand. "You don't believe in immaculate conception?"

"You're saying your sister is the Virgin Mary? Take your hand off the vent. You're going to burn yourself."

I held it there. "No, I'm just pointing out that it's not impossible."

"So what's happening with baby Jesus?"

I ignored the sacrilege and took my burning hand off the vent. "Adoption. I don't know the details. My grandma is setting up some appointment with an agency here, I think, but I'm not exactly in the know now that Charly's cutting me out. She seems to have forgotten she can't even pick out her clothes in the morning without asking me what to wear."

Ezra was silent again.

"I'm not bitter," I said, not looking at him, but knowing he wasn't looking at me. "I just miss my life. My friends and my house and Charly, or the *old* Charly. And then a couple of weeks ago I found out I didn't get in to Columbia, and that was my big plan, you know? My way out of Tremonton." Why was I telling him this? It was like the words were forcing their way out, like rising bubbles. "Instead I'm chained to my screwed-up sister so everyone doesn't figure out how screwed up she really is."

Ezra opened his mouth, then closed it again, and in

the silence of his hesitation I heard myself. I sounded girly. And stupid and needy. Blood rushed to my face, completing the humiliation. Blushing.

"Who's everyone?"

"What?"

"You said *so everyone doesn't figure out*. What does it matter what people think?"

I paused. "I guess . . ." He had no idea what it was like being the pastor's daughter, being Charly's sister, being constantly scrutinized. "It's less about what people think, more about her. I can't just abandon her."

"I get it."

Probably not.

"You don't think I do," he said, "but I do. She's your lost cause. You can't let her go."

The door opened and a woman with two children came in. They said hello to Ezra, then went straight to juvenile fiction.

Sometime between waking up and spilling my guts, my head had started to ache. It throbbed now. I pressed my fingers into the knot at the base of my skull, and pain shivered up into my brain. I'd had blinding headaches, but this wasn't blinding. It was sharpening. Bleary thoughts were becoming clearer and clearer, bringing all the ugliness back into focus. Like the chasm between Savannah and me. And Will engaged to Luciana.

"Maybe it's just too much for her to see it right now," Ezra said.

"What?" He had a way of doing that, I was noticing, of leaving silences so long that my thoughts had already moved on.

"Maybe your sister will thank you later."

Too simplistic, too tidy. This wasn't a movie. "I don't know."

"You'd still be here though, right? Even if she never gets how much she owes you for it."

Would I? And who was he to think he knew anything about me and Charly?

The phone rang, and Ezra picked it up. "Hello, Banff Public Library," and then in a relaxed voice, "Oh, hi . . . Yeah, but I can wait. . . . It's already eight, right? . . . Mom, I won't die if I don't eat for another couple of hours . . . Yeah, I'm doing them right now. . . ."

He pulled a second box of books out from under the desk, cradling the phone between his shoulder and his ear. I studied his face, looking for a hint of American Indian. Or Canadian Indian, or whatever. It was in his eyes—so dark they were nearly black.

"Hungry?" Ezra asked me, holding the mouthpiece to the side.

"Starving." Just saying the word made my stomach groan. Aside from the two handfuls of Skittles and one

bite of cold, too-salty shepherd's pie, I hadn't eaten anything since lunch.

"Can you bring extra?" he said into the phone. "Bree's
niece . . . Yeah, she has two . . . Till summer . . . The States . . .
No, I don't know why she never told you . . . Again, I have
no idea . . . Another good question for Bree . . . Uh, maybe
because she thought you'd ask her a million questions . . . I
was just kidding . . . I thought I told you when I picked them
up for her at the airport a few nights ago . . . I don't know,
I guess I didn't realize you'd want to know?"

His tone was surprisingly patient.

He stared at me, and said into the phone, "For a book,
I guess."

I waited. This was when he'd tell her I'd come stum-
bling in, hypothermic, nearly frostbitten, barely cognizant.

"Yeah, don't do it yourself. You'll hurt your back
again. I'll shovel them when I get home . . . okay . . .
okay . . . okay . . . bye."

He put the phone back on its cradle. "My mom's dropping off lasagna. She thinks I might starve to death if I
have to wait till 9:30."

"Thank you," I said.

"You can thank her yourself. She'll be here in about
two minutes."

"No, I mean about not telling her, you know, how I
came in here."

"The hypothermic stupor?"

"It wasn't that bad."

"Actually, it was. You know that's one of the signs of hypothermia? Thinking you're okay when you're not?"

"Seriously, not that bad."

Ezra shook his head. Our moment of camaraderie was clearly over. "I'm still not sure whether or not to mention it to Bree."

"Tell on me? What are we, ten? Why would you do that? It's not like I'm going to do it again."

He squinted at me, his eyes like caves. "Promise you won't."

"Okay."

He turned back to the computer. "I spend all day rescuing people from their own stupidity. You'd think ski patrol is about saving people from the big scary mountain, but it's not."

"Very compassionate of you."

"I just recognize that people cause their own injuries. That doesn't mean I'm not compassionate. Last week alone I pulled in a broken leg, two broken collarbones, and a concussion—all people skiing runs beyond their skill level. I missed you guys stopping by on Saturday for collarbone number two."

I squirmed, recalling how I'd assumed he was just an unreliable idiot. "I get it. Walking around town without a jacket is beyond my skill level. Lesson learned."

"Good."

He was quiet for a moment, then continued. "A month ago we had to dig a body out of an avalanche."

A body. Murdered by snow. I forced myself to picture it, Ezra tunneling through ice into a frozen face, or maybe a twisted limb. I wanted to ask him if the search had been frantic—if there had been hope of finding the victim alive—or if they'd had to search knowing it was already too late. Like dragging a lake. I'd seen that done last summer for a drowned boy, and there was nothing frenzied about it. Just methodical and hopeless.

"I'm sorry." The words weren't right, but I didn't know what else to say.

Ezra sat perfectly still, like he was reliving it in his mind. "It wasn't even his fault, actually. Some idiot skiing higher up the mountain started it, one of those thrill-seeking midlife-crisis tourists, skiing out of bounds. The run was supposed to be closed until we could blast for avalanches, but this guy—" Ezra broke off and shrugged.

Everything I could think of saying was too ordinary. "That's horrible," I managed.

"Yeah. Senseless. And it makes it hard to keep doing ski patrol, seeing people pull the same stupid stunts, putting themselves and everyone else in danger."

"Why do you do it, then?"

He didn't respond. He could do that apparently—just block out what he didn't want to hear. It was annoying. "So why do you do it?" I repeated.

He stood slowly and stretched his arms out to the side, like a hawk preparing for flight. "It's complicated." He dropped them back to his sides, and winked.

I looked away. The wink wasn't playful. Certainly not flirty. It was dismissive, like I was a child, still in high school, still too wrapped up in sister-fight drama to understand the complexities of *real* life. Why had I spilled my guts to him of all people?

"Where's the bathroom?" I asked, pulling myself to my feet. My knees trembled a little, but I hid it, steadying myself against the wall. I needed food.

He wasn't looking at me anyway. "There's a washroom back there," he said, pointing to the back room. "Behind the office."

Washroom. Whatever. I'd add it to the list of words. I went to find the *washroom*, passing through the office, which turned out to be more of an all-purpose living room. The clutter was systematically arranged but still clutter: a corduroy love seat with too many throw pillows and a granny square afghan; a mini-fridge topped with a coffee machine and at least ten mugs; a desk hidden beneath knickknacks and tidy stacks of books; and walls covered with crookedly hung photographs.

I paused to examine the pictures, wondering who took them—Ezra or his brother or someone else maybe. There were at least thirty, all black-and-white, magnified images. A wildflower. An icicle. A blade of grass. A leaf. A pebble. A feather. Moss. And on and on.

No people.

When I got back from the bathroom, Ezra's mom was standing behind him with one hand on his shoulder, the other pointing at the screen.

"It's that one there you need to change so it matches the others," she was saying, but stopped when she heard the door close.

"Well, hello," she said, with an open smile. She had a slight gap between her front two teeth. "I'm Naomi."

"Hi," I said, eyeing the rope of silver-streaked hair, thick at the top of the braid and wispy at the tail end. It went all the way to her waist. Beautiful, maybe. In a mountain-woman sort of a way.

"So you're Bree's niece?"

I nodded. "Amelia."

She squinted at me. She looked older than I'd have thought, not as old as Grandma, but older than my friends' moms. It was her skin, papery and pale.

"I'm trying to see a family resemblance," she said, "but you don't look much like Ginny."

My breath stopped in my chest. Mom's name was Virginia. Dad called her Virginia. Grandma called her Virginia. Why hadn't anyone ever told me she went by Ginny? And why did this stranger get to know it, but not me?

"I look like my dad," I said. "My sister looks like her, though."

"Well, we'll have to have the three of you over for dinner. It's been a while since we've seen Bree. I miss having her come around. How's she doing?"

"She's good." I didn't really know if that was true. I didn't know Bree well enough to say, but Naomi didn't have to know that. "She's busy, with nursing school and work."

Naomi nodded, arms folded, knees locked. She didn't look much like Ezra, but that stance was the same. Not aggressive, not exactly. It was more like she was just waiting for me to keep talking and say something stupid.

"So you and your sister are just visiting?"

I hesitated, trying to remember Ezra's phone conversation with her earlier. He hadn't told her about picking us up at the airport, so he definitely hadn't told her about Charly's pregnancy. "We're here for the semester," I said cautiously. "We wanted to get to know our mom's side of the family a little better."

I tried not to look at Ezra, but his expression was

burning itself into my peripheral vision. His eyes were narrowed, and his lips pressed into a thin line. This was new—lying to someone's mom right in front of them. But I wasn't lying.

Naomi smiled, a network of creases stretching across her face. Smile lines. But there was a weakness in Naomi's smile, like it was one sad thought away from fading.

"That's nice," she said. "Family is important."

Ezra pointed to the bag. "So, lasagna?"

Naomi peeled the Tupperware lid off a container, unleashing an explosion of smell: hot garlic and tomato and parmesan. I was salivating immediately.

"Take it back there, will you?" she suggested. "I know it's dead out here, but it *is* a library. I'd stay and eat with you two, but the group is meeting tonight at nine. In fact, I'd better run or I'll be late." She glanced at the clock, then said in a bright and shiny voice, "You'll phone me if Quinn phones, won't you? Or if he stops by?"

"Of course," Ezra said, already on his way into the back room. I followed the food.

"All right." She paused, then called after us, "And if he stops by, you'll try to get him to stay until I'm back?"

"Of course."

"And remember to turn off all the computers, even that one behind the study carrels."

"Yes."

"Monitors, too, and lock up both sets of doors."

"I always do."

"I know." There was an understanding in her voice and his responses: The nattering was unnecessary and they both knew it. "Thanks, Ezra."

Ezra found forks while I tried to decide where to sit. There was a chair at the desk, but the work space was covered with tidy stacks of opened mail. And there was the love seat, but it seemed, well, like a love seat.

"Take the couch," Ezra said, reading my mind as he handed me a plate of lasagna. He sat down on the floor with his back to the wall, plate on his lap.

I couldn't talk for the first few minutes. I could barely think, it felt so good to have warm food in my mouth, my throat, my stomach.

"This is amazing," I said finally.

"I'll tell her you liked it. Not that you could actually be tasting any of it, inhaling it like that."

"I haven't eaten since lunch." Sitting in the cafeteria, wiping the mayo off my bread slices—that seemed like days ago.

We finished eating, and Ezra rinsed our dishes in the small sink. I watched him while he turned off computers and lights and locked the back door. I followed him out the front door and waited in the cold lamplight while he locked it. He'd grabbed a fleece from a closet in the back and he wasn't shivering, but he still had to be freezing. I felt vaguely guilty, but not enough to give him his coat back.

"Who's Quinn?" I asked, drawing an arc in the snow with my toe.

"My brother." He finished with the door and turned away. I followed. Our feet crunched and squeaked over the packed dry snow as we walked toward his car.

"So you should come by again," he said, pulling open the car door for me.

I climbed into the SUV and buckled up. "Okay."

"You don't have to be on the verge of freezing to death."

"Okay."

He slammed the door shut and drove me home. No, not home. To Bree's.

It was hard to tell which made sleep more impossible: the snoring or the stench of burnt popcorn.

The snoring had come as a surprise—did all pregnant women do it? On TV it was all morning sickness and sore backs and stretch marks. Then again, why would a pregnant woman complain about snoring? *She was asleep.*

Charly was already at it when I got home, in so deep she didn't wake up when I pushed her head off my pillow and rolled her onto her side of the bed so I could get under the covers. That was new too. She was done with covers. Hot feet. Twitchy legs. Whatever.

I closed my eyes and tried to sleep, but I could feel her choking on the air between us. Sharing the bed was too much like sharing a body. Her, me, baby.

As for the popcorn smell, I'd already fished the scorched bag out of the trash. Charly must've chucked it before falling asleep. I'd put my boots and coat back on and run it out to the dumpster, but the whole apartment still reeked.

But all that was nothing compared to my churning brain. So many things to be pissed about, but it all came back to me. Tonight something had changed. I kept seeing Charly's face, right at the moment I'd called her a slut. Something in her had broken. Only the tiniest flinch showed on the outside, but I knew it had happened and I'd done it.

That feeling was worse than being shut out by Will and Columbia and Dad. Worse than snoring and stinking burnt popcorn.

I'd done it.

Chapter 14

I survived week one on my own.

Charly ate in guidance while doing odd jobs for Ms. Lee, and I ate in a library study carrel that smelled like tuna. Technically, food wasn't allowed in the library, but the media specialist clearly had no sense of smell and didn't give a crap about what went on in the dark corners. It stunk, but not as badly as eating alone in the cafeteria. The carrels were the perfect haven for social misfits and people so desperate to make out that the tuna smell didn't bother them.

My reward for making it through to the weekend was meeting Richard.

"You guys are going to love him!" Bree squealed as she shoved dirty dishes into the oven. "I'll do these later."

Both of those statements were unlikely to be true.

I'd grown to love the idea of him just fine—essentially he'd bought my winter clothes and was paying for my room and board. What wasn't to love? But meeting him was a sure way to ruin that affection. Couldn't I just love him from a distance?

I didn't share that with Bree, though. And I'd probably end up doing the dishes later.

That morning, Charly had taken a five-second break from the silent treatment she'd been administering all week, just to instruct me on how to act.

"Don't be a total douche bag to this guy, okay?"

"Sure thing. Wait, does that mean I can't ask him why he thinks it's okay to have a twenty-six-year-old girlfriend when he's older than dirt?"

She didn't answer.

Aside from that one little breach, Charly's silent treatment was surprisingly thorough. Void of scowls and glares, it was the most emotionless piece of passive aggression I'd ever seen from her. I hadn't known she'd had it in her. It was impressive.

Richard, however, turned out to be less impressive. He was painfully nice—like a grilled cheese sandwich on a rainy day, or new socks, or watching reruns of 90s sitcoms—but not any of the things I'd have wanted in a boyfriend. Not smart. Not funny. Not hot.

Yet Bree sat beside him on the couch and looked at him like he was a god, played with the curly grey hair at the nape of his neck, laughed at his flat jokes like he was the funniest man alive. And she seemed to mean it.

Charly sat across from them in the chair, smiling for the first time in a week, so convincingly that only I knew it was fake. And I sat at the island and chatted politely, making every effort not to be a douche bag. It was exhausting.

The upside to Richard's visit was that Bree left with him for the rest of the weekend. At least they recognized the studio was officially too crowded to be their love nest. Thank heaven for Canadian decency.

"Amelia, may I speak to you for a moment?"

I turned from my locker to see Ms. Lee. Charly's Ms. Lee. I examined her: She was petite, with delicate eyes and hair so black it was almost blue. And she was young, probably still in her twenties, and dressed like a Club Monaco mannequin. Charly probably idolized her for the clothes alone—not that Charly had said a word about her to me. Two weeks since battle royale, and I could count the number of words we'd said to each other on one hand.

Ms. Lee didn't repeat her question, but watched my face patiently.

"Sure."

"Come into my office," she said. "You have a free period now, don't you?"

I glanced at the clock. I did, but I'd been planning on using it to email Savannah. I'd written her several emails since we'd talked on the phone, and deleted every single one of them before sending. The things I wanted to tell her—that I was lonely, that I didn't want to be here, that I didn't get into Columbia, that Charly had gestational psychosis that had turned her into the meanest person on the planet—could not be said. That meant I had to make stuff up, more lies and stories about my great Canadian adventure, and apparently the cold had sucked all the creativity out of my veins, because I just couldn't do it.

"Amelia?"

I nodded and followed Ms. Lee into her office.

I don't know what I'd been expecting, maybe a couch and a Sigmund Freud bust, but there were only the same worn upholstered chairs as in Ashton's office. It smelled nicer though. Lemons as opposed to eau de tar and coffee. Ms. Lee had curtains and a little row of cactuses in square white pots across the edge of her desk.

"Do you want to sit down?"

Not at all. I sat. So this was where Charly had been eating lunch. Much nicer than my tuna-reeking study carrel. "I'm assuming this is about Charly."

Ms. Lee tucked a wall of glossy black hair behind her ear. "No. I just wanted to see how things were going. Being the new kid in a small community like Banff can be difficult. Are you making friends?"

I squinted at her. Girl talk? Was I really supposed to believe that was why she'd hauled me in here? Charly had spent hours in this room gabbing about her life, which meant gabbing about my life, which meant this woman probably knew more about me than my own father. "I'm fine," I said, getting to my feet.

"We're not done yet. Sit, please."

I sat.

"I see you're doing well in all your classes so far, although you don't exactly have a difficult load."

I snorted. "My classes are a formality."

"And friends?"

"I'm sorry, but why are you asking me this? I'm sure Charly is an excellent source for info if you want to know about my life."

She refused to look annoyed or offended. "I don't want Charly's opinion on how you're doing. This has nothing to do with Charly."

I rolled my eyes. "Everything has something to do with Charly. And I'm fine. I'm not going to lie and tell you I've made a ton of new friends, but I've got plenty back in Florida. So no, you don't need to put me on suicide watch.

And no, you really don't need to assign someone to hang out with me."

"Don't worry. I wasn't planning on it. Do you talk to your dad and grandma much?"

"My dad calls on Sundays to make sure we went to church, and my grandma sends me spam about once a day. Usually about protecting myself from rapists."

She didn't skip a beat. "Do you miss them?"

I held my breath. Neither of them deserved to be missed.

When I didn't answer, she went on to the next question. "So what are your plans for next year?"

"Are we really going to do this?"

"What do you mean?" she asked. The innocence in her eyes was maddening.

"Are we really going to just pretend that Charly hasn't told you everything about my life?"

Ms. Lee put both hands on her desk and leaned forward. "I really don't know what else I can do to make you believe me, Amelia, but Charly doesn't come in here to talk about you."

An embarrassing silence followed, then I heard myself speaking. "I have no plans for next year. I only applied to Columbia, but I didn't get in. I'm supposed to be applying to Florida schools right now, but I can't seem to make myself do it because I don't really want to go to any of them. That leaves moving back to Tremonton, and bagging groceries at Winn-Dixie for the rest of my life. So I guess that's my plan."

"I've seen your transcripts," she said, leaning back and folding her arms. "Obviously you don't really mean that."

I shrugged. "Maybe I do."

"That sucks."

"Yes, it does."

She raised an eyebrow. "Well, you've missed a lot of the deadlines for Canadian universities, but there's still Mount Royal University in Calgary, or—"

"I'm not staying here." I stood up. We were done.

"What about a smaller school back home?"

"I'm not going to some community college so I can learn how to answer somebody's phone or highlight hair."

"That would be *vocational* school, and that's fine if you aren't interested, but I was talking about—"

"No, thank you." I put my backpack on.

She stood unnecessarily. I didn't need to be shown the door.

"You know, Amelia, the world isn't quite as black and white as it might seem. It doesn't have to be all or nothing. People aren't that way either, and if you try to hold them to some perfect standard, you'll only alienate yourself."

I stared hard into her face. Neither of us blinked.

"I'm sorry, I thought you said Charly had nothing to do with this."

Just a second of embarrassment crossed her features, then she reset them into their perfect calm. "She doesn't."

Without a word, or a thought, or a moment's hesitation, I reached for the cactus on the far left side of her desk and knocked it off. The sound of the explosion, the square white pot shattering on the tile, was by far the most satisfying moment of my day. No, my week. Possibly my life. "Oops. Sorry."

Ms. Lee didn't flinch or speak. She just stood there while I walked out.

"So we're both going to ace our tests today, right?"

I squinted into Bree's face. Her smile was all *I know you can do it* optimism and BFF solidarity. Her dimples were like craters. She had no clue about what I'd done in Ms. Lee's office yesterday. Nobody did. I'd spent the rest of the day waiting to be summoned and reprimanded—assigned detention, paddled, publicly flogged, or whatever Canadians do to people who smash defenseless cactuses—but for reasons unknown, Ms. Lee had let it go.

"It's a quiz and I just have to label a diagram of a camera," I said, regretting I'd even mentioned it.

The smile didn't fade, not even a little. "Great. It should be easy then, eh?"

I stepped out of the car and gave Bree a nod good-bye. My skin was so tight I couldn't have smiled if I wanted to. Charly and I had been slathering on the moisturizer morning and night, but we were still molting like reptiles in the dry mountain air.

"Good luck with the anatomy test," Charly said as she climbed out of the backseat. "Remember, the leg bone's connected to the hip bone."

"What would I do without you, Charly?" she asked, then waved, honked the horn, and pulled away from the curb.

"So is it hard to turn the ice off and on like that?" I asked Charly, watching Bree's tires spit chunks of snow as the car pulled away.

She didn't answer. She still wasn't answering.

"Because it seems like it would be tricky. Remembering who got sugar and who got battery acid."

"Not tricky at all," she muttered.

Ha. I forged on. "School's terrible enough without having to worry about whether my own sister is plotting my death or not."

"It's not terrible at all and you know it."

"Maybe not for you."

But she was right. School wasn't terrible. It was too bland to be anything but boring and pointless.

If people had snickered or stared at Charly I would've

had somewhere to focus my anger, but Banff Public High's student body had gossiped indifferently for one day about Charly and me—mostly just Charly—and now they'd moved on. They had their own permanent lives: best friends, ex-boyfriends, extracurriculars, weekend plans. Aside from Ezra, maybe, I hadn't met a single person worth the effort, and it'd been a full week since I'd seen him.

"So I'll meet you out front after school?" I said as she turned left to go to her locker, still not sure if she'd answer me.

She shook her head. "Doctor's appointment."

Right.

She walked off.

My classes were agonizingly slow, except for CALM. CALM was the most fun Canada had yet to offer me, but only because it wasn't supposed to be. We were taking yet another personality test and I spent the entire period trying to convince the computer that I was a sociopath. So un-Amelia. I'd never screwed around in class before and definitely never intentionally messed up an assignment.

I am open about myself to others. On the five-bubble scale I chose the one on the far left. *Very Inaccurate.* A straight-up lie, but only because the last few months of my life didn't count—forced secrecy didn't make me a seclusion freak.

I care more about the happiness of others than my own

happiness. Ah, yes. The hallmark of sociopathic behavior. *Very Inaccurate.*

I get upset easily. Easy. *Very Accurate.*

I am highly theoretical. Um, *Very Accurate?*

I seek out patterns in the universe. Sure. Why not? *Very Accurate.*

I talk to many people at parties. Did it matter? It seemed like sociopaths could be either introverts or extroverts. *Somewhat Accurate.*

It was empowering. It was the kind of thing the old Charly would've done.

Then I ate lunch alone.

"Hey, Georgia. Wanna come skiing?"

I heard his voice before I saw him, but I kept walking. His SUV rolled beside me, crunching over the strip of snow between the road and the sidewalk. His arm hung out the window and his fingers tapped against the red, salt-crusted paint.

I forced myself not to smile. "I'm from *Florida.* And is skiing still an outdoor sport?"

"Yeah."

I looked over at him, then couldn't break away. His eyes were like magnets.

"Come on, get in."

"I don't think so. I'm almost home anyway."

"Nice try. I know where you live."

I shrugged and kept walking. I had a good ten minutes to go.

"I'm surprised you don't even want to try it. You look pretty athletic."

"I *am* athletic. That doesn't make me want to strap planks to my feet and hurtle down a vertical sheet of ice."

"What sports do you play?"

"Field hockey. Soccer. Cross-country."

"Cross-country, as in running?"

"No, as in bowling."

He pulled right next to the curb and put it in park. I stopped too. "You want to try cross-country skiing? It's flat—no vertical sheets of ice. And there are trails all over the place too, so we wouldn't even have to drive out to Lake Louise. If you're up for the workout, that is."

Truthfully, my body was dying for some solid cardio. I'd been doing the handful of Pilates moves I knew in Bree's apartment every night, but that crap wasn't cutting it anymore. But the cold. I shook my head. "I almost froze to death last week. Remember?"

"So that's a no."

"That's a no."

"Where's your sister?"

My stomach muscles tensed, bracing for the punch after it'd already come. Why did that have to be the defining question in my life? I pulled my eyes away from his and looked up the street.

"Somewhere else," I answered.

"Cryptic. So you're coming?"

I took one step toward the car. "I don't want to ski."

He shrugged. "Okay."

"And I don't want to talk about my sister."

"What sister?"

I was close enough to hear the music in his car now: a moody, indie rock song I didn't recognize. "And no snow-shoeing, or snowboarding, or ski jumping, or anything even remotely related to any of them." One more step. The wind moaned and I leaned into it, my bones aching.

He nodded to the passenger side. "I'll take you some-where warm."

Magical words. I forced myself to walk, not run, around the front of his car. I'd spent the last week replay-ing our conversation at the library, wondering how much of an idiot I'd really been. But it couldn't have been that bad. He was here. I climbed in and dumped my backpack over the seat.

"How was school?" He pulled out into traffic.

"Um, fine." His car smelled like the wintergreen air freshener hanging from the mirror.

"Really?"

I hesitated. Fine was the *leave me alone* answer for Bree. I shrugged. "It's just kind of nothing. Not terrible. Not good."

"I hated that place."

I played with the zipper on my jacket, waiting for him to elaborate. Different kinds of people hate school for different kinds of reasons. Dumb kids, social misfits, stoners. I didn't want Ezra to be any of those. "Why'd you hate it?"

"Boring," he said. "And people were always trying to pressure me into things."

"Like drugs?"

"No. University."

That was moronic. We drove on in silence, leaving town on a road climbing up, past cabins and more vacation properties, higher up the mountain.

I stole a glance to the side. Ezra was wearing a sky-blue T-shirt over a navy long-sleeved shirt and jeans. "Where's your coat?" I asked, not hiding my smirk. "Don't tell me you wander around in the winter without a coat on."

"No coat is not above my skill level."

"Funny."

"I'm serious," he said. "But my coat is in the backseat."

I looked over my shoulder. It was.

"So what's Florida like?"

I sighed and wished I hadn't. I hated sighing, hated sighers. "Warm."

"That's it?"

He tucked his hair behind his ear, and I noticed the

cracked skin on his hands. Red and angry. More proof this place was uninhabitable for everyone. "No," I said. "It's just hard to describe. The people are different. Everything's more . . . colorful."

He raised an eyebrow, but didn't jump in to deny the bleakness all around us. "I've never been there. Never been south of Colorado, actually, but the people didn't really seem that different there. Probably because I was in Vail. Skiers are skiers."

"I haven't really traveled either, but I think it's the South. People are really friendly in a loud way."

"You don't seem that way."

I paused. Maybe it was an insult, but it wasn't *not* true. "I guess I'm not. The town I'm from is small too, and it's really insular, you know? Everyone knows each other's business and goes to the same church and the same grocery store and the same doctor."

"Same gene pool?"

"No, that's Kentucky."

He almost smiled. It was just that way with him, I was starting to realize. The *almost* smile was as good as it got. I wanted to keep looking at his face, at the way his upper lip curved and dipped, and the tiny scar above his left eye. But he glanced at me, and I had to look away.

"It's insular here too," he said. "Maybe small towns are just small towns."

"It feels different being on the outside, though. Tremonton is suffocating, but being away from it is . . . I don't know."

"Lonely?"

I wasn't going to admit to that. "Disorienting."

Out my window, I recognized the bridge spanning the frozen river ahead. I took a deep breath and held it. Habit. In Grandma's car, we held our breath for bridges and made a wish.

"Are you holding your breath?" Ezra asked.

I shook my head no, but kept my lips pursed, breath safely intact.

"Should I speed up or are you going to make it?" He slowed slightly and watched me, waiting for a reaction.

I puffed out my cheeks and waited. The bridge was short, so we were at the other side in just a few seconds.

"Southern superstition?"

I let the air rush out. "What, Canadians don't make wishes?"

"We don't need to. We're Canadian, what more could we want?"

I rolled my eyes.

"Kidding. We throw pennies in fountains. What did you wish for?"

"You can't tell people what you wish for. And everyone throws pennies in fountains."

"I didn't take you for the superstitious type."

I shrugged. I wasn't. I hadn't even made a wish. I had a million things to wish for, but I didn't believe for a second that I could make any of them come true. Not by wishing. Probably not by trying either. "When we were little, Charly always commandeered my wishes."

"I don't think wishes can be commandeered."

"Trust me, they can. Once she ordered me to wish that the girl who lived across the street would fall into a hole or get leprosy before the *Wizard of Oz* auditions."

"I'm guessing that didn't work."

"No, but she did forget her lines." Why was I talking about Charly?

"So I should be putting wish requests in, then. Can you make it snow?"

I narrowed my eyes and smiled. "I won't use my wishing powers for evil."

"Of course not," he said. "Wishing leprosy on a little girl—that's not evil."

"She was kind of a brat. Where are we going?"

"Surprise."

I hated surprises, but at the moment it didn't seem to matter. The car was warm. I was warm. Talking to Ezra was easy enough that I could almost forget how mad I was at Bree and Charly.

Ezra stopped at a stop sign, and without warning

he reached out and touched my cheek with his finger. "Speaking of wishes . . ."

It felt like fire where he'd touched me.

"Eyelash," he said, and he held out his finger. "You get another wish, just in case you squandered the one from the bridge on leprosy or something."

"Let me think."

I looked at my lash on his fingertip, a single black curl. The arc of his palm was so close I wanted to touch it. Why bother wishing for something impossible? *I wish Charly had never gotten pregnant. I wish I'd gotten into Columbia. I wish Will was full full full of regret for losing me. I wish I could tell my best friend the truth instead of having to cover for Charly. I wish Dad cared that I was gone. I wish Bree wasn't a better big sister than I am.*

None of that was going to happen.

So I closed my eyes and wished Ezra would touch my cheek again. Then I blew the lash away.

A horn blared behind us.

"Settle down," Ezra muttered, and we started moving again.

My surprise: hanging in a glass pod over an icy crevasse.

"You lied," I said.

"What?"

"You said you'd take me somewhere warm."

"I think I said warm*er*. It's at least a couple of degrees warmer in here than outside."

The gondola rocked back and forth in the wind and I silently cursed myself for getting talked into this. "How far up do you think we are?"

"Not that far. Fifteen meters?" Ezra sat beside me, both of us backward, watching the town shrink as we moved up the mountain. Another gust of wind came and I tightened my grip on the metal bench. He glanced down at my hands. "You aren't afraid of heights, are you?"

"No." I wasn't phobic—I just didn't seek out gravity-defying experiences. Or enjoy them in the least. "And I don't speak metric."

"Oh. About fifty feet."

I stared up at the cable. It was out of place, a skinny, man-made thing stretched across a chillingly vibrant sunset. We were suspended like a single pearl hanging from a chain. One tug and *snap*. Below us ice and rock waited. The gondola car would explode like dropped crystal. "Rock-a-bye baby," I whispered to myself.

Ezra shifted his weight beside me, jostling the gondola. He was close enough for me to feel the warmth of his body, to smell the candy in his mouth.

He held out a Starburst pack. I took one.

"So what do you think?" he asked.

I looked down to the forest again, ice-crusted and

shimmering, then twisted around to the summit of Sulphur Mountain behind us. Pretty, but the magic was in the sky. The clouds were tangerine and violet and every shade in between, the sun smoldering behind the mountains. "The colors . . . ," I started, then didn't finish.

"I know. It's like the sky is burning."

"And the trees look purple. I hadn't noticed that before."

"Up close you only see the green. You need distance to really see them."

Distance. He was right. From far away they looked entirely different, purple and gold shining beneath the green. I took a deep breath, forcing my muscles to relax.

Distance from Charly, distance from home, distance from *everything*—was that supposed to make it all less ugly? If so, it wasn't working. Maybe I wasn't far enough away. Maybe I couldn't get far enough away.

"Look," Ezra said, leaning across me and pointing.

I looked without leaning, trying to keep the gondola level.

"Elk. Do you see them?"

"No."

"Down there." He put one hand on my shoulder, the other on my hip, and slid me over to the edge of the bench. The gondola tilted and I willed myself not to gasp. I exhaled shakily onto the glass, my breath fogging a small circle. He pointed again, but beyond his finger there was only white. White ice, white snow, white breath. Then I saw them. There were four, tan and brown, with broad grey antlers, ambling through the trees.

"Yesterday I pulled in a guy with a concussion, a Japanese businessman here on vacation. He didn't know, or maybe just couldn't remember, much English, but kept saying the names of animals he'd learned. He came to hunt."

"What do people hunt here?"

Ezra knocked on the glass with his knuckle. "Those. And anything else that moves and that they can pull the skin off to mount on their walls and show how manly they are."

"I take it you don't approve."

"That's a nice way of saying it."

I sat back as our car slowed. We'd reached the top, a station to disembark. Ezra twirled his finger in a loop and the attendant on the platform waved and nodded. "Unless you want to get off and wander around the mountain in the cold for a while?"

"No." Then after a pause, "This is nice."

His lips curved upward, but it was gone before it could become a smile. Our gondola car followed the cable track, making a U-turn and starting its way back down.

"You don't like to smile, do you," I said.

"Not true. I just save it for when I mean it. I know

people who smile all the time and it means nothing."

Bree came to mind. "Some people say it's the smiling that makes you happy. Endorphins or whatever."

"Ah, the smile-*until*-you-mean-it people."

"Yeah, them."

"That seems like something people say to excuse being fake. You don't smile all that much either."

"Not out of principle," I explained, suddenly self-conscious. "I just don't have much to smile about at the moment."

We sat in silence, gliding backward down the mountain. That side of the sky was ocean blue and darkening.

"Thank you," I said.

He looked down, tapping his boot on the slushy metal floor. "Don't thank me. Thank Yukon."

Yukon. The dreadlocked hippie at the gondola ticket office who had given Ezra a hug and insisted we "ride as many times as you freakin' feel like, eh?"

"No," I said, feeling almost embarrassed, but not enough to stop. "Thank you for being so nice to me. I don't really deserve it. I haven't been . . ."

Ezra looked at me, his face unreadable as always. Or maybe not. That blank calm was starting to mean more, like maybe he understood me. And maybe he was about to kiss me. I could imagine him leaning into me, putting his lips on mine. I wanted him to.

He didn't.

We rode the gondola until the colors darkened and the sky turned black.

"Where've you been?" Bree asked. But she wasn't even looking up. She was leaning over Charly, who was leaning over an open photo album at the island, her finger tapping a picture.

That was fine. I didn't want to tell them, or at least not Bree, because it'd meant something. I didn't want anything from the last two hours I'd spent with Ezra stolen in the telling.

A photo album.

"Are those pictures of Mom?" I asked, taking a step toward them. Hadn't I been waiting for this, for Bree to lug out the evidence? I'd known she'd have pictures, stories, memories linking her to Mom. So why the dread? Or was it anticipation?

"No," Charly said, and closed the book. "They're from the adoption agency."

I stopped, feeling like I'd been slapped. "You're choosing parents."

Charly didn't say anything, but slid the book off the table into a bag by her feet. There were several more albums in the bag.

"We just picked up a few of these profile books that couples who want to adopt put together," Bree explained.

"Oh."

"Where've you been?" Bree asked again.

Charly was choosing people to be her child's parents and she didn't want me to see. I was too disoriented to lie. "With Ezra."

Bree looked up, startled, then grinned. "Really? Doing what?"

"Riding the gondola."

"Seriously?"

Did she think I was lying? I nodded.

"*Nice*," she exclaimed. "So, since when has this been going on?"

I sat on the bench by the door and unzipped my boots. "I don't know. I guess it's just starting now." What was I saying? Was something really starting? My insides swirled at the thought of Ezra, his sinewy arms and black eyes, his silence.

"Ha. You're blushing." Bree elbowed Charly, who didn't respond. "Look, she's blushing."

"My cheeks are red from the cold."

"Sure they are. So what happened?"

I glanced at Charly. A few months ago she would've cared that I'd spent the last few hours with a guy. She was staring across the kitchen, avoiding eye contact.

"Nothing," I said. "I mean, we talked."

"So did he call or something, or did you guys just bump into each other?" Bree pressed.

"No. He picked me up while I was walking home from school."

"Like he just happened to be driving by, or he knew you'd be walking home?"

"I didn't ask him. He didn't say."

Bree shook her head. "I did *not* see that coming. You and Ezra . . ."

Did she not realize that was insulting?

"Ezra's a good one, by the way," Bree said. "He's a genius, not to mention the sweetest kid in the world. Naomi would totally be in the loony bin without him."

"Sorry, a genius?"

"Yeah, he had a scholarship to University of Toronto last year. Some math or engineering thing, but he turned it down to stay here in Banff."

"What? *Why?*" I asked, watching Charly slide down from the stool, collect the bag of adoption binders, and head up to our room.

"His mom. I'm guessing he didn't tell you about Quinn."

"No. I mean, I know you dated him."

"*Dated.*" Bree rolled her eyes, opened the fridge, and pulled out a bowl. "I don't know if that's how I'd describe it. Tabbouleh? Charly and I already ate." She placed the bowl on the island and retrieved a clean plate and fork for me from the dishwasher. "If sitting in his basement, smoking weed, and occasionally making out counts as dating, then sure, we dated. That was before he started doing the serious stuff, though."

"Serious stuff."

"Meth. Crack too, but mostly meth. I can't say I emerged unscathed, but at least I got out. No thanks to my mom."

I took the seat Charly had just left, the rush of being with Ezra draining out of me with every word. Too many questions cluttered my thoughts. *No thanks to my mom*—I knew almost nothing about her mom, *my* grandmother, the woman my own mother had moved across an entire continent to get away from. I knew what Grandma muttered under her breath about Fiona Goodwyn when asked about her—words like "tramp," and "manipulator," and "princess." And on the one occasion that I asked him, Dad had described her as "difficult." Then he'd changed the subject. He was excellent at not speaking poorly of people.

"Why? What did your mom do?"

"When I was seventeen I got busted trying to buy drugs and she used it as an excuse to kick me out." Bree dumped a few spoonfuls of tabbouleh on my plate, then pushed it toward me. "But it wasn't about the drugs. That was just good timing. Her boyfriend wanted her to move to Montreal with him, and I was cramping her style."

I took a bite so I didn't have to look Bree in the eyes,

so she wouldn't see me looking horrified. What kind of mother would do that? Hopefully I'd inherited only a bare minimum of her genetic material. And as for Bree—sitting around smoking weed, busted for buying drugs? Seriously?

"They're still together, surprisingly enough. They live in France though, and I see her about once a year. That's plenty. You like the salad?"

I did. The mixture of garlic and lemon and mint was different, but good. "I've never had it before."

"It's Mediterranean."

I nodded, my mind pulling back to Ezra. "But Quinn . . ."

"Quinn's just . . ." She paused for words. "Sad. He's a cautionary tale, you know? Total junkie, in and out of rehab and jail since high school. I heard he just got kicked out of some intense detox program up north of Edmonton. He stops by his mom's every once in a while to beg for cash or steal something, but luckily he doesn't come find me anymore. Not since I moved in here. Not since Richard."

"It doesn't make sense," I said, thinking aloud. "Ezra staying, I mean. Why wouldn't he want to get as far away as possible?"

Bree took a wet rag from the sink and began wiping the countertop. "He stayed for his mom. Not that she didn't want him to go, but she's kind of, um, unstable.

Depressive. After Quinn got sent to jail for grand theft last year, she had some kind of mental breakdown and ended up in the hospital. She's sweet and all, but—"

"I met her," I interrupted.

"Naomi? Really? When?"

"Last week at the library."

Bree stepped back from the island and put her hands on her hips. "Wow." Her face was a mixture of surprise and admiration. "So you guys really have been hanging out, then. I'm glad he got over Taylor so quickly. They've been on-again, off-again for so long."

The mention of Taylor made me feel queasy. Had I forgotten about her or had I consciously pushed her out of my mind? Or maybe it was the digging into Ezra's secrets that made me slightly nauseous. He was so private. I knew I should let it go, but curiosity pushed me onward. "Back to last year. What happened with Naomi?"

Bree sighed and tried to look like she didn't love having all the answers. "She took a bunch of pills." Then she stared into my eyes and paused for effect. "And it was Ezra who found her."

I was too stunned to hide the revulsion that rolled through me. I shuddered. He'd found his own mother trying to kill herself.

"That was last winter, so probably right around the time he was offered that scholarship to U of T," she continued.

I tried to hold on to the words, but they slid by me. All I could think of was Ezra finding Naomi cheek-down in vomit, calling 911, doing CPR, riding in the back of the ambulance. Anyone would've been out of their mind with fear, but what did a terrified Ezra look like? Did he cry? I couldn't even imagine it, but clearly I didn't know him at all.

"After that he wouldn't consider going to school anywhere, not even Calgary. He barely got through that last semester of high school, and supposedly, the teachers just let him graduate out of pity or—"

"How do you know all this?" I interrupted.

She shook her head. "Banff is small."

Yes, it was.

"It's one of those things. Everybody knows what happened."

And now I did too.

"You've really never had tabbouleh?" Bree asked. "I got the recipe from Richard's sister. She's a *real* chef at this swanky restaurant in Bragg Creek, which makes impressing Richard impossible. Once I tried to make this soufflé . . ."

She nattered about eggs and air, while I pushed tabbouleh around on my plate. My mind turned Bree's words over and over, looking for something to grip, something that made sense, but it was all too slippery. If Ezra's too-cool-for-school persona was just an act, if Ezra was a mathematical genius tied to his unstable mother and screw-up brother, if he spent every day wondering if his mother was going to commit suicide—then he had to be the most miserable person on earth. And I hadn't seen any of it.

". . . and he's super excited to take us all there this weekend."

"What are you talking about?" I asked, suddenly sick of her voice.

"I said Richard's coming again on Friday. And he wants to take us to his sister's restaurant. The one in Bragg Creek."

"Oh. Sure. I've got homework I should be doing."

Bree bit her lip, covered the bowl with Saran Wrap, and put it back in the fridge.

Why did she have to be so needy? I just wanted to be alone, and to think about Ezra. "I'm excited to go to the restaurant too," I said.

She gave me a sunny smile. "Good."

"Night," I said over my shoulder.

"Good night."

The light was off. Charly had burrowed under the covers as part of her pretending-to-be-asleep routine, so I sat at the desk and flipped on the reading lamp. Then I stared at the cover of my photography textbook.

Ezra had beautiful eyes. Dark and warm.

Except I had no idea what was behind them. I thought I knew, but clearly that was only what he'd wanted to show me. Or what I'd wanted to see.

But Ezra the math genius, Ezra the dutiful son, Ezra the dream-broken hero—why hadn't I been able to see any of that on my own? Was I that bad at figuring people out?

I forced myself to do the photography questions, then put on my pajamas and got into bed. Charly's breathing was louder now and her foot and arm hung off the side of the mattress, which meant she wasn't faking anymore. I stared at the back of her head in the dark. She'd forgotten to take her hair clip out.

Charly. I sighed, gently removed the clip, and placed it on my bedside table. Then I got out of bed to tuck her limbs back in, and finally went to sleep.

Chapter 15

Throwing the CALM personality test had been stupid. Fun, but stupid. Now I had a list of careers I was supposed to research that looked like serial killer day jobs: coroner, lighthouse operator, medical transcriptionist, security guard, pathologist. Clearly, my file had been tagged DOES NOT PLAY WELL WITH OTHERS.

I pushed the stupidity of my school situation from my thoughts as I left the building after the final bell. Bree had the day off school, which meant she was at the apartment, which meant there was no way I was going there. So I was going to the library, as long as I didn't chicken out before I got there and end up at Rocky Mountain Coffee House instead.

Charly had an after-school study group with some people from her biology class. That's all she'd said. Probably the girls I'd seen her talking to in the hall before class this morning. Or maybe the tall guy with the glasses I'd seen her outside the cafeteria with yesterday. I guess she didn't have Ms. Lee every lunch hour, but I didn't really know. I was still sneaking lunch in the library.

As for dealing with me, Charly had realized that profound silent treatment was too complicated. So we got by on a relaxed version that allowed for basic communication. *Yes. No. Hurry up with your hair—I have to pee. Get your own ice cream.*

I unzipped my jacket to let the breeze in. It was inexplicably balmy again. Not that I was complaining, but the nonsense of it all—deathly cold one day, nice the next—was unsettling.

People were wearing T-shirts and throwing snowballs in the parking lot, a situation Dr. Ashton had only herself to blame for. She'd started the school day by giving a five-minute lecture over the PA system about the dangers of throwing snow (corneal abrasions, concussions, car accidents, wet hair) and the response was an all-out snowball war. I had to assume she was inside slapping another couple of nicotine patches onto her arm because she didn't appear to have snapped and expelled everyone.

At first I just watched my classmates pack the slush

with bare hands and lob it at each other, cars, the side of the school. Then out of solidarity, or maybe just curiosity, I threw one too. Right smack at the *P* in the Banff Public High School sign. It didn't feel nearly as satisfying as I'd thought it would.

I crossed the street, hopping over a huge pile of slush. My legs were taking me to the library, but I was distracting myself by thinking about my newest CALM assignment. I had to write a response to the list of careers by answering a bunch of questions: Do you agree with the assessment and the careers suggested? What did you learn about yourself from this? Do you think the test overlooked specific traits or talents that you have? *Do you give a crap?*

The last one was my own, and the only one I had a solid answer for.

Prepping for disappointment seemed safest, so I was telling myself Ezra wouldn't be there. It wasn't like I knew his schedule. Or the library could be busier than last time, or maybe he worked with other people. Naomi could be there. And I didn't even know if Ezra would be okay with me just stopping by again. He'd said I could, but maybe he was just being polite. Maybe "come again" was Canadian for "good-bye."

The walk was shorter than I'd realized, and I was suddenly there. What was I doing? I scanned the parking lot for the red, deer-dented Pathfinder. There it was. I flattened the flutter in my stomach and walked almost calmly down the steps to the library entrance. This time I didn't have to worry about slipping, since the ice was slush now.

I took a deep breath and reminded myself, nothing about the way he'd treated me so far suggested Ezra was *interested* interested. He'd been nice. Friendly. No flirting, no checking me out, no touching, or not really. So coming to the library like this, I wasn't pursuing him, I was just doing what everyone kept bugging me to do, which was make a friend.

I pulled open the door, suddenly wishing I hadn't tried so hard—my green sweater was too fitted, and based on my reflection in the window, my lip gloss was too red.

Ezra was sitting behind the desk reading a book. He looked up, but didn't smile. I shouldn't have come. "Let me guess. You're looking for a winter sports guide."

"Guess again." I tapped the toes of my boots on the mat, knocking the clumps of slush off of them, and looked around. Empty, aside from two middle school–age boys at the computers and a woman perusing the romance paperbacks.

"How about something girly and Canadian, like *Anne of Green Gables*," Ezra said, closing the book he was holding and shoving it under the circulation desk. Then he slid off the stool and put both palms on the counter. He was wearing a black T-shirt, the words WE HAVE COOKIES in cursive and a green lightning bolt on the front.

"You have the most random T-shirts. What does that mean?"

"Thank you, and it's hard to explain."

I shook my head. "Did you say girly and Canadian? Seriously?"

"Kidding, but how about *angry* and Canadian, like *The Handmaid's Tale*?"

"Thanks, but I'm already angry and Canadian enough."

Finally, he smiled and everything inside me sighed. "So what's up?" he asked.

"Nothing. This place is dead," I said, glancing around. The two kids had finished at the computers and were tugging on the woman. She was still trying to browse.

"It's the chinook. Everyone's outside."

He was right. The sidewalks had been packed with people. Crazy people. People without hats. People in shorts.

"Coat?" Ezra held out his hand.

At least he'd assumed I was staying. I wiggled out of the parka and handed it to him.

"You must've been roasting out there," he muttered. "Do we need to have another talk about dressing for the weather?"

"I didn't *know* it was going to get this warm," I said. "Yesterday it was minus twenty."

He raised an eyebrow. "Look at you, speaking Celsius."

"I'm practically fluent now," I bragged.

"Really?"

"No. Not even close. I know water boils at a hundred and freezes at zero, and I know that for the purposes of chemistry experiments, room temperature is twenty-five."

"Impressive."

"Oh, wait," I added, "I also know that I start getting really angry when it's below minus ten."

"And hypothermic at minus twenty."

"Is that what it was that day I wandered in here?" I asked. That number actually meant something to me now. The memory was equal parts painful and embarrassing.

"Without a coat." He shook his head, like it was still just as unbelievable. "And now you know the locals break out the beach wear when it's five degrees."

The romance novel woman had appeared at the desk and was piling her books in front of Ezra. Her children were poking each other with pushpins from the cork-board by the door. I watched Ezra as he checked her books out for her and asked nicely for the boys to put the tacks back. He was only a few inches taller than me, but he was thick, muscular. And there was a tightness to his arms, his neck, his shoulders, and a rigidness in his features. I wanted to ask him if his nose had been broken or if it was naturally crooked like that.

Ezra thanked the woman for coming and she left.

"You want to come sit down?" he asked me, already

walking toward the back room. "I usually hang out in the back when nobody's here."

I stepped around the edge of the desk, suddenly nervous. It felt nice to be talking to someone. I'd spent the last week wandering through the crowds at school encased in my foreigner bubble and frozen out by Charly. Lunches were silent. The apartment was silent, unless Bree was home, in which case the silence would have been preferable. And Savannah must've had a busy week, because she'd only emailed once.

Talking to Ezra was exactly what I wanted to do.

But there was something about the way he was looking at me that made my stomach churn. He looked hungry, and for the first time in forever I felt pretty. Was I imagining it? Maybe I was actually lonely enough to dream up someone wanting me.

I followed him in, glancing at the book he'd shoved beneath the circulation desk. *Amusements in Mathematics*.

From there, my eye moved along the progression of framed photographs on the wall. I hadn't thought I was learning much in my photography class, but I found myself seeing them differently this time. The detail was shocking, forcing me to step in closer to inspect the swirling grain on a cross section of wood, the glisten on the surface of dew.

"Who took these?" I asked, examining a black-and-white close-up. It took me a minute to see what it was:

a petal with a torn edge, wilting and shriveled along the fissure.

"My mom." Ezra sat down at the swivel chair in front of the cluttered desk.

"She's a real photographer."

"Yes."

"Hmm." I sank into the love seat. "So what do you usually do when this place is empty?"

"Nothing. Listen to my iPod."

Liar. But I knew instinctively not to call him on *Amusements in Mathematics.* "Your mom doesn't care? You aren't supposed to be reshelving books or whatever?"

He shrugged. "I do that stuff too. She's mostly just happy to have me manning the desk."

"What kind of music do you listen to?" I asked, wishing immediately that I hadn't. Music was the topic of at least half of Charly and Bree's conversations. Bree's band, Charly's voice, Bree's new guitar, Charly's range, Bree's favorite ballad, Charly's love for Bree's favorite ballad.

"Um. Audiobooks, actually."

"Really? I love to read, but I can't listen to books," I said. "My mind wanders."

"Maybe you're just listening to the wrong books." He stood and went over to the kitchenette.

Maybe they had been the wrong books. I'd only ever tried listening to novels assigned for school: *The Scarlet*

Letter and *Call of the Wild*. Both attempts had been complete failures, possibly because I'd been trying to work out at the same time. "What would the right books be?"

Ezra didn't answer, just handed me a mug. I took a sip before I realized he hadn't even asked me if I wanted coffee. It was just as disgusting as last time. I took another sip and tried not to make a face. "My sister likes her coffee strong like this," I said.

He gave me a confused look. "So you have a sister again? I thought you two were dead to each other."

I fiddled with my birthstone necklace. It was last year's birthday present from Grandma and Dad, a tiny emerald on a white gold chain. Charly got the same necklace with a ruby for her birthday in July. She'd lost it by August. "Not dead to each other. Just not exactly talking."

Ezra waited for me to go on, his face revealing nothing.

"This whole . . . pregnancy thing," I stumbled on. "It's been hard. She's different. Everything's different." The words felt like betrayal. Talking about Charly's pregnancy with anyone hadn't been an option, and as much as I'd wanted to tell Savannah the truth, it was only for the immediate relief. Lying hurt. Telling would relieve some of the pressure.

But I hadn't wanted anyone to actually know and judge.

"Sometimes different just takes a while to get used to."

I shook my head. "But things will never be the same. And it seems like she should be able to ruin her own life, but not mine too." I let go of the emerald. "I miss stuff."

He stared into his mug. "Your old life."

"Yeah. My friends and my family and school." But as I said it, I realized that wasn't it. I missed Charly. "I keep thinking that I could pick up the phone and end this whole stupid thing. Charly could stay and I could go home. Nobody is going to guess that adorable little Charly Mercer is knocked up, and she doesn't need me here. She's got Bree. She won't even talk to me right now."

"Seems like it should be the other way around," he said.

I couldn't tell him. I'd treated her like garbage. I'd called her a *slut*. She'd deserved it, but that didn't make it any less ugly. "I don't know. Collateral damage isn't supposed to bite back. I bit back. Don't you ever want to tell your brother to go to hell?"

His eyes filled with shock.

My words echoed around us before silence swallowed them. The seconds slowed. Stopped.

"Not really," he said finally. "He's already there."

What he didn't say filled the space between us: *You have no right to talk about him. You don't even know him. You don't even know me.*

Blood rushed to my face. I shouldn't have come. What was I thinking, baring my self-centered soul to Ezra? His brother was an addict and a criminal, his mother was sui-cidal, and he was chained to both. By comparison, I was living a Disney Channel sitcom.

"I'm sorry," I mumbled. I rubbed the raw skin on my thumb where I'd picked at a hangnail. My fingers were covered in them, and half were bleeding. I looked around for an excuse to leave. Maybe I could pretend I'd left a book at school or something.

"It's fine," he said.

"I shouldn't have said anything."

"It's fine."

It wasn't fine. It couldn't be unsaid or prettified, so I sat and willed my cheeks to stop burning. "Have you been here all day?" I asked lamely.

"No, I spent the morning throwing boosters."

"I don't know what that means."

"We have packs of explosives called boosters that we use to clear the mountain for avalanches. Little bombs."

"You're screwing with me."

He looked at me and grinned. "No."

The fluttering in my stomach came back. "Seems like bombs would *start* avalanches."

"That's the point. We make little avalanches so people don't start big ones."

I thought about it for a minute. "But what stops the boosters from setting off big ones?"

He shrugged. "You get pretty good at predicting what the mountain is going to do. And at least when we're clearing a run, there isn't anybody on it. We do it before the slopes open and most of the time, like this morning, we're just blasting away snow that's built up and getting ready to slide. You look like you don't believe me."

"I'm still grappling with the information that you actually ski with explosives."

"A backpack full. Jealous?"

I had to laugh. This felt good again. "No. But you've got a scary glint in your eye. I don't know if I trust you to be throwing bombs."

"Oh, we don't always throw them. Sometimes we use a little cannon to shoot them."

"But I thought ski patrol was mostly first aid. Pulling people on the stretcher-sled thing."

"That's just the part I have to put up with."

"Isn't playing Superman every little boy's dream?"

"No," he said. "Explosives are. Trust me. And I'd rather save people *before* they hurt themselves. People break their legs on the bunny hill all day long, but if ski patrol wasn't out there blasting, avalanches would kill a lot more people than they already do."

Avalanches. Killing people. A fragment of conversation struggled to the surface of my memory. Had we talked about avalanches last time I'd come here? We had.

When my brain was blurry from cold. I closed my eyes and tugged at the memory, and suddenly I saw the way he'd looked, his glassy stare and set jaw, when he'd said it: *I dug out a body.*

"A few patrollers died last year in British Columbia," he said, his voice softer now. "They were throwing boosters, taking a cornice off the back side of Fernie Mountain. They started a few small slides and they figured that was it, so they skied over the fresh powder and that triggered a big one. It took their ski patrol team two hours to dig out the bodies."

Being swallowed and crushed by snow—when would blinding white turn to pitch-black? "How long does it take to freeze to death?"

"You don't freeze to death in an avalanche. You suffocate. And that takes anywhere from fifteen to forty-five minutes, depending on injuries and if there's much of an air pocket around your head."

Subconsciously, I held my breath. Then stopped. "You can't dig your way out?"

"No. You're entombed in ice."

I shivered and rubbed the raw hangnail again. "I can't believe you go out there every day knowing all that. I can't think of a worse way to die."

"Sure you can," Ezra said. "Fire would be worse."

"No, I think I'd rather burn."

"Spoken like a true preacher's daughter."

"He's a pastor."

"Sorry. Pastor. You know, they probably aren't that different. Either way you're asphyxiating, right? I mean, it isn't the heat or the cold that kills you."

"Nice conversation."

"Sorry," he said. "I didn't mean to upset you."

"I'm not upset."

For at least a minute, neither of us spoke. The heater whirred. The computer monitor made the softest buzzing sound. I stared into my empty mug, wishing I could be whatever it was Ezra needed.

He broke the silence with a command. "Come here."

I looked up from my hands. Something about his voice made me feel weak.

He was leaning back in the swivel chair, shiny, dark hair covering one side of his face. He tucked it behind his ear. "I don't bite."

"I'm not scared of you," I heard myself say. I stood up. I wasn't, but I couldn't tell what he was thinking either. I walked over to the desk and rested my fingers on its surface to steady myself. I was still a couple of feet from him, but I couldn't close the distance. "What?"

He leaned forward and grabbed hold of my arm, his fingers sliding up under the sleeve of my sweater. I stared at his hand, feeling the heat from his skin radiate through me. "I'm glad you came today."

I couldn't trust my voice. The pressure of his thumb on the inside of my wrist made my whole body ache. Nobody touched me anymore. Not even casually. Not Charly, not Grandma, not Dad. Not Will. When exactly had I become untouchable?

Ezra stood and gently pulled me toward him. I let him. Our bodies met and every inch of mine sang. He felt warm and firm and I wanted to stay like that, not moving, just breathing. It felt like coming home. He paused, looking down at my lips, then leaned over and kissed me.

Everything bad melted away. It was only us, his lips on my lips, his hands on my back then down to my waist, like he could hold me together with just his touch. I was only vaguely aware of being moved backward, the room swirling around me, but then I felt him lower me onto the couch, but rising up too, like I was sinking and floating at the same time. His hands were in my hair and touching my neck and sliding—

Ding.

Ezra was off me before the sound could register in my brain as anything more than noise.

Ding. Ding. Ding. Ding. Ding. Ding. Ding. Ding.

The service bell. I gasped, panic gripping every muscle in my body. What was I doing? I was practically in public, in a *library*, making out in a back room with the door wide open. I twisted my body around to the open door, but thankfully, the love seat was too far over to be visible.

Ding. Ding. Ding. Ding. Ding. Ding. Ding. Ding.

I released the breath I was holding, and let my head fall back into the cushion. This looked bad. Worse than it was.

"Coming," Ezra called, already halfway to the door, running a hand through his hair.

My heartbeat was scaring me. What was I doing? I barely knew Ezra. I'd known Will for ten years before we'd kissed. Not that ten years was normal, but Ezra hadn't even taken me out on a date.

Ezra gave me a sheepish grin over his shoulder and pulled the door not quite closed behind him. I felt weak. The shock and shame of nearly getting busted were nothing compared to what I wanted. Him. Back on the couch with me.

A female voice on the other side of the door pierced my thoughts. "Nice lipstick."

I tensed. It was shrill. Almost familiar.

His response was too low and muffled to hear.

I shuddered, pressing my palms to my cheeks. They felt hot. I felt nauseous.

"Who's back there, anyway?"

Again, I couldn't hear Ezra's reply.

"Not my business? *Seriously?*" The voice was getting louder. She'd either started shouting, or she was—

The doorknob *clicked* and twisted, and I realized too late that I did not want to be lying on the couch when the door opened. I scrambled to my feet, vaguely aware that my sweater was twisted, my hair was a mess, and I had gloss smeared around my lips.

Taylor. It took a moment to recognize her without the braids and snow pants. Her hair was loose and curled, and she wore a low-cut sweater and belt over leggings. Our differences glared at me through that outfit—she had more curves and style and raw feminine power than I would ever have. And she was pissed off.

"Give me a break!" she moaned, then turned her back to me. "This is moving on?"

"Leave her alone," Ezra said, and tried to close the door, but Taylor stood in the way, her arms folded over her chest.

"No, you leave her alone," she shot back. "What is she, fifteen? Last time I checked that was illegal."

"She's in grade twelve, and again, not your business," he said.

Her lips twisted with disgust. "So all that *I've changed* crap, that was actually code for *I want to screw little girls?*"

Little girls. I could feel myself shrinking. I couldn't move, not even to blink or breathe. Soon I'd be nothing at all.

"Calm down, Taylor." Ezra tried to close the door

again, but this time she grabbed it and shoved it back open.

"You know you could do better than little Miss Trailer Trash of America here, right? What is it, the Southern drawl? It is! It turns you on, doesn't it!"

My tongue felt dry and thick. Another word and I might actually be sick.

"But seriously, look at her," Taylor said, pointing at me like I was a mannequin in a window. "She's got the body of a twelve-year-old. Don't tell me you'd rather be with—"

"*Stop!*" he muttered through clenched teeth.

I had to get out, but I couldn't make myself walk. My legs were frozen. Plus, Taylor was still blocking the exit, and she looked capable of throwing punches.

"You need to go," Ezra said.

I looked up, terrified he was talking to me. But he wasn't. He put his hand on Taylor's shoulder and tried to turn her away from me, but she shrugged it off.

"*Don't* touch me!" she spat, and shot him a wounded glare. "You don't get to ever touch me again!"

I looked away. That well of pain in her eyes—that wasn't for me to see. This wasn't my fight.

Ezra's hand dropped awkwardly to his side, and the three of us stood motionless. Like statues. Blood pounded from my fingertips to my temples. He hadn't even stuck up for me.

Taylor sniffed, and I felt an unexpected surge of pity

for her. But then she turned to me again, a snarl on her lips. "Oh, and just so you know, you aren't the first girl to feel the earth move on that couch." The snarl became a grin, showing a row of perfectly white teeth like squared pearls. "And not just me. No way, not our Ezra. This boy's had more girls back here than you American girls can even count. It's the hair, I think." She reached out and ran her fingers through Ezra's long bangs.

I wanted him to grab her wrist but he didn't. He just stared at the floor, jaw set, the veins in his neck bulging.

Taylor continued, one hand on her hip. "Feels good, though, doesn't it? Especially the way he puts his hands—"

"*Enough!*" Ezra shouted.

Taylor smiled. Satisfied.

I had no choice—it was either sit back down or have my knees buckle and crumple to the floor. I sank into the couch.

She whirled around, her beautiful red hair like a blur of fire behind her. Ezra and I stayed perfectly still, our bodies lifeless. The door clanged shut behind her and we still couldn't move. Or speak.

Finally, Ezra found words. "I'm sorry." His voice was barely above a whisper.

He was sorry. What was I supposed to say? Or do? Or feel? The range of emotions I'd felt in the last five minutes was too large. I'd been spun too hard, was too dizzy to walk in a straight line or even see what'd just happened.

Was I supposed to say it was okay? Nothing about that was okay.

I absentmindedly ran my hand along the well-worn upholstery beside me. Well-worn. Was I just somebody to make out with? Had I forgot everything Grandma had drilled into my head about guys? I wasn't sexy like Taylor, or pretty like Charly, or even cute like Bree. I was the girl next door. I was a warm body.

"We broke up a few weeks ago, but we were together a long time, like three years." He was leaning against the doorway and staring at the carpet, like he was scared to come closer. "She's not . . . you know . . . taking it well."

I laughed, and the sound echoed oddly around me. It wasn't funny. But I couldn't think of any other response. Then I put my hands over my face and started to cry.

"Don't," Ezra pleaded, coming toward me.

He'd said all the right things today. He'd been exactly who I needed him to be, dug through all the layers to get to me. Why couldn't he really be that guy?

It didn't matter. If he was just looking for action, Taylor was right. He could do better.

He sat down beside me and tried to pull my body toward him, but I pulled away. He let go of me.

How far would I have gone if Taylor hadn't barged in? What was the matter with me?

I stood up. "I made a mistake."

"Don't leave angry." He went to take my hand, but then stopped himself. "Nothing she said was even close to true."

"It's not about what she said," I lied. She'd made me feel like I was just some worthless skank. "This just isn't me. I need to go."

He didn't try to stop me. I took my jacket from the hook by the door and escaped into the afternoon twilight.

Chapter 16

knew what pregnant women looked like. Obviously. And I knew what Charly looked like, so I had no right to be surprised when it started happening.

But in my mind I'd superimposed her face on a raindrop-shaped body. I didn't think about the transformation. If I had, I'd have realized she was going to swell like the slowest filling balloon in the world, and it would start with just a tiny bulge.

"What are you looking at?" she asked.

I shrugged. We hadn't said more than *pass the milk*, and *get your stinking clothes off my side of the bed* in weeks. I hadn't even told her about what happened with Ezra.

I hadn't told anybody about Ezra, and now there wasn't anything to tell. It had been three weeks and I hadn't heard a word from him.

"Seriously, stop staring at me!" she snapped. She was turned sideways, her hands in her hair, smoothing it into a ponytail. But her body in profile was just too much—I couldn't look away from the curve of her belly.

She grumbled something under her breath and left the bathroom, leaving me to finish slathering on lotion alone.

According to Bree, Charly could've been showing much sooner but wasn't because she was young and this was her first pregnancy. The wardrobe helped too. She'd been wearing big sweatshirts and walking around with the top button of her low-rise jeans unbuttoned, to avoid dipping into the clothes Bree had bought her.

"Why don't you just wear the maternity clothes?" I yelled after her.

"Because I don't need them yet! Why don't you stop bossing me around?"

I took a deep breath. I *didn't* boss her around. Or not anymore, at least.

"She's nervous," Bree whispered to me as I laced up my boots. "She's got an ultrasound today."

I pressed my lips together so something honest wouldn't come flying out. As far as Bree was concerned, I was already the worst sister in the world. No need to add fuel to that fire.

Bree dropped us off at school and I pushed through my day without thinking about Charly. Almost. I had to take a brief hiatus over lunch to silently call her every swear word I knew. She'd earned it. I'd seen her through the window into the cafeteria, eating with three normalish-looking girls while I was on my way up to my stinky little corner of the library to chew on my contraband bagel and listen to people suck face. She'd definitely earned it.

After I was finished with the silent cursing, I wasn't hungry. I rolled my pen down my notebook, then pushed it up again, then did it again. And again. I'd planned on using the lunch hour to email Savannah back, but it felt like too much work. That needy panic I'd felt between her emails during the first few weeks in Canada was gone. It wasn't like she was sitting around waiting for my reply, anyway.

Last night's missive had contained a full report of everything I could've wanted to hear and more: Everybody's least favorite cheerleader, Libby Portier, got a brutal nose job; the varsity girls' soccer team destroyed Baldwin 6–1; Sebastian got promoted from bagger to cashier; and best of all, Luciana accidentally dropped a Tampax super plus out of her purse in front of half the football team. It didn't get any better.

So why didn't I still hurt? Those first few emails from home had made me ache all over. The homesickness had tasted sweet and metallic, like I'd sliced my tongue on a candy, but with this one I'd felt nothing. I should've at least been happy for the team and for Sebastian, but that just seemed like too much effort.

Tremonton was fading, and there didn't seem to be any point in holding on. Email reports and memories weren't enough, and I wasn't ever going back, or at least not to PHS. How long would I even be back in Tremonton before I went on to whichever second-rate college I decided on? A month. Maybe two.

That was if I managed to actually apply. Last week I'd made it through exactly half of UCF's application before Bree's computer crashed. I took it as a sign. Not that it mattered yet—their rolling admissions policy meant I had months to get it together. If I wanted to get it together.

I glanced around the library, ignoring the giggling from two carrels down, and tried to picture Ezra here. He didn't fit. He was so much deeper than this blandness, he must have stuck out as odd. Or maybe he and Taylor had subsisted in their own little universe.

I'd been trying so hard not to think about him. Remembering the humiliation hurt too much, but I couldn't keep it shelved. He kept reappearing in my thought patterns like he belonged. And remembering the way he tasted, the warmth of his hands, it just made me mad. I couldn't retrieve those memories without pulling with them the things Taylor had said and feeling like some cheap skank.

How "over" were they, anyway? I tried to replay the conversation between Bree and Taylor at the Lake Louise lost and found, but it was over a month ago now. I thought Taylor had said they'd broken up and then later Bree had suggested they'd been off and on for years. But what if it was the opposite? What if they really *were* still sort of a couple and Ezra was just a . . . I stopped that thought. I didn't want him to be a cheater. A disgusting, typical, filthy, common cheater.

It hadn't felt like that. Or at least not for me.

I stood up, brushed the sandwich crumbs off my lap, and wandered over to the yearbooks. Last year's was black with a snarling, gold-embossed buffalo on the front. I flipped through the pages, scanning for Ezra. His head shot was a good one, and my stomach lurched just a little, remembering the way he'd looked at me right before he kissed me.

I blinked and flipped the page.

Aside from his head shot, he was in three other pictures. In the first two he had his arm around Taylor. In the third he was giving her a piggyback, her legs and arms clamped around him, her chin digging into his shoulder, her red hair masking half his face. He was smiling. In all three pictures, he was smiling.

I snapped the yearbook shut, put it back, and returned to my tuna-scented refuge.

Now I could forget about him.

"Amelia, wait."

Crap. I'd only made it to the third step in the spiral. When I'd walked in and seen Bree curled up on the couch with an open anatomy textbook on her face, I'd hoped for the best. Apparently my stealth was no match for her killer surveillance skills.

She twisted around, her hair all spiky from sleep. "I need to talk to you."

I didn't move. Maybe it'd be quick. "What."

She rubbed her eyes and squinted at the microwave clock. "Where have you been? It's almost eight."

"I ran laps around the gym at school for an hour. Then I went shopping."

She looked at me.

What, was I supposed to produce sweaty running shorts? Bags? Receipts? If I'd have known she'd be here for an interrogation I'd have actually bought something, rather than just sitting and reading in the shopping plaza food court.

"I thought you were working tonight," I said.

"I have a big test tomorrow, so I asked for the night off to study."

I raised my eyebrows. Bree's studying looked intense. "I'll let you get back to it, then."

"Wait." Then in a whisper, "Your sister had an ultrasound today."

I looked up to the loft. The light was off, but that didn't mean she was asleep.

Ultrasound. So what? And if Charly no longer wanted to feed me every grotesque detail of her visits to the obstetrician, I sure didn't want to hear them from Bree. I came back down and stood beside the couch, arms folded.

"I don't know if she'll want to talk about it," Bree continued, "but she was kind of upset. She cried afterward."

"Why?" A chill ran through me, flushing the annoyance away. "Is there something wrong with the baby?"

"No. It's a girl."

A girl.

"It was kind of amazing, actually. They had one of those 3-D ultrasound machines and you could see her little knees and elbows and fingernails."

A girl.

I could feel Bree staring at me, trying to coax a reaction out of me, so I gave her nothing. I blinked a couple of times. "Okay. Good night."

She didn't answer.

I turned to leave and this time she didn't stop me.

Sleep. Ha.

First I listened to Charly breathing. Then I listened to Bree dawdle through the mindlessness that was her evening: sweep the kitchen floor, hum show tunes, talk on the phone with Richard, make herbal tea, brush and floss with the bathroom door open.

When it was finally quiet, I wished it wasn't.

A girl. She was here in this bed with us. Did she look like Charly? Like Mom? Or maybe she'd inherited Charly's latent Mercer genes. Maybe she looked like me.

It didn't matter though, because I would never know her. She wasn't ours. She couldn't be a Mercer, never had been, not from the insignificant moment she was conceived to the moment she would force her way out of my little sister. So why did I feel this aching hollowness like somebody was ripping something out of me? It wasn't even my body she was sharing.

Charly rolled into the center of the bed and started snoring. Defeated, I took my pillow and the extra blanket Charly had already kicked to the floor and went downstairs to the couch.

I couldn't force my mind from her. Not Charly. *Her*— the real, live, human girl with a beating heart and fingernails and earlobes and cheeks and eyelashes and *everything*, all inside of Charly.

What else was there to think about?

Ezra. I'd forced him out of my thoughts completely, but just for tonight, I needed him. I could let myself imagine that things had happened differently. I deserved the distraction, even if it was a lie. His voice, his eyes, his warm hands on my back—I closed my eyes and pretended that all that was actually mine to dream about.

For a while.

But I've always sucked at pretending. Reality can't just be turned down like volume. When we were little it was Charly who created the make-believe worlds and forced me to play along. I did, but halfheartedly.

With Ezra the facts were screaming-loud and my volume knob was busted. Pretending meant forgetting the fact that Ezra hadn't called or stopped by or anything since that night. It all just confirmed what Taylor said: He was a player, and I was a warm body. A warm, lonely, needy body. And what she hadn't said, but implied—that I was a slut—made my whole body burn with shame and anger. I couldn't even defend myself.

The couch wasn't big enough to really roll over, so I

flopped onto my other side like a fish on a dock, praying for mercy, that someone would pity me and kick me back into the water. Or maybe just put me out of my misery.

When I finally did drift off, a nightmare seeped its way in.

I dreamt it was me who was pregnant, not with a girl, but with some grotesque monster. A doctor pulled it out of me, greenish-black and writhing snakelike. I tried to scream but I couldn't push the air out. Then I saw it wasn't a doctor but Charly, and she was holding the thing, rocking it like it was her baby. She wouldn't even look at me. I was trying to tell her it was a monster, but she turned away like she couldn't hear me. Like I didn't exist.

I forced myself awake with a gasp.

3:49. The kitchen clock glowed green. I shivered, my heart racing, then pulled the blanket tight around me and waited for my mind to clear, to remember what was real and what wasn't.

It took a minute or two, but eventually my heart slowed and the panic dissipated. And then all I could feel was emptiness.

"Where's Charly?" Bree asked.

I pointed a finger loft-ward.

"You didn't want to wake her up?"

I put my cereal bowl in the dishwasher. I wasn't

gratifying that question with an answer. Waking Charly up was like poking a hibernating grizzly with a stick— nobody wanted to do it. And more to the point, it wasn't my job.

She took her keys from the hook. "Ready to go?" Little lines creased the skin between her eyes. She was ticked, but I totally didn't care. *She* could go and wake Charly up. *She* was the one who convinced her to go to school in the first place. I'd told them both this day would come and I'd been completely ignored.

I slung my backpack over my shoulder.

"Did she say anything about the ultrasound last night?" Bree asked.

"No."

"Hmmm. I hope she doesn't sleep all day. Yesterday she said something about a math test after lunch."

"Charly doesn't give a crap about a math test." I followed Bree out the door and down the stairs.

"Well, she should."

"Well, she doesn't."

We walked to the car in silence.

"I just don't want her to start slipping. School is important."

"Really?" Why was I resorting to sarcasm with Bree? "Listen, when things get rough, Charly holes up like a mole. You can't lecture her out of it. It's just what she does. She gets bored of things or stressed out or upset and just shuts down. Honestly, I'm surprised she lasted a full month at school." I climbed into the car while Bree went to town on the windows with her scraper. It was violent, but the windows were frost free in less than a minute.

Bree got in the car, giving the door a good slam. "I just think if you were to help her out a little, you know, try to keep her motivated, it would really go a long ways."

I stared out the freshly scraped window and felt my heart thump. Backing down would be smart. Patience would be smart. At this point, even putting my fingers in my ears would be smarter than what I really wanted to do. And she was just so deserving of a push.

"Back when you were so eager to have Charly in school," I started, "you both thought that I was the mean one. Never mind that I'm the girl with lifetime front-row tickets to the Charly show. I mean, it's great how gung ho you are about education now, but maybe you should have channeled your own high school dropout days before convincing her she could handle high school pregnant."

Bree flinched.

I sat, arms folded over my chest, trying to keep from shivering. Neither of us said a word the rest of the drive.

She pulled up to the school and I got out, but before I could shut the door she asked, "So what happened with you and Ezra?" Her voice was peaches and cream as usual. She was too good to let even a hint of a smile bend her lips, but there was a glow.

I slammed the door shut.

I fully expected Charly to still be in bed wallowing when I got home from school, but she was sitting on the couch, dressed in one of the new maternity tops and stretch-band jeans, hair curled, makeup on.

"You're up."

"Yeah."

"Bree had her panties in a bunch about you missing school."

"I'll talk to her."

I went straight to the kitchen. My lunch had been rudely interrupted by an impromptu library walk-through by Dr. Ashton. Mr. Langer may not have cared that people ate in the carrels, but apparently she did. She'd disentangled the make-out couple two carrels down, then taken my lunch.

"What's with the makeup?" I said, taking a block of cheese and some deli meat from the fridge. There was maybe a fifty-fifty chance she'd answer me, versus telling me to go to hell. I thought it best not to mention the fact that she'd broken and finally put on the maternity clothes.

"There's a couple driving in from Calgary to meet me."

I grabbed a loaf of bread and started making a sandwich. A couple. It took my starving brain a moment to realize she was talking about people wanting her baby. An adoption interview—that was why Bree had been so tense about Charly spending the day in bed. She'd been worried Charly wouldn't get it together. And of course she couldn't have just told me, seeing as I wasn't a part of their little circle of trust.

"When?"

She glanced at the clock. "Hour and a half."

"Here?" I asked, shocked that she hadn't shut me down yet.

She shook her head. "I'm meeting them at a restaurant."

I took a bite of my sandwich and chewed about thirty times.

A restaurant. She wouldn't even tell me the name of the place, like she honestly thought I was going to crash her little dinner. Was this a done deal or just an interview? I couldn't ask. I couldn't ask *anything*, but how on earth did Charly know what to ask them?

A thousand questions flooded my mind: *Do you just hand over the baby and never see them again? Are they smart? Do they go to church? Are they dog people or cat people? Do they vote? Do they recycle? Do they floss every night?*

I swallowed and took another bite of my sandwich. I couldn't ask a single one.

· · ·

I was alone in the apartment when the phone rang. I hunted under throw pillows for it. Bree always called home at least once during her evening shift at McSorley's, just to make sure we hadn't burned down the apartment or been abducted. On the one night I'd dared to let it go to voice mail, she'd freaked out and come home early.

I found it after the sixth ring, and pressed talk before I noticed the caller ID display. Banff Public Library. *Crap.*

"Hello."

"Hi."

It was him.

"Amelia?"

"Yeah."

"It's Ezra."

"Yeah."

One second. Two seconds. Three seconds. Then he said, "How are you?" at the exact same time I managed to spit out, "How's it going?" We followed that up with a simultaneous, "Fine/Good," and another few seconds of awkward silence.

"So, I haven't seen you in a while," he said.

No, you haven't, not since your beautiful and psychotic ex verbally abused me. "I've been busy."

"Yeah?"

"Yeah."

"I need to apologize," he said. "For the other day."

"Don't." The other day? As in three weeks ago. The statute of limitations on an apology was long gone.

"You didn't deserve to be the target of Taylor's wrath."

"It's fine."

"No, it's not. I shouldn't have let it happen, and I definitely should've called you sooner. I've been feeling like an idiot for the last two weeks."

"Three."

"Right, three weeks."

"That's a long time to be feeling like an idiot for. Poor you."

He ignored my sarcasm. "I thought you didn't want anything to do with me. From the sounds of it, I wasn't wrong."

"No."

He paused. "No, I was wrong, or no, I wasn't wrong?"

"I was embarrassed. I've never been in that kind of situation before."

"Yeah, Taylor really lost it."

"No, I mean, I'm not the kind of girl who gets caught making out in a library. Or anywhere. Ever." Great. Now he thought I was a prude.

"Too fast, then."

"Yeah, and you disappearing didn't help anything."

"I'm sorry. It's not like I planned to hook up like that."

That sounded terrible. Like he'd kissed me and couldn't for the life of him figure out why.

"And I definitely didn't plan on Taylor dropping by."

"Are you two even officially broken up?"

"Of course." He sounded insulted. "We haven't been together since before Christmas."

My stomach churned, a mix of excitement and anger and shock swirling around. I'd spent the last three weeks convincing myself I'd never hear from him again. I couldn't believe we were actually talking.

"I feel bad that *you* feel bad," he continued. "You didn't deserve that. And the things Taylor said to you, and about me—none of that was true."

"But you still didn't come find me."

More silence. Every piece of me wanted to let him off the hook, to be one of those girls who giggles and ignores whatever needs to be ignored. But I was still me, and he'd still kissed me till I was dizzy and then let me think I was nothing to him for three whole weeks.

"You don't let a guy off easy, do you?"

"Guess not."

"Any suggestions for me?"

"I might be willing to negotiate some sort of penance."

"I'm listening."

My brain stalled. What did I need from Ezra? It wasn't like he could undo what had happened. "I don't know," I said. "Maybe you should just start trying to impress me and I'll let you know if I decide to forgive you."

"At least give me a hint of what would impress you."

"I could really use some Florida sunshine right now."

"Great. That should be easy to arrange. How about Florida orange juice instead?"

"No dice."

He sighed. "Okay, I'll work on it."

"Good luck," I said, wondering if he could hear the smile in my voice.

"So how's life at Bree's?"

Bree, my favorite subject. I opened my mouth ready to complain, but stopped myself. Ezra had it worse than I did. At least I didn't walk around feeling responsible for anybody else's mental health, and as much as my situation sucked, it wasn't permanent. "Okay. Things are starting to feel normal. We've got our routines so we don't get into each other's hair too much. How are things with you?"

"Nothing new. I'm actually about to close the library up and hit the road. I'm going to Calgary for the weekend. What are your plans?"

I wasn't about to admit my plans revolved around Charly, Bree, and Richard, or more specifically, avoiding Charly, Bree, and Richard. But they did. "Not solidified yet. What are you doing in Calgary?"

"Not much."

"Just so you know, part of your penance is actually answering an occasional question."

He laughed. "Fine. I'm staying with some friends at U of C."

"In the dorms?"

"No. They live in a house just off campus. We all went to high school together."

I couldn't ask if they were guys or girls without sounding jealous, but the thought of him playing sleepover with a bunch of girls was mildly annoying.

"Most of the guys I hung out with moved to Calgary last year after graduation," Ezra said.

"But not you."

"Not me."

If our conversation was a bike tire, we'd just rolled up to the lip of the curb and were now rolling backward. But that didn't make it a complete failure. He'd answered a question or two, and had actually volunteered information without having to be grilled.

"So how's school?" he asked after a moment.

"Not bad. CALM's lame, but kind of funny. Today Ms. Hill talked about how racial slurs are not nice."

"Oh yeah, I forgot about that unit that's like diversity for bigots. What else are you taking?"

"Photography is the only other interesting class, but I suck at it. The tests at the beginning were easy, but I'm kind of a spaz at the picture-taking part. We have this huge assignment coming up that might actually require me to go sit in the snow for an hour or two."

"Good thing you love the snow so much."

"I know."

"If you need any help with the photography you should ask my mom."

"Oh. Yeah." I'd forgotten. "She wouldn't mind?"

"Are you kidding? She'd love it. She loves you."

"What? She doesn't even know me. She met me once for like two minutes."

"She loves anyone who isn't Taylor."

The *T* word. The ensuing pause was our longest and most awkward yet. "Maybe I'll call her then," I said finally. I'd said it with just enough noncommittal enthusiasm to keep the conversation from dying completely. But I wouldn't call Naomi. It was the muddled inverse of the whole thing with Will, and I wanted to be loved because I wasn't Taylor about as much as I wanted to be unloved because I wasn't Charly. So, not at all.

"Okay," he said. "I guess I'll see you around."

He hadn't said to come by the library to see him. "Sure."

"All right. I should go."

"Drive safely," I said, "and pull over if you're tired." Hearing Grandma's words come out of my mouth filled me with a sudden pang of homesickness. Tears welled unexpectedly before my eyes. I blinked them away, relieved he couldn't see me.

Ezra laughed. "It's only an hour. I think I'll be okay."

"How do I know you're not narcoleptic? And laughing at me is no way to start your penance project, by the way."

"That's right. I have Florida sunshine to find."

"Good luck."

"Good night."

I hung up and hugged my knees to my chest. I wanted to think about Ezra, to just lie on my bed and analyze every word he said, picture his face and his mouth as he said them. I could believe him.

But then there was the other voice, the cruel one saying cruel things. It was Taylor's but not Taylor's, because at some point my mind had melted her words and poured them into a different mold. It was my voice now.

I almost faked sleep when Charly got home. I could have. I was already in bed, reading some corny self-help book I'd snagged from Bree's bookshelf, when I heard her come in. She'd done it to me enough times lately, always making sure she was spread from corner to corner of the bed. I'd started to feel like the couch was home.

But I wanted to talk to her. No. I wanted her to talk to me.

"Hey," I said.

"Hey."

She took the headband out of her hair and flopped down on the bed beside me, sighing like her lungs had been holding it in all night.

"That much fun?" I asked.

"Yeah. No. I don't know."

So that's where we were. I turned to the next page of my book and went back to learning how to grow my inner goddess.

"Actually, it was pretty good," she said softly.

Her back was to me, but I didn't look at her, just to be safe. It was like trying to feed a squirrel—eye contact would be a mistake.

"They were nice. Really nice."

"Yeah? Was Bree there with you?"

"No. I went alone."

Hallelujah. Except if Bree had been there, at least the basic questions would've been asked. On her own, Charly very well may have spent the entire interview on junk food preferences and favorite bands.

"At first I wasn't so sure about them," Charly offered. "She's kind of odd-looking, and her eyebrows are plucked to almost nothing and then drawn in, you know?"

"Yeah."

"But then she turned out to be pretty cool."

Nice and cool. She could've been describing a Pop-sicle. *Please, Charly, please say you got more than just that.* My own list of questions was flying through my brain, but Charly was too skittish for me to just start firing. She'd clam up.

But if I could only get away with asking one, which one? What did she need to think about that she hadn't already?

I was about to open my mouth when she started up again. "Her name's Summer. She's a nurse at an assisted living center for old people, and he's something geeky to do with computers. I don't know, I stopped listening. But she wants to quit her job and stay at home after the baby's born. If . . . you know.

"Anyway, she ordered rainbow trout, which I thought was weird, but whatever, and then when it came I could totally tell she didn't like it." Charly stopped to think or to breathe or maybe just to make me wonder where this was going. "Except she didn't say anything. Maybe because she didn't want to seem like a snot in front of me, or maybe because she's just the kind of person who doesn't complain when they get gross food. I don't know. But then he traded with her. Ryan. His name's Ryan."

Another pause. I pictured the scene: the geek husband quietly sliding his plate toward his wife, her painted-on eyebrows rising in surprise and then appreciation.

"So Ryan ate her nasty rainbow trout," Charly said, "and she ate his ravioli."

"That's kind of nice," I said.

"Yeah. Amelia?"

"Yeah."

"I'll pay you a million dollars if you brush my teeth for me and give me a foot rub."

I chucked the self-help book on the floor and grabbed one of Charly's feet. "I'm not doing your teeth."

"Okay."

Chapter 17

The envelope was tucked beneath the wiper on the passenger side of Bree's car.

"Holy crap!" Bree screamed, doing a little spazzy dance. "Which one of you darlings snuck out and scraped the car? Best. Monday. Ever!"

"Honestly," I said, "it's never even occurred to me." It hadn't. Charly and I'd sat shivering in the car while Bree had scraped every single morning since we'd gotten here. And until this moment, it hadn't seemed that selfish.

"Wasn't me," Charly said, sliding the envelope out from under the wiper. "Oooh, it says *Amelia* on it." She waved it in front of my face, then pulled it away as I reached for it. "And it looks like *man* writing."

I snatched it out of her hands and put it into my backpack.

"Are you kidding me?" Bree squealed. "You're not going to open it?"

"I'll open it later."

"But I need to know who scraped off my car so I can love them for the rest of my life. Isn't the curiosity killing you?"

"I know who it's from." I willed my mouth not to smile, but Charly laughed and the smile won.

Bree lifted her eyebrows. "You and Ezra are still happening?"

"They never *were* happening," Charly said. "Then they were never *not* happening. And now they're never happening all over again."

"Are you even speaking English?" I muttered. "And what makes either of you two think you know anything about me and Ezra? We're just friends. Again."

"Works every time," Charly explained to Bree. "I just have to start spewing nonsense, then she gets mad and tells all." She turned back to me. "Since when do you make out with your friends?"

I didn't take the bait. She had no way of knowing about that.

Charly shrugged and said to Bree, "Okay, so maybe not every time."

Bree dropped us off at school and I made my way to the photo lab, the green envelope burning a hole in my backpack. I was early enough for class to take my time, so I pulled it out and turned it over, memorizing the softness of the envelope beneath my fingertips. *Amelia.* Charly was right. The writing was masculine: all caps, hurried but not messy, no slant.

If there hadn't been people all around me, I might've smelled it too.

It wasn't sealed, so I slid my finger easily inside and pulled out a folded piece of lined paper. I opened it. Something fell out and fluttered to the ground before I could catch it. It was a sun. A sticker. I bent over and picked it up. No, not a sticker, a temporary tattoo, a gold disc surrounded by triangles, wavy like they'd been bent by heat. A tight gold swirl began at the center of the circle and coiled its way outward.

I read the note:

Not exactly Florida sunshine, but the best I could do.
  Ezra

I reread it. And then again. I would've kept on doing it, but Mr. Klein finally wandered in and told us to take out our cameras.

"What's up?"

I turned to the goth guy wearing black nail polish on my left. Why was he talking to me? Nobody ever talked to me in this class. "Nothing."

"What's with the smile?"

"Nothing."

He gave me a look, then went back to defacing his textbook. "Freakin' crazy Americans," he muttered.

I let it go.

It was colder again. I'd wrapped my scarf tight around my head, but the water droplets from my breath kept freezing in the wool around my mouth. I'd already rewrapped twice, moving the icy circle to the back of my head both times, but I only had so much usable scarf.

Snow squeaked beneath my boots. Who'd have thought snow could squeak? It did, though, if it was cold enough and if it was the dry kind. I made a mental note to tell Savannah. Emailing her was easier when I found little details to talk about, things I didn't have to lie about, but things that didn't totally suck. Like squeaky snow.

It had to be below minus twenty degrees. Maybe closer to minus twenty-five. There was a big electronic sign that displayed the temperature in red lights, just past the halfway point between school and Bree's. I'd gotten surprisingly good at gauging degrees Celsius based on the amount of pain I was in. I didn't know exactly what minus twenty-five converted to in Fahrenheit, but I'd come to the realization that it didn't matter. At all. Only the *feeling* mattered, and that wasn't something anybody back home would understand.

Today I wasn't going to pass the sign anyway.

The deer-dented Pathfinder pulled in front of me just as I was about to step into a crosswalk.

"Where are you going? I almost couldn't find you."

Ezra. I tried to smile normally, like I wasn't melting inside.

"Errands," I said. "Hey, you know you're officially Bree's favorite person in the whole world?"

"Bree's? Shoot. Get in so I can roll up my window."

I hurried around front. It was way too cold to play hard to get.

"If you had your own car I could've scraped that off."

"You're saying Bree's car was an afterthought?" I pulled off my gloves and covered the vents with my palms. "Don't tell her. She's probably baking you brownies as we speak."

"Not an afterthought. Just a second thought."

I thought I could feel him looking at me, but when I glanced over his eyes were on the road. "If I had my own car," I said, "you wouldn't have an excuse to keep kidnapping me like this."

"It's not kidnapping if I let you pick the destination. Where are we going?"

"Shopping."

"Can you be more specific?"

I watched pedestrians scurry along both sides of the sidewalk. Nobody was sauntering anywhere today. "It's kind of embarrassing."

"As in zit cream, or as in bras? Because I would be willing to help you shop for either. I mean, I'd prefer the latter, but whatever."

"Neither, idiot." I looked away so he couldn't see me blush.

"You've never called me idiot before."

"Not out loud."

He laughed again. That was twice now. "I kind of like it."

I leaned forward, putting my frozen cheek in front of the vent.

"So not zit cream or bras."

"I need to buy a cactus."

He did something funny with his eyebrows—one up, one down. "Now that *is* embarrassing."

"Well . . ." Was I seriously telling him about the cactus incident? "You know Ms. Lee?"

"Yeah. Guidance."

"Right. So you know those cactuses she has along the front of her desk?"

"I think so."

"Well. I, uh, kinda broke one."

"How'd that happen?"

I gave him a sheepish look, then turned my face away to give my other cheek vent time.

"Seriously?" He laughed. *Again.* Was that three? "So what, you picked it up and threw it?"

"It was more intentionally dropping than throwing. And I was having a *really* bad day," I added, like that was a justifiable excuse for violent vandalism.

"I should thank you. That woman drove me crazy."

"Ms. Lee?" Even mid–temper tantrum, I wouldn't have taken her for anyone's nemesis. "Why?"

But the minute the question was out of my mouth I knew exactly why. Of course Ezra would've been forced in there to talk about Naomi's suicide attempt, his scholarship, his brother. He would've been Ms. Lee's project of the year.

Thankfully, he just shrugged and lied. "She had a problem with me skipping school to ski. So cactus shopping, eh?"

"Cactus shopping."

Ezra took me to Cascade Plaza, the closest thing to a

real mall, and we trolled the stores until we came up with something close enough.

"The terra-cotta will totally wreck the feng shui thing she has happening," I said to Ezra as the gift store woman wrapped the box with a red ribbon.

"Nah," Ezra said. "It's the thought that counts."

"Oh, I almost forgot. Thank you for my sun," I said, pulling up the sleeve of my coat to show him the skin on the inside of my wrist where I'd put the tattoo.

"Nice." He took one hand and held my wrist, tracing a wavy sun ray with his thumb. "Do you feel warmer?"

I blushed, remembering the last time he'd touched my wrist like that. In the library.

"Yeah." I looked at the tattoo. "It's perfect."

By the time Ezra dropped me off in front of Bree's it was already dark, but the art gallery lights were still glowing and the dinner crowd at the sushi restaurant was just starting to trickle in.

"So am I forgiven?" he asked.

I held my breath. Was he asking because he wanted to kiss me? Was all this effort just to get me back on the couch? "No."

"But I helped you find a cactus. In *Canada*."

"I'm impressed. I am. And your request for forgiveness is officially under consideration."

He nodded and tapped his thumbs on the steering wheel, a satisfied look on his face. "Good enough."

I delivered the cactus to Ms. Lee during lunch the next day. The plan was to drop it by her empty office, but apparently I wasn't the only antisocial one. She was eating a salad and reading a novel at her desk.

She took it out of the box, examined the succulent, terra-cotta pot and all, then put it where the old one had been. It looked ridiculous next to the others.

"I'm sorry," I said, hoping she wasn't one of those people who required groveling and explanations too.

"I accept your apology," she said, her tone warm. She smiled.

I looked away. Acting like a child was embarrassing. Apologizing for acting like a child was brutal. Being smiled at like I was a child? Time to leave.

Her voice stopped me on my way out. "At the risk of losing another cactus, I'm going to repeat my previous offer. My door is open anytime."

"Thank you."

She went back to her book and I left.

"Hello?"

"Did she like it?"

"Who is this?" I asked into the phone.

"Very funny. Did she like the cactus?" Ezra repeated.

"Hard to tell. She's kind of distant like that. Why don't you say hello or good-bye when you're talking on the phone? I thought you Canadians were supposed to be polite."

"Only to each other. Americans get the special treatment."

"But I'm Canadian, too."

"No, you're not."

"Yes, I am. My mom was Canadian. I have both passports."

"Sing the national anthem."

I sang the first two words of *O Canada*.

"Is that all you know?"

"Maybe."

"Are you one of those people that already knows that they're tone deaf, or do you need to be told?"

"Already know. So where are you? Is this your cell?" The number on the caller ID wasn't the library number.

"Where are *you*?"

"At Bree's. Where you called me. The only place I can receive calls in my cell phone–less existence. So back to my question: Where are you?"

"Are you really going to make me ruin the surprise?"

"What surprise?"

Knock, knock.

I stared at the door, hung up the phone, and said the first four-letter word to come to mind.

"Totally wish Grandma had heard that," Charly called from the kitchen, where she was eating ice cream out of a bucket on the counter.

"How do I look?" I whispered.

"Like you're not wearing a bra."

I swore again and jumped off the couch. "Answer the door!"

"But I'm eating."

I was halfway up the spiral stairs, doing two at a time and trying not to trip. "Answer the door or I'll delete every single episode of *The Bachelor* on the DVR."

"You wouldn't dare," she said, but she'd already abandoned the bucket on the counter and was making her way over to the door.

Up in our room, I examined my Saturday afternoon self in the mirror: plaid pajama pants, glasses, bush-girl hair. *What is the matter with that boy? Who just stops by?* I rifled through my clothes, pulling out skinny jeans and the only clean long-sleeved shirt I could find. Saturday was supposed to be laundry day. Thank goodness Bree wasn't around. She'd never stop pumping me for girl talk. My heart was beating like an apoplectic hummingbird, but I couldn't slow it down.

"Strawberry ripple?" I heard Charly ask from below.

"I'd say yes, but I'm freezing." The sound of Ezra's voice made my stomach flip.

Charly's response was muffled, then he said something else I couldn't hear and she laughed.

That *laugh*.

I froze. How had I forgotten? It turned guys into slobbering idiots. I'd seen its mind-melting effects too many times. I'd seen it with Will.

We had to get out of here.

I twisted my hair into something I hoped looked messy-chic, rubbed lip gloss onto my lips, and took a deep breath. *Calm. Down. Amelia.*

I repeated the words in my mind, then walked quietly to the top of the stairs and willed myself to stop. Fingers curled around the railing, gripping for dear life, I waited. Everything inside me was screaming to hurry down and take him away from here and from her, but I couldn't.

I had to watch Ezra and Charly. Just in case.

Charly was still anchored to the island by her spoon, but Ezra was leaning back against the counter, arms folded. She was the one doing the talking—in between bites, waving the spoon around, oblivious as it dripped a trail of pink dots onto the countertop.

No denying it: She was adorable. The yoga pants and long, tight T-shirt clung to the curve of her belly, but it wasn't repulsive like I'd imagined it'd be. No bloated whale, no shapelessness, no swollen cankles. TV and movies were full of crap. She looked like herself with a cantaloupe under her shirt and that was it, like one of those girls, no *women*, on pregnancy magazine covers.

I forced my eyes to Ezra. He was listening politely, his body pulled back and his face down—not so much away from her, as into himself.

He looked bored. I wanted to kiss him. Hard. Now.

Like he'd heard me, he turned his head, looked up, and smiled. "I didn't know you wore glasses."

Crap, the glasses. I started down the stairs. "I don't. This is an optical illusion. Give me a minute to put my contacts in."

"No, don't. They look good on you."

I reached the bottom of the stairs and wallowed in awkwardness while Ezra stared at my face. Now was I supposed to go put my contacts in or not? I settled on not.

Out of the corner of my eye I could see Charly, just behind Ezra, with one eyebrow cocked, grinning like an idiot. I forced myself not to look at her so he wouldn't turn around.

"I brought you something," Ezra said, and reached for a Starbucks cup on the counter beside him.

I took it and our fingers touched. His were like ice, despite being wrapped around the piping-hot cup.

"What is it?"

"Taste it."

Charly batted her eyelashes and made pouty lips at me. Mentally, I gave her the finger.

"Thank you," I said.

"It's hot."

"Aren't you going to tell me what it is?"

"You really can't handle surprises, can you?"

"No," Charly said, "she really can't."

I glared at her and took a sip. It was the most divine hot chocolate I'd ever tasted—creamy and sweet and cinnamony. "This is good. Thanks."

"You're welcome," he said, and turned to Charly. "I'm sorry. I should've got you one too. I wasn't thinking."

She took the spoon out of her mouth and shook her head. "No worries. I'm all about the ice cream lately."

"Do you want a sip?" I asked him.

"No, I drank mine on the way here. I was going to wait, but I spent all morning outside and just needed to warm up."

"All morning? Are you kidding me?" Bree had read us the weekend forecast last night—below minus thirty and with a windchill factor of minus sixty—so Charly and I had determined not to leave the apartment unless it was on fire. Bree had gone to a band rehearsal, but she was clearly lacking in judgment.

"Yeah, conditions are kind of a mess up there right now with the warm-up last week and now it being so cold. We had to clear a lot of snow off this morning before the runs could even open."

"I can't believe you spent hours outside in this," I said. "That sounds horrific."

"It kind of was," he admitted.

"Can I take your coat?"

"Thanks." He unzipped the coat and handed it to me. He was wearing a wool sweater, the neckline showing at least two shirts layered beneath.

I laid his coat over the edge of the couch and made my way back to the kitchen and my hot chocolate. "Well, at least you survived."

"Yeah, but I have to head back out there for night skiing. I'm working three till close."

"Three? So you have to leave soon."

"In an hour."

I hid my disappointment in another sip. I'd just assumed he had the rest of the day free. Although, he had come here. He'd come all the way *back* here.

"That's a long drive for just an hour in town."

He shrugged. "Maybe I had something I had to do in town. Maybe I really wanted some hot chocolate."

"Because hot chocolate at a ski resort—that would be impossible to find."

Ezra looked at Charly. "Help me out here. Is she always this mean?"

"Pretty much." Charly put the lid on the ice cream and put it back in the freezer. "Half the time it's because she really is mean, and half the time it's because she's clueless. I think right now she's just clueless."

Another sip, this time to hide the smile on my face.

"And as much as I'd like to help you out," Charly continued, "I have a date with Bree's bed and *The Bachelor*. Wait, not like that. Not the actual bachelor. You know what I mean."

I waited for the wink-wink, nudge-nudge, I'm-leaving-you-two-alone glance, but in what may have been Charly's most self-controlled moment ever, she walked to Bree's bedroom without saying or doing anything embarrassing. Not even a grin. She just closed the door behind her. I'd never loved her so much.

Bree's TV blared behind the closed door, and Ezra looked up at me, arms still folded.

"So."

"So."

"I changed my mind," he said. "Can I have a sip of your hot chocolate?"

I held out the half-empty cup and he took it from me. But this time his hand was warm and he held it around mine.

"I have a question for you," he said.

"Shoot."

"Your dad's a preacher."

Not the direction I thought we'd be going. Not even close. "A pastor, and that's not a question."

"So does that mean you're super religious?"

I thought about it for a second. Being religious scared guys. Being a pastor's daughter scared them even more. "Depends how you define that."

"That was vague."

"Thank you."

"And not a compliment."

I crossed over so I was beside him, leaning on the counter, hip to hip, our elbows touching. Conversations like this went better without eye contact. I took a deep breath. He must've showered after his shift because I could smell his shampoo or his aftershave or whatever it was that was making it so hard to concentrate. "Fine," I said. "I'll be less vague. I am religious. I mean, I actually believe the stuff my dad preaches. Are you?"

"Religious? I don't go to church or anything. My mom's Anglican, but she doesn't go to church either. But, I don't know, I don't think I'm *not* religious. I mean, I think about things a lot."

"*Things*," I said. "And I'm vague?"

"Like death. And I think I probably believe in God.

Most days. Organized religion just isn't for me, no offense to your dad or you. But, yeah, I think about why things happen and what happens after we die all the time. So does that make me religious?"

"According to my grandma, no. According to me, maybe."

He smiled with half his mouth, like I'd said something amusing. "You talk about your grandma a lot more than your dad. You must be really close."

"I guess we are. She's there more than my dad. He's kind of permanently elsewhere. In his head, I mean."

Ezra shrugged. "My dad's elsewhere physically."

I waited for more, not sure whether we'd progressed to the point where I could ask. "As in Australia?"

"I wish—my summer visits would be so much cooler. No, as in Whitehorse."

The blank look on my face gave me away.

"Capital of the Yukon."

I couldn't help it. Another blank look.

"The territory above British Columbia?"

"Got it."

"You should really sit down with a map of Canada sometime."

"Sure," I said. "And after that I'll quiz you on the capitals of all fifty states."

"Bring it," he said, and elbowed me gently in the side.

"So when you're at home do you hear your dad preach every Sunday?"

"Yeah, but . . ."

"But what?"

"Why are you asking me about all of this?"

The look on his face was tight, thoughtful. I could see him trying to think through every word. "That day at the library, when we were, you know, before Taylor showed up . . ."

"Yeah."

"Yeah. That was nice."

My stomach was churning. Could he hear it?

"But I don't want you to feel like that's why I'm here. I mean, it isn't *not* why I'm here—"

My brain attempted to unscramble the double negatives, but he was already moving on.

"—but I don't want you worrying about what Taylor said, about me getting a lot of girls. That's not why I want to be with you—"

I was trying to decide how insulted to be by this, but he was already moving on again.

"—or it isn't the *only* reason, 'cause I'm not going to lie, I've been thinking about that, and that would be . . . Anyway, I know that after everything happened you felt really bad, but not just about Taylor, about us, too. What you said about things going really fast and me getting the wrong idea—I just want you to know that I'm okay with where you're coming from. You and your family. I know you're all going through a lot with your sister right now."

Words. Why couldn't I think of something to say? I had to say something, but everything I felt was flowery and ridiculous, and anything less wasn't enough.

I turned my head, then my body, toward him and tipped my forehead to his shoulder. He lifted his arm and I slid into him, breathing his clean, foresty scent. "Thank you," I mumbled into his chest.

"I think that was thank you, so you're welcome."

We stood there like that, with me curled into his body, listening to his heart beat against my cheek for a minute before he asked, "So do you miss going to church?"

How did he know what to ask? "Yeah. But it's ruined whether I'm there or not. I used to feel like my dad was talking to me—he doesn't do the whole hellfire and damnation thing. He isn't that kind of pastor. I used to really love his sermons. I used to love everything about church, actually. But then Charly got pregnant and everything was different."

"I thought he didn't know."

"He didn't. Doesn't. I guess I'm the one who changed. I've been so mad at him, and I know it's not his fault, but I can't help but think that if he were a different kind of person, a different kind of dad, we'd have been able to tell him."

Ezra's chest rose and fell, my body moving with it.

"Maybe he wouldn't have freaked like you think he would've."

"Maybe," I said, not believing it. "But we weren't worried about him being angry. We were worried about it breaking him."

"Oh."

The word was full of sadness. I reached down and touched his hand, his skin rough and warm beneath my fingertips. I opened my mouth to ask about him and his mom, then closed it. He was so private. I didn't want him to pull away from me now, not after pouring my heart out. "And it would've been the scandal of the decade in Tremonton. If sadness didn't kill him, the humiliation would."

"But there are worse things than getting pregnant," he said. "Maybe your dad would've been okay."

I looked away. "Charly's the special one. Everyone says she's exactly like my mom."

I let the words settle and prayed he wouldn't try to tell me I was special too. Savannah always responded to my hinting around this truth with self-esteem boosting comments, like telling me how much my dad loved me meant anything.

He turned his hand around, lacing his fingers through mine. "That sucks."

"And after Charly got pregnant and I knew I was leaving, sitting and listening to his sermons was hell. I don't miss that. But now I feel guilty for not going."

"Yeah, you don't seem like you've got much of a rebellious side."

I smirked. "You think having a tattoo makes you the expert?" I traced the bear on his forearm with my fingertips.

He watched my fingers travel over its head and back, around each leg and back up to the head. "The tattoo doesn't count. My mom supported it. If you want to piss off your parents, you do the *opposite* of what they want."

"In my case, that wouldn't work. Satan worshipping is so extreme."

"Good point."

"And the sight of blood makes me sick, so animal sacrifices are out."

"That's a relief. I can't see us hanging out if you were busy skinning house cats. Plus, chicks who wear black lipstick scare me."

"That makes two of us."

His stomach grumbled audibly and I laughed. "You're hungry. You should have said something."

He shrugged. "I figured I'd drive through somewhere on my way back to Lake Louise."

I walked over and opened the fridge. "Leftovers à la Bree?"

"If you're offering."

I pulled last night's pork chops out of the fridge and started heating up a plate for Ezra. "So I feel like I've talked your head off," I said. "It's kind of embarrassing. You probably won't believe me, but I don't usually do that."

"No, I believe you. You've got closed book written all over you."

"Me?" The microwave beeped and I took the plate out and slid it over to Ezra. "What about you? You ask me question after question, but you never talk about yourself."

He took a bite of food.

"Sure," I said. "Eat instead."

He chewed. And chewed. Then swallowed and took another bite of food.

"My point exactly." My smirk, my tone—they only hid so much.

Finally he spoke. "So what do you want to know?"

So much. But I didn't want to ask for it. I wanted there to be something magical about me that dissolved his stone-faced filter that held everything in. I wanted him to shake his head and wonder why he found himself saying things to me, things he couldn't tell anyone else. "I want to know why you read a math textbook at the library and hide it when people come in."

"I like math."

"And the hiding?"

"I don't like people bugging me about liking math."

"That doesn't seem a little sixth grade to you?"

"No, and it's called *grade six* here. I don't know why you're pretending you don't know anything about me. Like Bree hasn't told you everything." A ragged edge had crept into his voice, something sharp beneath the surface. He looked at the cupboard above the sink and pointed. "Mind if I get myself some water?"

"Go ahead."

I folded my arms and watched him. *Let it drop, Amelia.*

He drank, then put the glass down. "If someone asked you about your college plans right now, would you feel like talking about it?"

"Of course not. Last time *someone* insisted on discussing the wreckage that is my future, I smashed a cactus."

"Exactly."

"But I'm not just *someone*." My vulnerability stung with all the rawness of skin under a ripped nail.

He needed to reassure me. Now was the time for him to say something ridiculous like, *No, you aren't just someone, Amelia. You mean so much more than that to me.* If he said it softly and kissed me hard right now, I'd completely ignore the gag-worthiness of that kind of declaration and the fact that I'd fished for it, and I'd believe him. With everything in me, I'd believe him.

"I need to go," he said.

And I'd just bared my pathetic soul.

I glanced at the clock. "So you were kidding when you said you didn't have to be there till three o'clock."

"I forgot I have to stop for gas."

"Yeah." *Shut up, Amelia.*

"What is going on?" The irritation in his voice just made me madder. "You want to go check the gas gauge?"

I kept my voice calm and low. The last thing I needed was to be called emotional. "Yeah, I'd really love to go out in minus six hundred degrees to prove you have a full tank. If you'd rather lie and duck out than have a real conversation with me, whatever."

"How has this not been a real conversation? We've been standing here talking for almost an hour."

"No, twenty minutes. And *I've* been standing here talking. You've been refusing to share anything that might make me feel like I might actually know you."

His body stiffened. "You know me. I'm just shy. So what?"

"But you're *not* shy! Shyness wears off when you get to know somebody, and this is definitely getting worse. You just don't trust me."

"It has nothing to do with you."

"Exactly. It never does. Sorry for not being thrilled about it, but I've had enough of that recurring life theme."

He looked me in the eyes and I saw layers of ice cracking, something simmering underneath. "Fine. You win.

My mother is bipolar and occasionally suicidal. My brother is a junkie and a criminal. My father is gone and I don't blame him, because if I could run away without the entire world exploding, I would too. What else? Oh yeah, the girl I was with for three years hates me because I couldn't love her enough, whatever that means, and the girl I can't stop thinking about insists I don't trust her. And she's right, because I don't trust anyone anymore. Happy?"

The air rushed out of me like I'd been kicked in the stomach. *Happy?* No. Needy. Egomaniacal. Ashamed. But definitely not happy.

"I'm going to be late," he said quietly.

I looked down at my feet. Was I supposed to apologize? He'd been trying to do something nice and I'd crushed it like glass under my boot. Stomp and twist. But it was true—he pulled further into himself the more time we spent together and it felt like rejection.

That made us wrong for each other.

"Thanks for the hot chocolate," I muttered.

"You're welcome."

I walked him to the door, fighting the churning in my stomach with every step. I wanted to hug him and apologize, but I couldn't. He might not hug me back. He might just stand there with my arms around him.

"You want your pork chop for the road?"

He shook his head, and I wished for the millionth time

his eyes weren't so unreadable. I leaned against the wall, watching him put on his boots and bundle up. "So, don't freeze to death."

"No promises."

The door was only open for a couple of seconds, just long enough for him to slip out and cold air to force its way in. I stood perfectly still, leaning into the closed door, letting the cold and the silence swallow me.

Chapter 18

need to talk to you."

"Gimme a minute," I mumbled. Midsentence, mid-thought, mid-email—did she always do that intentionally, or was it some kind of interruptive radar she'd been born with?

At least she was still talking to me, though. And the way she'd cleared out when Ezra had stopped by yesterday had been surprisingly thoughtful.

I sighed and pushed back from the keyboard, gliding across the hardwood.

"What?"

"Well, actually . . ." Her voice trailed off. She was

sitting sideways in the armchair with her legs dangling over the edge, scissors in one hand, a braid in the other. She'd freaked out this morning about the static making her hair stick to her neck, and begged me to give her two French braids. The effect was very Swiss Miss.

"Wait, what are you doing?" I asked.

"Trimming split ends. It's so freaking dry my hair is turning into straw."

"Cutting your own hair is mental-patient crazy. Put the scissors down."

Oddly, she obeyed. And I could see nervousness in the set of her mouth and lines between her brows.

I folded my arms and waited.

"Actually it's Ms. Lee who wants me to talk to you," she said.

Ms. Lee. Charly had all but moved into the counseling office—wasn't that enough for that woman? "You can tell her I'm doing fine," I said, "and I'm not coming in."

"No, not like that. She wants me to, like, *talk* to people. She wants me to tell people things, and I told her I'd start with you."

Things? Was Charly actually gearing up to tell me off? Because if so, I had a few choice words for her too. "So talk, then."

Charly sighed. "Jeez, Amelia." Her voice was shaky.

"You don't have to make this so hard. I just need you to listen to me."

It was the way she said my name. Something in it startled me. Then it made me ache, like she was going to cry and it was going to be all my fault.

"I'm sorry," I mumbled. "I'm just ticked at Savannah."

"Maybe we should just talk later, then."

"No. Really, I'm sorry. Go ahead."

She took a deep breath and the bulge of her belly rose and sank with it. "Well. Back in the fall, at home, I sort of let people believe things. Things that weren't exactly true. At first I couldn't explain, and then once everyone had already assumed things, and I'd already disappointed everyone, those things kind of became true to me—I mean, what everyone thought, instead of what really happened." She was pulling her braid like she was milking a cow, like she could coax sense out of it. "So I kind of stopped believing that the things that everyone thought were true *weren't* actually true."

"Charly." I took a deep breath of my own. This warranted being annoyed, but I didn't feel annoyed. I felt afraid. "I have no idea what you're talking about. I need you to replace pronouns with nouns, and 'things' with other words."

"I can't remember the difference between a pronoun and a noun."

I closed my eyes. "Are you kidding?"

"Maybe?"

"Okay, but you know what I mean. I really *do* want to listen to whatever it is that Ms. Lee wants you to say, but you're not making sense."

She nodded, her eyes big and focused on mine. "Okay." She dropped the braid and started tugging on the other one. "Okay. So you know in the fall, before home-coming?"

"Yeah."

"You know that party I went to on that night when I didn't—"

"Of course I know," I interrupted, trying to keep my voice patient. "The night you didn't come home, the night"—I waved my hand in the air at her—"this happened."

"Yeah, that night." She swallowed. "Well, I drank a little bit."

I remembered. She'd arrived home looking like the hangover poster child. "A little bit?"

"A little bit. One wine cooler. But I don't remember most of that night."

"Yeah, but what did you drink after the wine cooler? I saw what you looked like when you came home, remember?"

She just shook her head. "I only had the one drink. I swear."

"So then you got high?"

She shook her head again, her lip trembling. "No. I don't remember."

The twinge of fear in my stomach was swelling, but I couldn't stop it. "What are you saying? You don't remember getting high or you don't remember anything?"

"I remember Ty's cousin bringing me a wine cooler and—"

"Was it open?"

"Yeah, and I remember sitting with the guys on the porch and drinking it because it was too hot and sweaty inside, and then it gets . . . harder to see. Blurry, kind of, and more just flashes, and even then I don't know if it's because I'm trying too hard to remember something. Voices. Somebody's shirt in my face. That feeling of being picked up, hoisted and upside down, you know? Like over a shoulder?"

"Charly, look at me." It was my voice that was trembling now.

She wouldn't. Somewhere midstory she'd trained her eyes on the window to where snow was blowing sideways. The wind howled like wolves.

"*Look at me.*" My voice cracked in the middle, a sob escaping my throat. "Why didn't you tell me this?"

She sat perfectly still, like I hadn't even spoken to her. What was she thinking? Was she lost in horrific memories or was the murkiness too thick?

"When I woke up I was soaked. They'd left me outside, in the grass behind the bushes by the house. They didn't even put my pants back on."

I had just enough time to get to the sink before the vomit forced its way out of my throat. I retched and retched and when I was done, my throat burned and the sound of it rang in my ears.

I turned to Charly.

She'd swung her feet around to the ground now and was sitting upright, still staring out the window.

I opened my mouth to speak, but nothing came out. With a thousand words screaming to be first, how could I say nothing? I wanted to beg for forgiveness and promise to protect her and scream at her all at the same time.

Instead, I turned on the faucet to rinse the vomit down.

I tried again, but this time barely a whisper came out. "Why didn't you tell me?"

Finally she looked at me, the answer, an accusation, glimmering her eyes: If I was a different type of person, a different type of sister, she could have.

She didn't say it though. She bit her lip and looked away. "At first? I didn't tell because it was so *disgusting*. And so humiliating, waking up like that and not really knowing, except *knowing* what they . . ." She shook her head. "If nobody knew, then I could pretend it didn't even happen. I mean, I had bruises and some scratches and a bad headache and a few disgusting half-dream-half-memories, but I could hide all that. Plus, everyone was so mad at me for being gone so long and not calling."

Everyone? *I'd* been so mad, worse than mad, and meaner than I'd ever been to anyone in my entire life. To Charly.

I turned back to the sink, wanting to retch again, the taste of vomit still burning my throat and mouth, but I couldn't. I closed my eyes and saw the faces of the losers, with their slimy grins that'd made my skin crawl from day one, with their skinny faces and greasy hair and dirty finger-nails. They'd touched her with those hands and she hadn't even been awake. That was enough. I threw up again.

"What about them?" I said once I was finished. "Those pigs need to be in jail. Rape is a crime, Charly. You were a victim of a *crime*."

"You sound like Ms. Lee," she said. "Like them going to jail would make something better for me. It wouldn't. I don't even know who or how many or . . . I can't prove anything."

"Look at yourself!" My voice was too loud, but I couldn't control it now. "You've got DNA evidence grow-ing inside you!"

"Evidence of what? They'll say sex. Whoever the father is, and all his friends, they'll say I got drunk and had sex."

"But if you can't even remember it and you only had one drink—"

"Yeah, but nobody's going to believe me. Especially now, months later. You honestly think I haven't thought this through?"

I had a whole lifetime of Charly not thinking things through to point to, but I didn't. I hated everything she was saying, but I knew, between the pounding of my pulse in my skull, that she was right. They'd never be convicted of rape. Or not Charly's rape. I shuddered, picturing them still out there, doing the same disgusting thing to other girls, no thought to what they were breaking and the lives they were ruining. People's sisters and friends and daughters.

"See?" she asked. Her eyes were on my face, and I realized she'd been watching my reaction. The vomiting, the shuddering, the anger and revulsion. "I didn't want people thinking about it and me like you are right now."

"But I'm not thinking about you like you did something wrong, I'm just thinking about how evil and disgusting they are."

"It would all be the same in people's heads though. For the rest of my life, people would hear my name and think, *Oh, the wild pastor's daughter who got drunk and screamed rape after she woke up half-naked in the bushes.*"

Again, I wanted to tell her she was wrong. But she

wasn't. She knew, like I knew, because Tremonton was both of our tiny worlds. Maybe a big-city girl could get lost, be anonymous, but Charly would be the victim of small-mindedness forever.

"Still," I said softly, "*I* didn't need proof."

"I know. I don't know why I couldn't tell you. I didn't want to be different to you."

I dropped my hands to my head. She'd been afraid I'd judge her for being raped? How could she think that?

"It was just easier." She paused and stared at her stomach like it didn't belong to her, somebody else's skin stretched over somebody else's horrible mistake. "Then when I realized I was pregnant and it was too late to prove anything, I thought you might not believe me—"

"*What?* Of course I would've believed you!"

"—but if you hadn't, it would've been the worst thing in the world." She stopped, her voice faltering. It looked for a moment like her eyes might fill with tears, but she blinked them away.

"*No,*" I groaned, pushing off from the sink. I felt my own tears streaming down my cheeks as I moved toward her. I wanted to pull her up and hug her so hard she'd feel how wrong that was, but something stopped me. She looked so injured and untouchable at the same time, like a wounded wild animal. Instead, I sank to the floor beside her chair. "I'm sorry," I said, through my own sobbing.

"I'm sorry that you thought that, and that I was so cruel. But how was I supposed to know?"

"You weren't." Her voice was calm but distant. "It's not your fault. And for the longest time I thought it was my fault." She held up her palm to stop me before I could start. "You don't have to tell me it doesn't make sense. I've already heard it. It's Ms. Lee's mantra—*not your fault, Charly, not your fault!*—but it doesn't help that I know if I'd listened to you about those guys, and if I hadn't gone to the party, none of it would've happened."

I choked back tears, trying to muster enough composure to talk. "That doesn't make it your fault, though."

"No, but regret and guilt don't feel all that different."

It was true. My brain raced through memories of the last few months, tripping over every mean word I'd said to her, every scornful look. I'd been so unforgivably vicious. Why? Not just once either, but again and again and again. Each memory felt like a pinprick. Did it matter whether it was regret or guilt? Collectively, they felt like fire either way.

A much older memory pushed its way to the surface. I was seven and I'd stepped in an anthill at a church picnic. I will always remember looking down and seeing hundreds of fire ants pouring through the cracks between my toes, over the straps of my sandal, swirling up my calf, and over my kneecap. I was too mesmerized to save myself. But I'd been lucky. Grandma had picked me up and sprinted for the lake, throwing me in before I could think to hold my breath. Altogether, I'd had sixty-seven bites, but when the pain set in, I couldn't feel the individual stings. Just the burning of dozens.

I looked up at Charly. Her hand hung limply over the arm of the chair. I pressed my forehead against the back of it, feeling the coolness of her skin. I was burning up.

But she took her hand away, and I pulled back, ashamed. This wasn't about me.

Charly pushed her shoulders back and straightened her spine, like a marionette being called to attention. "Ms. Lee says that it will take a while, but that I'll feel better if I tell people."

"People?" I asked. Grandma? Dad? Bree?

Bree. Had she already been told? *Before me?* I couldn't say the words without seething jealousy.

"People," she repeated. "But I don't know if she's right. You're the first person I've told."

A sigh of relief escaped before I could stop it. "Are you going to tell Grandma?"

A long pause followed, so long I assumed she wasn't going to answer. Outside the wind picked up, the howls becoming more like whines.

"Would you?"

What was she asking? If I were her, would I tell

Grandma? Or was she asking me to tell Grandma *for* her? I was trapped either way. There was so much I owed her now. "I don't know," I said. It was true for both questions.

If we told Grandma, she might insist we tell Dad, and there was no predicting what he would do. He'd be devastated and furious and everything in between. He didn't even know she was pregnant. I inadvertently looked to Charly's belly. We'd already come so far. If we just stuck it out, we'd never have to experience the small-mindedness and cruelty waiting for us back home.

I took a measured breath and began. "I think we should—"

"*Stop!*"

The venom in her voice stung.

"But you asked—"

"I know," she said, quieter now, but just as firm. "I shouldn't have. I forgot. It's not *we*. I need to decide on my own, and then I need to do it on my own."

I felt winded, like she'd kicked me in the stomach. Our whole lives had been *we*. "Is that Ms. Lee talking?" I asked, noticing the bile from round two of throwing up still sour in my mouth.

"No, that's Charly talking. From now on it's going to be all Charly talking."

Fine. That sounded right. It just felt wrong.

Suddenly exhausted, I rested my head against the

brushed suede of the chair. I knew better than to try to touch her again, so I just listened to her breathe. It was so shallow. The panting of squished lungs. I tried syncing mine to hers, but the pregnant-girl pant left me breathless and on the verge of hyperventilating.

"Are you going to be all right?" I asked finally.

"I don't know."

What if she decided to tell Grandma and Dad? Dread and relief twisted themselves together inside me. Would that mean we'd be going home?

"What if I can't do it?" she continued. "I mean, I know I will, because I can't keep the baby and be a mother right now. I know I can't, but I think about actually giving her away and I feel so sad, I can't . . . Too sad to explain. I think it might break me."

It took a moment to realize that she wasn't talking about surviving the telling. It was the losing. I hadn't even considered it. I had no insight to offer, no possible way of understanding how she could feel that kind of love for something she'd had forced on her. It was too illogical.

But she was wrong. "It won't break you."

"You don't know that."

"Charly, you got drugged, raped, treated like trash by the people who love you most, kicked out of your home, and exiled to the coldest hell on earth. You would've already broken."

She didn't answer. But then I felt her hand resting on the top of my head, gently, like she wasn't so sure she wanted it there.

"I'm sorry," I said, the inadequacy of the words burning my ears. "I'm sorry. I'm sorry. I'm sorry."

"Shhh," she said. "I know."

Bree came home to a quiet apartment. Charly was asleep upstairs and I was in front of the computer trying to read the latest email from Savannah.

"What'd I miss?" she asked, biting the fingers of her glove and yanking her hand out. "Did you guys even leave the apartment once today?"

I looked up at her from the screen. "No."

"Aren't you going stir crazy?" She rifled through the mail on the table, chucking an armload of junk mail into the recycling.

I didn't answer, just let my eyes gloss over Savannah's words for the third time. Their meanings weren't getting any less slippery, which was unfortunate because I didn't have a fourth attempt in me.

"Did Charly send that stuff to the Paysons?"

Bree's voice sounded less nasal than it usually did too. Had the entire world become less? Less vibrant, less annoying, less sharp? I clicked reply, and wrote *hey* and then deleted it.

"Earth to Amelia."

"I don't know who the Paysons are."

"The couple she met with. She told them she was choosing them and everything. You knew that, didn't you?"

Did I? I stared at the blinking cursor. No. But I'd assumed it, the way Charly had talked about them the other night. Even the gravity of that decision seemed lighter.

My little sister had been *raped*. I'd missed it. All the signs were screaming at me now, but I'd been too busy feeling wounded and punishing her because I'd missed a field hockey game. And a dance.

Bree just absorbed my silence like it wasn't rude. Why did she do that? Why had she put up with my brat routine for the last two months and why hadn't I noticed before?

"You look tired," she mumbled.

"I am." I closed out my email, unwritten and unsent. Savannah wasn't sitting around waiting for me to reply.

Bree started humming that annoying song from *Hairspray*, and I suddenly wondered how many times she'd seen me roll my eyes at her.

And then, with all the force of a slap to the face, I got it. She had to *hate* having me here. I was sullen, uncooperative, sarcastic. Pretty much the worst guest ever.

"Tea?" she asked, waving a packet of something undoubtedly herbal—ginger seaweed, or lemon dirt, or whatever.

"Sure. Thanks."

To her credit, the wide-eyed astonishment only lasted a second. "Orange spice or honey mint?"

"Honey mint, please."

Chapter 19

Ms. Lee had specifically said her door was always open. I remembered the conversation clearly. But she was either lying or speaking figuratively, because her actual door was *never* open.

I walked by the closed door every day for the next week, which was risky because Dr. Ashton's door was right beside it and never closed. One day she'd be offering chocolate-covered espresso beans to passersby, the next day she'd be threatening expulsion to the next juvenile who tracked snow into her office. Powder keg.

Finally I just knocked.

"Come in," Ms. Lee called.

I did it quickly, closing her door behind me.

"Amelia."

"Hi."

"Something going on in the hall?" she asked, frowning.

Apparently I'd come in too quickly. "No, Dr. Ashton is just talking with the UPS guy and I . . . didn't want to get in her way." Actually, she'd been feeling the biceps of the UPS guy while twirling her necklace, and I was grateful for the diversion. She'd taken my lunch twice this week already.

"UPS guy," Ms. Lee said, and punctured the skin of her orange with her thumbnail.

The smell of citrus hit me like a splash of cold water. I wondered if Dad's trees were actually growing fruit this year.

"The young one?" she asked.

"Yeah."

She rolled her eyes. "Sit down."

I did, taking in her desk. She had the remnants of her meal—an empty soup bowl, crumbs on a plate, a Diet Coke can (*Coke-Diéte* facing me)—plus a boring-looking novel with a withering flower on the cover, and the cactuses. Or was it cacti? My terra-cotta pot still sat at the end of the perfect line, looking ridiculous.

"So did you want to talk to me about something?"

"Yeah."

She finished peeling her orange and offered me a section.

I took it. "My dad has a few citrus trees in our backyard. Oranges and limes mostly. A few tangerines."

"Seriously?" she asked.

A snottier Amelia would have asked if people often told her lies about citrus. "Yeah."

"You know, I've never actually seen an orange on a tree," she admitted. "I mean, I've seen pictures. And the Minute Maid carton probably isn't lying to me, so I believe that's how they grow. That must sound crazy to you."

"About as crazy as never having seen snow would sound to you."

She grinned and I understood why Charly could talk to her. She was the perfect blend of quiet and open.

"Charly told me," I blurted out.

She put her orange down. Apparently she wasn't a multitasker.

"Good." Her pause was long enough for me to consider leaving. "And how are you feeling about it?"

"I . . ." I had no words.

Ms. Lee nodded and waited for more.

"Why couldn't she tell me?"

"She did tell you."

"I mean right after it happened. Or when she found out she was pregnant. Or anytime before now."

"Did you ask her that?"

"Yeah, and she said a bunch of things that made no sense. Like she didn't want me to see her differently, and she felt guilty, and I was so mad, and she was worried I wouldn't believe her. I can't . . . I can't . . ."

I put my palm to my forehead and held it there, hoping I didn't look as pitiful as I felt.

"I can't believe she thought I wouldn't believe her. We're talking about rape. We're talking about my sister. How could she think that?"

Ms. Lee looked out her window and then back to me. "You may not understand her reaction to what happened, but that doesn't mean it isn't genuine. She's not you. She's going to react to things differently than you would, and there are things about being a victim of sexual assault that you just don't understand."

"Like feeling guilty."

"Exactly. It's irrational. I know that, she knows that, you know that. But sometimes understanding logically that something isn't your fault isn't the same thing as feeling it. It takes time and hard work."

I sat perfectly still. I couldn't tell if she was talking about Charly or about me.

"Amelia, what do you want?"

I stared at her. Was she kicking me out?

"What do you want most right now?" she clarified.

That had to be the stupidest question I'd ever been asked. "I want this never to have happened."

She shook her head. "No time travel. What do you want *now*?"

I didn't hesitate this time. "I want her to forgive me. And I want to be a better sister."

Ms. Lee gave me a sad half smile. "You aren't a bad sister. From what Charly has told me, I think you're mostly a really good sister. Everybody does things they regret. I am getting the sense though, that you have a hard time accepting less than perfect. From yourself and the world, I mean. Am I right?"

"Maybe."

"That takes time too," she said. "Learning to see shades of grey instead of just black and white. Which reminds me, we need to talk about next year."

Next year. I was having a hard time thinking forward to next week.

"There are plenty of universities here and in Florida that are still accepting applications for fall, but you're running out of time and I get the sense—"

"I can't think about that right now. Don't worry, I'll get it together and apply to some second-rate school, but I'm clearly dealing with some stuff right now."

"This is one of those shades-of-grey situations," she said. "You gambled on Columbia and you lost, but it doesn't have to be all or nothing. When I look at your transcripts, I see a young woman who has cared deeply about her academic future for *years*."

I fiddled with my necklace and tried not to think about what she was saying.

"You're going to look back and regret throwing it all away because you didn't get exactly what you wanted." She glanced at her clock. "I have an appointment right now, but I think you should come see me again."

I didn't answer.

"And I want you to take a look at this," she said, pulling a book from her bookshelf. *Recovering from Rape.* The word screamed at me from the cover, and I realized it was the first time I'd seen it written since finding out.

"It might be tough to read, but it'll help you understand what Charly's going through."

I slipped the book into my bag and stood to leave. "Can you answer one question for me?"

"Of course."

"Do you think Charly should tell my dad and my grandma?"

"That's not for me to decide."

"But that's not what I'm asking. I just want your opinion. She needs my help, but I don't know what to tell her to do."

Ms. Lee shook her head firmly. "That's the problem,

though. You can't tell her what to do—it's not your decision or my decision. It's Charly's decision. Let her make it."

"But . . ." I heard my voice getting higher and tighter, inching me closer to crying. I hated this feeling, the losing control of my own body, feeling like someone's fingers were tightening around my throat. "But you told her to tell me, right? How is that any different? Why can't I tell her who else to tell?" My ears ached from the whine of my own voice.

Her face softened as she reached out to touch my shoulder. Wow. Did I really sound pitiful enough to warrant teacher-student touching? I didn't back away.

"I didn't order her to tell you. I told her talking to people would help the healing process. She chose you, Amelia."

That should've made me happy, but it didn't. It'd still been six months too late.

Ms. Lee opened the door and waited for me to shuffle out. The hall was empty. No sign of the UPS guy, and Ashton's door was closed for the first time this week.

Miss Lee gave my shoulder one last squeeze. "Think about what I said. About next year." Then she left me standing alone.

I needed, more than anything in the freezing world, to run into Ezra. No, actually, I needed more. An accidental encounter wouldn't be good enough. I needed him to come intercept my walk home like he used to do, or drop by Bree's again. It'd been a week.

"Are we going in?" Charly asked.

We were standing on the corner of Beaver Street and Caribou Road, staring at the snow-caked library sign. White on grey.

"No."

"Are *you* going in?"

"No."

"Are you sure? It's so much easier to make out with a guy when you're in the same room."

"I don't want to make out with Ezra."

"Liar. And did I say make out? I meant make up."

"We didn't fight."

She gave me the exasperated eye roll. "I spent an hour watching an episode of *The Bachelor* that *I'd already seen* so that you could be alone with him. If you didn't make out and you didn't fight, it was a total waste of an hour. For both of us."

The light turned green again and we stared at the flashing walking man.

"Let's go home," I said. I turned and started trudging back.

"Seriously?"

I kept trudging. I shouldn't have let Charly drag me

over here in the first place. If he'd wanted to work things out, he would've come by, or at least called, but he hadn't. More than that, the balance between us had been off from the beginning. I was always the vulnerable one, revealing more, feeling more, leaving myself perfectly poised for injury. I had to stop doing that.

"What are you so afraid of?" she called after me.

I didn't answer. It was hard to tell.

"Are you awake?"

I groaned.

"Sorry. I thought you were awake."

"Because I had my eyes shut or because I wasn't moving?"

"Sorry. Go back to sleep. Unless you really are awake."

"I am now," I muttered.

"I can't sleep."

"Probably because you're hissing in my ear."

And then I remembered.

Would it always be like this—the forgetting and then remembering all at once? No. It'd been the same way when I'd first found out she was pregnant. It'd only taken a few weeks of relearning the horror every morning before I'd been able to wake up already hating her for getting herself knocked up.

But going in reverse wasn't any easier. My default

mode with Charly had been set to pissed off for too long. I'd already snapped at her more than once before remembering everything wrong in the universe wasn't her fault.

"Why can't you sleep?" I asked.

"I'm too itchy. I'm so freaking itchy I want to rip the skin off my stomach."

"So put some lotion on."

"I've got an entire jar of jojoba butter on my stomach right now and I still feel like I'm covered in mosquito bites."

"Well, I'd stop scratching it unless you want some nasty stretch marks." I had no idea if that was true, but the scratching was seriously hampering my sleep. "Hey, do you remember when we had chicken pox and Grandma made us that oatmeal bath?"

"Vaguely," she said. "What was I, six?"

"Do you think that was actual oatmeal or some special oatmeal bath product?"

"No idea. I don't remember anything from first grade except you beating the tar out of Nathan Barnes."

"Little pissant deserved it for ripping the streamers off your handlebars. I wonder if Bree has oats. I'll go down and check."

I tiptoed down and rifled through the pantry.

"Any luck?" Charly asked when I returned. She'd pulled the covers off and had her tank top rolled up over her glossy white belly. Apparently she hadn't been kidding about the jojoba butter.

"No. Unless you think bathing in a packet of peaches 'n' cream instant oatmeal would do something for you."

She snorted and that rolled into giggling. "I could just make up a bowl and smear it on my stomach."

"Strawberry Shortcake's lesser-known friend, Knocked-up Peaches 'n' Cream."

She was laughing loudly now, so I plowed on.

"The doll every parent is clamoring to buy for their daughter. Comes complete with stretch-panel pants and a removable purity ring."

That killed her. It wasn't even that funny, but she was making those wheezing sounds she makes right before she starts crying. I had no choice but to push her over the edge.

"GED sold separately."

By the time Charly could breathe again, Bree was pounding her way up the stairs.

"Are you okay?" she gasped, both hands clutching the railing like she'd pulled herself up with arm strength alone. Her eyes were golf ball–size and her platinum hair looked like a punk-rock halo.

Charly tried to stifle a hiccup, but snorted instead and then started laughing all over again.

I shrugged. "It really wasn't that funny."

Bree groaned and threw herself onto the foot of the bed. "I hate you both. Do you realize it's three a.m.? Tomorrow I'm practicing IVs on you as punishment."

"I'm sorry," Charly managed, wiping tears from her cheeks.

"You'll be sorrier tomorrow. I was like zero for five at finding veins today. What was so funny anyway? And why does it smell like Sephora exploded in here?"

"Jojoba butter. And Amelia was . . ." Charly sighed. "I can't even tell you or I'll start laughing again."

I shook my head. "Again, not that funny."

Bree rolled over onto my legs. "Oww! You're too boney. Seriously, my heart's still racing. I thought we had a preterm labor situation up here."

Charly answered with another snort, which became another round of hysterical laughter.

"Not unless laughing like a hyena can bring it on," I said.

"I'm not a nurse yet, but I'm pretty sure that's a no. Good night, you guys." Bree pulled herself up and off the bed, then gave us a tired wave without looking back. "Wake me up again and you're both getting catheters."

"Speaking of," I said to Charly, punching my pillow and burying my face in it. "I don't care if you can't stop laughing—if you pee the bed I swear I'll kill you."

"Good night to you too."

• • •

It was another Saturday before Ezra came around. Not physically. Electronically.

> To: ameliamerc@gmail.com
> From: ezracmackenzie@gmail.com
> Are you busy?

I read it several times, taking inventory of what was missing: a subject line, a greeting, pleasantries, an apology, an explanation, a closing. Oh, and maybe some reference to the fact that it'd been a full week since he'd walked out of here all pissed off because I dared to ask him questions about himself.

I checked the time the email was sent. Just a couple of minutes ago. I typed a response into the chat box.

> A: I hate that question

I waited. Waited. Waited.
Ezra is typing . . . appeared, and I exhaled.

> E: Why?

> A: Really?

E: Really

A: No means I have to say yes to whatever you're about to ask me to do. It also means I don't have a life. And yes means I can't say yes to the follow-up without looking desperate. It also means having to come up with a good lie right now, because I'm watching field hockey drills on YouTube and you might not think that qualifies as busy. But it does to me.

E: Wow. Forget I asked.

No. No, no, no, no. He could *not* think I was being serious.

Was *he* being serious?

Crap, this was why Savannah was always harping on me about emoticons. Was it too late to send a ☺*just kidding!!!*☺ or what was that winky one?

The *Ezra is typing* . . . prompt appeared and saved me from humiliating myself.

E: Do you want to go to Calgary?

Calgary. I checked the time. It was four thirty, which meant if we left right away we wouldn't be there till six. Most stores closed at six on Saturdays.

A: Now?

E: That would be why I asked you if you were busy.

I typed my response, grateful Charly was upstairs so she couldn't make fun of the stupid grin on my face.

A: What's in it for me?

E: Unlimited hot chocolate.

A: Carnation mix?

E: Of course not. Starbucks.

A: Careful what you promise—I will drink your paycheck away.

E: It's taken care of. I tutored the weekend manager through Math 20

and 30. He owes me his high school
diploma.

A: Do you pay for anything in this town?

E: You're complaining?

A: Nope. I'm in.

There was a moment's pause before *Ezra is typing . . .*
reappeared.

E: You don't want to know why we're
going to Calgary?

A: Yeah. But I'm not going to ask.

My heart pounded in my ears while I waited for his
response. I meant it. I didn't want to force anything out of
Ezra. Or anybody anymore.

E: Pick you up in a half hour.

"Charly!" I hollered. She was in the loft doing a man-
datory tidy-up. I'd threatened to hide the iPod Bree had
lent her in a snowbank if I couldn't see the floor by the

end of the day. "Are you okay here if I go to Calgary with Ezra?"

"But who's going to spoon-feed me my dinner?"

"Hilarious."

"And my butt, who's going to wipe my butt?"

"I probably won't be back till late."

"Well, then you'll definitely need to hire a sitter to put my jammies on and rub my back while I fall asleep."

"How's the cleanup going?"

"Shut up."

Ezra drove faster than usual. Too fast. My stomach rolled with each curve of the highway, my mind picturing the SUV flipping over and over.

"So that deer . . . ," I said.

"What deer?"

"The deer whose body is imprinted on the side of your car."

"*That* deer," he said, shaking his head. "It came out of nowhere. I was on my way back from Jasper last year. The road was really slick and it was dusk. Kind of like now, actually."

"You don't think it had anything to do with you driving too fast?"

"No." He glanced at the speedometer. "And the dent is in the side of my car. So it ran into me."

"Okay."

He glanced at the speedometer again.

I didn't say anything as the car slowed slightly and he put the cruise control on.

"So how are things?" he asked.

"Things?" Things were upside down—not terrible, just confusing. But I couldn't talk about it with him. Charly hadn't told me to keep the rape a secret. *The rape.* I still couldn't think the word without everything inside me aching. But it wasn't my tragedy to share, and I was finished spilling my guts to Ezra.

"School's fine," I said. "Bree's chipper as usual. Charly gets bigger and crankier every day. Same old."

Ezra glanced at the clock and put his foot back on the gas pedal.

"Are we late for something?" I asked, and instantly regretted it. So much for not asking. "Like our own funerals?"

"Kind of. Not for our funerals, but I have something I need to drop off at U of C before six."

I nodded. *Something.* A love letter, a pipe bomb, a library book. The possibilities were endless and I still wasn't going to ask.

"You know it's Saturday, right?"

"Yeah. The professor that I'm giving this to said he'd be in his office today until six." He pulled a manila envelope out of the side door compartment and put it on my lap. It wasn't sealed—the flap was open, and the two little metal prongs were still sticking straight up.

I kept my hands by my side and forced myself to stare out the window.

"Do you want to see what's in there?"

"I don't know. Are you *asking* me to look in there?"

He half grinned. "You're a piece of work."

"Right back at you."

"Fine. Yes, Amelia. Would you please look in that envelope? And would you please read that top page and then tell me what you think without being a total brat? I'm kind of nervous about it."

"Well, only since you're begging," I mumbled, pulling out a crisp stack of papers.

On top was a letter, addressed to a Professor Matthis. I skimmed quickly. It was a request for a recommendation. "You know this professor?"

"I had an internship in his lab the summer after grade eleven. He's a physicist."

"A physicist with sixteen-year-old interns?"

"I was seventeen, and not usually, but it was a national scholarship program thing."

I flipped through the other pages. An application for University of Calgary, high school transcripts, a couple of letters from teachers at BPH, including Ms. Lee and Mr. Wozniak, the math teacher. I turned to the front page of the application. Fall semester. He was applying for fall semester.

"Ezra." It was all I could say. I reached out and squeezed his arm. I was so happy and relieved and jealous I felt like exploding.

"You think it's a mistake?"

"Of course not. Are you kidding? And is this paper application for real? I've never seen one that isn't online."

"I missed the deadline so I can't apply online, but last night I talked to Professor Matthis, and he insisted he could get me in if I brought it all in today for him. He's leaving town tonight, going to some conference in Dallas, but he said if he can get it on the dean's desk before he leaves I at least have a hope of being considered."

"This Matthis must love you."

Ezra didn't answer, just rubbed a hand over the stubble on his jaw.

My fingers walked through each page and envelope again. "Wait, if you just talked to him last night, how did you get your transcripts and these letters from Lee and Wozniak?"

"Lee and Wozniak were easy. I called them last night and then picked up the letters this morning."

"But the transcript."

"Yeah, getting Ashton to surface from her hangover and open the school for me was trickier. That's why I'm so late."

I raised an eyebrow. "Do I want to know what you had to do for that?"

He shook his head, his mouth grim. "Things I'm not proud of."

I dropped the packet. One of the letters slipped out onto the floor and I scrambled to get it while Ezra laughed.

"I'm kidding."

"I knew that."

"I *did* threaten to leave an anonymous tip with the RCMP that she kept the confiscated weed from locker checks in her desk, but that was just to wake her up. I think she knew I was kidding."

"Does she?"

"Keep the weed? Don't know, but it seemed likely enough to try it out."

I brushed the dirt off the back of the paper and slid it back into the envelope. "Sorry about that."

"No problem. I don't think dirt is going to matter. I was up all night writing those essays so they're probably full of mistakes anyway, but nobody in the math or physics department knows how to write a sentence."

"You're probably right." I watched as the foothills

leveled into white prairie and the sky blackened. It felt like riding on the moon. But then I saw Calgary lights glittering in the distance like fireflies, and suddenly I was sitting in the black walnut tree with Charly, legs dangling, fingers stained with strawberry juice.

I turned to Ezra, and before I could think and stop myself, I leaned across and kissed his cheek.

He didn't say anything. I didn't say anything. We drove on. We didn't slide off the road. Nor did we hit a deer, though we saw several bounding erratically alongside the highway. By the time we pulled into the faculty parking lot outside the Physics and Astronomy Building it was 6:16.

"Only two cars," I said, "and three lights on in the whole building. That's not good."

Ezra was too stressed to notice the annoying commentary. "He said he had to leave right at six to catch his flight. I probably missed him."

"Run. I'll stay here."

Ezra threw it into park and bolted.

My heart pounded in my chest as I watched him disappear into the squat brick building. Why was I so nervous? It wasn't like missing this guy really meant that Ezra wasn't getting in for fall semester, did it? But I'd never heard of professors making their own admissions rules at all, so maybe the strings being pulled could only be pulled so hard.

I watched the clock. 6:17. I listened to the car heater

rattle, fiddled with the door locks, turned on the radio. *Celine Dion again?* Turned off the radio. Snooped through the glove box—Smarties and a can of bear spray. 6:18. Why was my heart still racing? I turned on the radio again. *Bieber? Seriously?* Turned the radio off again. Finally, I just stared at the clock. 6:19. 6:20. 6:21.

When had he changed his mind? And when had leaving Naomi gone from a never to a yes? I'd been so overwhelmed by Charly's revelation that everything else— even that fight with Ezra—had faded.

The front door of the building swung open. Ezra walked out. Smiling. He turned and held the door open for a man, a man so nerdy I could see it through the layers of wool and fur and Gore-Tex and whatever else he was bundled in. He was smiling too. Ezra walked him to his car. They stood talking in the freezing cold, while Ezra swept the thin layer of snow that had fallen on the man's windshield. The man got into his car, started it, and just when I was sure they were done, he got back out and resumed the conversation. It ended finally with a handshake and a backslap, then the man got back into his car and Ezra jogged to the Pathfinder.

"So?" I asked.

"So." He was shivering through his grin. "That was him."

"I guessed. And?"

"And we should go celebrate."

Chapter 20

What are these called again?" I asked, mid-mouthful. The box sat open between us, the air heavy with the smell of sugary glaze and vanilla.

"Timbits. I can't believe you've been here this long and this is your first trip to Tim Hortons. Bree's dropped the ball."

"My dad would love these." I picked a chocolate hole from the box and put it in my mouth to melt. "How can you drive and eat these at the same time? These things probably cause more accidents than texting."

"Years of practice."

"You're still smiling," I said.

"No, I'm not."

"It's not a bad thing."

He gave me a quick glance, then looked back to the road. "I just can't believe it's going to happen, you know?"

Sort of. My life had become a jumble of the things I couldn't believe were going to happen. Not good things, though.

"What changed?" I asked. It wasn't a question I could've asked last week, but things were different now. The wall behind his eyes had dissolved.

"Nothing. My mom has always insisted that I should go away to school, but I don't really know if she's any stronger than she was last year when things got bad. I mean, she seems better." He chewed his wind-chapped lips and I waited, praying he wasn't about to retreat again. "But I've seen too many ups and downs to believe much. And my brother still reappears to make her life hell every few months. So, no. Nothing's different. I guess I just realized I couldn't stop it or fix it."

I looked away from him, out my window, but really just at my reflection. My skin was only a shade darker than the snow.

I wanted to believe him, and I wanted to believe that *he* believed it too. I just didn't. Turning it off wasn't that easy. Charly had spent her whole life needing me and I couldn't for a single second forget it.

"Do you remember that night at the library when Taylor barged in on us?" he said.

"Yes." Like I could ever forget.

"That sucked. I'm sorry. The worst part about it was watching you while she was going off. You were just soaking in everything she was saying, and there wasn't anything I could do about it. I couldn't explain it to you with her standing right there, and I couldn't make her stop."

"Why not?"

"Because it would've really hurt her. She's a jealous nut job, but I can't just not care about her. We were together for too long. It's complicated. I'm sorry."

"It's okay," I said. Caring about her feelings didn't make him a bad person.

"No. And after it was over you should've been mad at me. Or you should've wanted to pull her hair, claw her eyes out—I don't know, do whatever girls do to each other—but it was like you were too busy hating yourself. It was messed up."

"You don't know," I started, then stopped. So much of this story wasn't mine to tell. "I deserved it."

"What are you ta—"

"No, I really did," I said. "I said terrible things to Charly. Things so mean that I feel sick to my stomach when I think about them. And not just that. I spent months treating her like garbage. I'm so ashamed, I . . ." I swallowed, trying to force the lump in my throat down so I could push the words out. "When Taylor called me a cheap slut, or whatever it was she called me, I finally got it. *I* was the bad sister."

Ezra was mercifully silent. He kept his eyes on the road.

I turned back to my reflection and started counting stars so I wouldn't cry. There had to be thousands visible from my window alone. I hadn't reached one hundred when I felt his hand on the back of mine, his fingers circling my wrist. "You aren't," he said.

I rolled my palm to his and we rode toward the mountains, our fingers laced together, me counting stars for both of us.

The red glow of brake lights ahead brought me back to earth.

"What's going on?" Ezra muttered. We slowed, then came to a complete stop behind a long line of cars.

I craned my neck to see up a mile ahead where the cars snaked around a curve. "Nothing's moving."

"That's bad." He fiddled with the radio for a minute, then unbuckled his seat belt and put on his toque. "I'm going to go ask those guys." He pointed to a couple of men huddled together on the shoulder.

I watched him walk away in the snow and remembered what kissing him felt like. It'd only happened that one time, but the replay count was nearing a million in my head. Why hadn't he tried again? There'd been plenty of moments I'd seen it in his eyes, that he wanted to. That he was thinking about it.

He jogged back to the car and got in. "There's a semi on its side up there. They think it's some kind of spill. The TransCanada is closed."

"For how long?"

"They're guessing a few hours, but they don't really know."

"So what do we do?"

"What that car is doing." He pointed to a minivan turning around up ahead. I could see several more doing U-turns and starting back toward us. "We can stay with my friends in Calgary tonight. If that works for you. I'm supposed to work tomorrow morning at nine, so we'll have to leave early."

He took out his cell phone and made a call while I pictured the filthy frat-house couch I was about to crash on. I'd be lucky to survive the night without catching something.

He finished his call and held the phone out to me. "Do you need to call Bree?"

I shook my head. "She and Richard went to Jasper for

the weekend. She won't be back until late tomorrow, but I should try Charly. She might be asleep though."

"Seriously? It's nine thirty."

"Yeah. Either the baby is sucking all her energy, or she's turning into an infant herself. Including naps, she must sleep at least fourteen hours a day."

He laughed and I felt a twinge of guilt. I wasn't supposed to be making fun of her anymore.

"Maybe I will call her," I said, and dialed the apartment. It rang five times, then went to voicemail. I left Charly a message and gave Ezra his phone back. "So are these guys ski friends or math club friends?" I asked.

"Um, both. Why?" he asked.

"I'm just trying to picture whether we're going to be interrupting their Saturday-night kegger or their Star Trek marathon."

"Probably both." He took off his toque and put it in his pocket.

I laughed. "Your hair looks insane. It looks like it did the first night I met you. I thought you were homeless or something." I reached out and smoothed it down.

"Toque head is an occupational badge of honor. I wear it proudly." He messed it back up again. "I didn't have the best opinion of you that night either."

"What's that supposed to mean?"

"I thought you were one of those pretty, mean girls."

A compliment and an insult rolled into one. I let my hand linger on his neck for a second, then pulled it away. "I was really sad. And mad."

"I figured that out," he said.

"Sorry. Lame excuses."

"I know what that combination feels like."

I let my head lean against the headrest. He thought I was pretty. Nobody had thought I was pretty since Will, and to him I'd been pretty, but not quite pretty enough.

We pulled into a quiet neighborhood street. "This is not the frat house I was picturing."

"Leo's a clean freak," Ezra warned as we pulled into the driveway. "Totally OCD about germs, just so you know."

"So I shouldn't lick every fork in the utensil drawer?"

"No, you should not."

The house was a smallish bungalow, old, but freshly painted. "How many guys live here?" I asked as we walked up the sidewalk. It'd been freshly shoveled.

"Three. Leo, Nathan, and Mike. I know them from this summer mathletics camp I went to a few years ago."

I snorted. "Did you just use the word 'mathletics'?"

Ezra rang the bell and a tall blond guy with a reddish goatee answered. All he needed was a horned helmet and he'd be a Viking.

"What's up, man?" he said, greeting Ezra with a grin and me with a nod.

"Amelia, this is Nathan."

"Hey, nice to meet you," he said to me.

"Hi." I stared up at him.

"Nathan's on the U of C basketball team," Ezra explained. "It's where freakishly tall people go to feel less freakish."

"It's true," Nathan joked. "The basketball's a front. We're really a support group for the six-foot-five-and-over club."

"Seriously, thanks for letting us crash," Ezra said.

"No problem. I just checked the traffic report, and the TransCanada is still closed. They're not even sure they'll be able to clean it all up by morning. I guess it was a lumber spill."

"I'm glad we turned around," Ezra said, taking off his boots.

I did the same, then Nathan gave me a tour of the house that involved pointing instead of actually walking: three bedrooms, a kitchen, a living room, and a bathroom.

"This is nice," I said, looking around and trying not to sound too surprised. It was a pile of contradictions, was what it was—a spotless college pad full of athletes and mathletes.

"We're kind of lucky," Nathan admitted. "Leo's dad owns it, so he gives us a good deal on rent. Plus we get

Leo's OCD cleaning skills for free. Just don't go leaving an eyelash or anything on the couch."

"Where is he?" Ezra asked.

"Leo? In his room studying for his O-chem midterm. I wouldn't go in there if I were you, though. He was talking to himself last time I poked my head in there, on the verge of a freak-out."

"That's my boy," Ezra said, stretching his arms over his head, then collapsing into a chair. He looked exhausted, like the all-nighter writing those essays had caught up with him. "And Mike?" Ezra asked, midyawn.

"At Ashley's. I'd offer you his bed, but he'll probably be back later."

"That's okay," Ezra said. "I'll take the floor."

"I think there's an air mattress somewhere out in the garage," he said. "Amelia, are you okay on the couch?"

"Sure. Thanks."

Nathan went to go hunt for the air mattress while Ezra and I brushed our teeth with our fingers.

"What would happen if I used Leo's toothbrush?" I whispered.

"You'd be held responsible for his next mental breakdown."

"And this guy's your friend?"

Ezra shrugged. "He's cool. As long as he's taking his meds."

Back in the main room, Nathan had piled blankets on the couch for me, and was blowing up an air mattress for Ezra.

I waited until he was done, then asked, "I don't suppose I could borrow some sweats or something." It'd be a long night in jeans but there was no way I was sleeping beside Ezra in my underwear.

"Sure," he said, then to Ezra, "And for her sake I'll get you something too. Unless you're still doing the nude sleepwalking thing."

"Funny," Ezra said.

"Should I ask?" I wondered aloud.

"Better not," Ezra muttered. "What happens at math camp, stays at math camp."

The pajama pants were about a foot too long and about as sexy as one of Grandma's muumuus, but otherwise comfortable. I lay down on the couch while Ezra and Nathan talked about basketball and some argument between Mike and his girlfriend's brother. I closed my eyes, suddenly tired.

"Well, I should let you guys sleep," Nathan said, after a few more minutes of talking. Ezra climbed into the sleeping bag and Nathan flipped off the light. "Oh, and I was kidding about the eyelash, Amelia. I would much rather our couch smell like you than Febreze."

"Um, thank you?"

"Go to bed already," Ezra called from the floor.

Nathan laughed and closed the door, leaving us in pitch-black. The house was perfectly silent.

I waited for what felt like a few minutes, then whispered, "Are you still awake?"

"Yeah."

He was tired. I should let him sleep. "Nathan seems nice. If you get into U of C, is this where you'll live next year?"

"Hopefully. Mike might move in with his girlfriend and then there'll be an empty room."

"Hmm." I pictured Ezra living here, going to classes in the physics building, brewing his noxious bitter coffee in the spotless kitchen. "You'd make sense here."

"What does that mean?"

"I mean when I see you driving down Banff Ave or at the library, you don't make sense. Like you're living somebody else's life. You make more sense here."

The pause was long. Long enough to wonder if he'd fallen asleep. "I know," he said finally.

I listened to his breathing, steady and deep, and tried not to think about the ache in my stomach as it spread into my chest, down my limbs, throbbing in my fingers and toes. Ezra belonged here. I belonged nowhere—not in Banff or Tremonton, not in the present or next year, not even with anybody. Except Charly of course. I belonged with her, but that was like being stuck to a plastic bag in a windstorm.

"Thank you for saying that," he said quietly, and suddenly I wanted him to touch me so badly I could almost cry.

I swallowed, grateful he couldn't see my face in the dark. "That day in the library," I said.

"Yeah."

I clenched my fists beneath the blanket. "Why haven't you kissed me since then?"

This time the silence was absolute. No breathing, no *shh-shh* of sleeping bag against air mattress. "I thought you didn't want me to."

That didn't make any sense. Except I'd pulled back. The horror of being caught so vulnerable had made me curl inward, and I'd kept him at a safe distance ever since. "But you kept coming by," I said, thinking aloud now. "If you thought I wasn't interested, why did you keep coming by?"

"I thought we could still be friends," he said.

Friends. That sucked. Not only that, but it contradicted pretty much everything I'd been told about guys and their ability to be just friends with members of the opposite sex.

"Screw it," he said. "That's a lie. I was just hoping you'd change your mind."

How could I have changed my mind? I'd never stopped wanting him in the first place. I had to say something, but everything was too needy, or too cheesy.

"Ezra," I started, then stopped. I couldn't do it.

But he didn't make me. I heard the sleeping bag rustle, the floor creak, and then the fall of bare feet on the carpet, coming toward me. I didn't have time to feel anything but elation. Cold air rushed in as he lifted the blanket, and then his warm body was alongside me.

I shifted onto my side to make room, letting his hand rest on my hip and his legs lace with mine. I closed my eyes. This felt perfect, facing each other, his breath on my neck. Like heaven.

His fingers found my cheek in the dark and traced the line of my jaw. Seconds felt like hours. He had to feel my pulse racing, but he didn't say a word.

"You're hard to read," he whispered finally.

"Am I?"

"Yeah."

"You aren't exactly an open book eith—"

His lips stopped mine, the kiss slow and gentle, his warm hands suddenly around my waist pulling me closer. It felt good enough that when he pulled away, something inside me collapsed. I could get addicted to that feeling.

"We should sleep," he said.

"Probably."

"I'd hate to get in trouble with a pastor's daughter."

"Trust me, it's my grandma you don't want to mess with."

He laughed. "Should I go back to the floor?"

"No." I put my cheek on his chest and listened to his heart pound, breathing in his scent. It smelled like his ski jacket. Pine needles and smoke. The mountains.

We left early, before anyone else was up.

Neither of us said anything about waking up tangled around each other. We didn't need to. He reached out and brushed my hair out of my face as we walked out to the car. I let him see me smile about it.

"Nobody's on the road," I commented as we pulled out of the neighborhood.

"Typical Sunday morning."

Typical Sunday morning. I looked at the clock and added two hours. "My dad's at the pulpit right now."

"Do you go to a church in Banff?"

I shook my head no.

"There's a Methodist church just down the street, I think. You're Methodist, right?"

"Yeah. I've seen it, and I've been meaning to go, but . . ." I shrugged, trying to decide whether to change the subject or just say it. "My dad asks every time we talk on the phone. He wants to know if I've called the pastor he knows in Canmore, or attended a service here in Banff. Anyway, that's why I can't go."

"Because he asks?"

"Because it's the only thing he asks."

We drove for a little while in silence, then Ezra said, "That's kind of sad."

"Why?"

"Last time we talked about it you told me how much you loved church before everything with your sister happened. Losing that—it's sad."

"I guess. I'm just too frustrated with him."

He didn't ask why, which was good. I couldn't explain. I was mad because I wasn't important enough for my father to really know, not as important as Charly, or his congregants, or his faith. I was mad because he was so unreachably idealistic that his own daughter couldn't tell him that she'd been raped.

"I'll go with you sometime if you want."

Was he serious? "That night in the kitchen, you told me organized religion is a joke."

He wrinkled his brow. "I think I said it wasn't for me, but it's obviously important to you."

"It was. But it's not that easy, separating him from church."

He shrugged. "Seems like geography's already done that for you, though."

That was only partially true. Obviously, Dad wouldn't be at the Banff First Methodist Church next Sunday, but I wasn't so sure I could sit there and feel what I used to feel—good and happy and peaceful—without him at the pulpit.

"Sorry," he said, reaching over and taking my hand. "I'm not trying to upset you."

"No, I know." His hand felt warm and a current went up my arm. The feel of his lips on mine flooded my memory. Ezra would go with me if I wanted him to. That meant something.

The ride home was smooth, all evidence of the lumber spill gone, the rest of the world still sleeping under the Sunday-morning frost.

"Do you want to come up and grab some breakfast?" I asked.

He hesitated, his fingers holding the key in the ignition.

"Actually, that would be great." He turned the car off and slid the key out.

He followed me up and leaned against the doorframe while I fiddled with my key.

"I'm guessing sloth-girl is still asleep," I said softly and pushed the door open.

I could smell the dirt immediately. No, not dirt. Herbal tea. Bree sat at the island with her fingers wrapped around a mug, staring into a cup of sand-colored water.

She looked up, eyes even rounder than usual. "Amelia."

Everything about her voice was wrong. Nervous, staged, somber—like my name was the first line in a play, and she'd been sitting here rehearsing for hours.

"I thought you were staying in Jasper till tonight," I said.

"Hey, Bree," Ezra called from behind me. I moved aside so he could come in and shut the door.

"Ezra."

Why did she sound so irked? She couldn't possibly be getting parental on me now. I was almost eighteen and she liked Ezra. But the way she was staring at him now said he wasn't supposed to be here. Whatever she'd been planning was for me alone.

"Sorry I stole Amelia," Ezra said. "We got stuck in Calgary last night. There was a semi—"

"The lumber spill," she interrupted. "I know."

"What's going on?" I asked, hanging our jackets in the front closet, suddenly impatient with the mysterious act.

"I need to talk to you about Charly." She glanced from me to Ezra, then back to me, and my stomach dropped down, down, down. Something was wrong.

"Oh, I was just leaving," Ezra said.

I reached out and grabbed his arm, feeling suddenly like the world was spinning. "Don't go," I said, begging him with my eyes.

He nodded, but I didn't let go of his arm.

"Isn't she here?" I looked up at the loft. "She was here when I left."

Bree bit her lip.

No. Charly had gone into labor. I should never have left her. But she wasn't far enough along, so was the baby dead? It had to be. Not *it*. She. And Charly—women died having babies with nobody to help them. Where was she? I'd left her here alone, nobody to drive her to the hospital, nobody to call for help. I didn't even know if 911 was the same in Canada, which meant she definitely didn't know. Why hadn't I bothered to find that out?

"She's not here," Bree said.

"The hospital?" My voice was strangely calm, considering my screaming thoughts.

"No. She went home."

"They discharged her? So she's asleep?" My eyes went up to the loft again. The light was out.

"No, she didn't go to the hospital. She's fine. The baby's fine. She went *home*."

Home.

Bree sighed, and I noticed for the first time the mascara smudges under both eyes. Her eyelashes were clumped together like crooked spider legs. "Florida."

Florida. Charly went *home*.

Without me.

Bree's voice floated on, and I felt Ezra's warm hand

on my back between my shoulder blades, but the rest of the room seemed to melt, the colors all bleeding into each other.

She'd gone home without me.

"She called me from the airport and told me she'd decided to tell your dad and grandma everything."

But she couldn't do it with me there. She had to go alone.

"She said to tell you don't be mad," Bree was saying. I pulled myself toward the sound of her voice.

"Mad."

Was I? It hadn't even occurred to me. Mad didn't hurt this bad. Mad didn't feel like my lungs were being squeezed. I'd never been so mad I couldn't breathe. Tears filled my eyes and I didn't bother blinking them away or wiping them.

"It didn't have anything to do with you," Ezra whispered in my ear.

But it did. Charly was like an appendage, how could it have nothing to do with me? I took a careful breath. Ezra shifted beside me and I realized I was still gripping his arm. But I couldn't let go.

"Are you okay?" he asked.

"Okay?" I asked shakily, and then again in a firmer tone, "Yeah. I'm okay."

"Don't be mad," Bree repeated.

"I'm not mad," I said. I didn't have the energy for mad anymore.

Bree slipped off her stool and came toward me, then pulled me into a hug.

"When is she coming back?" I asked.

"What?" Bree asked.

I was about to ask again, but stopped. She'd heard me.

Bree bit her lip, and suddenly I knew Charly wasn't coming back.

I let go of Ezra and sank into the sofa. Deliverance. I was getting exactly what I'd spent my whole life wishing for. The choking duty of making sure Charly didn't kill herself or screw up her life had been lifted, and by *her* of all people. She didn't need me anymore. The shock of it felt like an explosion—all blinding light and shrapnel and confusion. We'd been shackled to each other since birth, and she'd been the one to finally turn and snap the chain?

Even stranger, I wasn't floating to the surface now. I was sinking—sinking and realizing that all this time I'd had it backward. She wasn't the anchor. I was.

Chapter 21

The airport was busy. All around us people flowed, but we stood frozen in front of the arrival/departure screen. Ezra was behind me, his hands in my belt loops, chin resting on my shoulder. No jackets. It was a good ten degrees above freezing—good weather for May, according to Ezra—so the natives were wearing halter tops and drinking frappuccinos. I'd opted for short sleeves myself.

"Nervous?" Ezra asked.

"No. Are you?"

"No."

"You should be," I said.

"Then yes."

I turned my head and looked up at him. He was staring earnestly at the screen with that look of concentration I loved. "She's kind of a force to reckon with," I said.

"I handle you all right, don't I?"

"Barely."

He pointed to the screen, the concentration holding his face still. If he'd let me, I would sit and watch him read his math textbooks for hours, but I was a focus killer, or so he claimed. He was months from the start of fall classes, but Professor Matthis already had him reading ahead. Or catching up. I wasn't sure.

"It's just arrived," he said. "It'll take her at least twenty minutes to get her luggage and get through customs."

"Let's go wait by the gate," I said, pulling him by the hand. "I don't want her to have to wonder if we've forgotten her, like you did to us when we flew in."

He smirked. "That's the *handling* I'm talking about."

"Trust me. My grandma's way harder to win over than I am."

A crowd had gathered around the glass doors where international arrivals came through, so we waited side by side at the edge, in front of the metal cowboy statue.

"I can't believe how much has happened since the last time I was here," I said, more to myself than Ezra. "I remember staring at this statue thinking two things: One, it was the ugliest thing I'd ever seen, and two, my life was over."

"And now?"

I shook my head. "It's just the ugliest thing I've ever seen."

The backs of Ezra's fingers grazed the backs of mine.

"And just so we're clear," I added, "all touching must cease and desist the minute she walks through those doors."

He laughed. "I thought you said you weren't scared of her."

"I said I wasn't nervous, and I'm not nervous because I know not to do anything stupid, like make out, for example, in front of my grandma."

"My fingers touching your fingers is making out?"

"Trust me. This woman kills chickens with her bare hands."

"Seriously?"

"No, we aren't that rural. But she totally could if she had to."

"Okay. No fingers accidentally touching until she leaves."

"Good."

"When does she leave again?" He'd taken my hand now and was drawing me into him.

I pulled back but let him keep holding it. "One week. Maybe we should go over appropriate topics of conversation."

"Right, because otherwise I might bring up my career as a porn star or those years I spent in juvie."

"I'm serious," I said and tugged my hand away from his. "Don't mention Mount Royal University."

The smile faded. "You haven't told her yet?"

"I will. I just thought it would be easier in person." That was not even close to being true. Insubordination was not something Grandma appreciated, over the phone, by email, in my thoughts, or to her face. Telling her I'd chosen a Canadian school wasn't going to be received well.

"Wait, so she still thinks you're coming back after graduation?"

"Probably."

He sighed and folded his arms. "Okay, so I don't mention Mount Royal. What else?"

I thought for a second. "That's it, actually. Unless you would consider hiding your tattoo?"

He looked down at his bare arm, then back at me in disbelief.

"Just kidding?"

He took a box of Milk Duds out of his pocket, poured himself a few and handed it to me. I took some too. "And don't feel bad if she lectures you about your candy habit. In fact, maybe you should try to cut down for just this week."

"I can try."

"And don't feel bad if she lectures you about any-thing, or starts ranting about socialist healthcare. She can't help it."

"I've got thick skin. And I'm guessing I'm not sup-posed to tell her what I think about your dad canceling his flight last week."

"Definitely don't do that." I sucked on my Milk Dud. I was over it. "Besides, it's better that he stays with Charly now, right?"

Ezra didn't answer, but his silence was full of judg-ment. I knew him well enough to hear the unsaid, and I couldn't blame him for being annoyed at Dad. For weeks he'd listened to me plan all the places I was going to take them and things they had to see. And then he'd been there to see me suck back tears when Bree had delivered the news that Dad wasn't coming.

"No, it really is better," I said. "I was upset, but the fact that he's staying with Charly means something, you know? For her. I know it does."

His eyes rested on my face, waiting for me to admit I was trying too hard.

"She needs him right now," I said. Whatever disap-pointment I felt, that at least was true.

According to Savannah's last email, Charly had become Wonder Woman on a suicide mission. She was walking around Tremonton like she'd never left, massive belly and all. Everyone knew that she'd marched into the police station with Dad and Grandma in tow and filed a sexual assault report. She did it, and I was so proud of her it hurt. She did it like there was a chance in hell of charges actually being made, which we all knew there wasn't.

Without actually saying it, Savannah's email hinted around what I'd known: People didn't believe her. Maybe not everyone, but enough of them. They were talking, shaking their heads, raising their eyebrows. I could practically hear them—*crying rape is awfully convenient, don't you think? What pregnant pastor's daughter wouldn't?*

Also according to Savannah, Charly was even sitting in our pew every Sunday beside Grandma, pretending she actually enjoyed listening to Dad preach. I almost wished I could see it.

"How's Charly doing?" Ezra asked, bringing me out of my thoughts.

"Good." I thought about our last phone conversation. She'd been happy, full of complaints about Grandma's bridge party cheese tray stinking up the house, and willing to describe the phenomenal hotness of Matt Kilner's cousin who was staying with the Kilners for the semester. She'd been herself. "She misses things—Canadian chocolate and Bree and that repulsive fries-cheese-gravy concoction she always got at A&W."

"Poutine."

"Yeah, poutine."

"And you," Ezra added. "She misses you."

"You read her mind?"

"I just know."

I knew it too.

The glass doors slid open and the first couple of bedraggled passengers emerged.

"One more of these," Ezra said, taking one last Milk Dud and pocketing the half-empty box, "and one more of these." He leaned down and kissed the side of my neck.

I closed my eyes. The bliss of being wanted trickled through me, and inexplicably, amidst all things foreign, I made sense.

ACKNOWLEDGMENTS

My favorite delinquents:
Dave Low, thank you for being stupid enough to hit flaming golf balls, and, Jen Low, thank you for being insane enough to take a bite out of a formaldehyde-soaked frog. Your stories made Charly perfectly crazy. I can't believe you people have never served jail time. I hope your own Charlotte is just as fun, but more law-abiding.

My favorite professionals:
Anica Rissi, you are a brilliant editor, and you're turning me into a spoiled writer. Mandy Hubbard, there's nobody else I'd rather have in my corner. Thanks for the hand-holding, cheerleading, and wise words. I sometimes feel like I stumbled onto the publishing gold mine with you two. I'm lucky to call you both friends.

Family shout-outs:
Josh, thank you for your ski knowledge. Don't kill yourself doing backflips off cliffs. Amanda, thanks for listening to me hash out the plot while we ran together. I love you, even if you have always made me look like the mean sister. And of course, Mom and Dad, thanks for loving me more than your other kids. Come on, you know you do. Okay, maybe just Dad.